THE LAZARUS CULTURE

A ZOMBIE NOVEL

THE LAZARUS CULTURE

A ZOMBIE NOVEL

PASQUALE J. MORRONE

To my children

THE LAZARUS CULTURE

A *Living Dead Press* book.
Published by arrangement with the author.

ISBN   Softcover ISBN 13: 978-1-935458-24-1
                    ISBN 10: 1-935458-24-8

For more info on obtaining additional copies of this book, contact:

www.livingdeadpress.com

Edited by Anthony Giangregorio

PROLOGUE

Doctor Marlene Peterson was a doctor in a small community in Maryland. Like all the others before her, she took an oath to save lives. Looking at the man lying before her, an emaciated being who only stared at the ceiling and groaned once in a while, she had her doubts. He was rapidly evolving into something far from a normal human being. There was a heartbeat, but it was slow with a strange form of arrhythmia. Cat scans showed brain activity, but they also showed a shadow of something that covered the brain stem and partially covering the brain itself. If it was cancer, it was a strange new form of tumor.

There were others with the same affliction, and all had the same pattern shown by the CAT scans. There currently weren't any deaths with whatever plagued these people, but it was taken under advisement that none of them should share a room. Each patient was placed in medical solitary confinement. Not for even the minutest amount of time did these patients share the same space with others suffering from either the usual or natural ailments.

She turned and walked to the next bed. Once again the chart showed identical symptoms. These people were too sick and too weak to be scheduled for surgery. She couldn't figure out how the blood was getting around in the veins and arteries. It was thick and seemed to coagulate immediately upon being drawn from the body. It was a hell of a thing, but she wished one of them would expire. An autopsy would expose whatever it was that assaulted the brain. There was a possibility that it could actually save lives.

Feeding any of these individuals intravenously was rapidly becoming a lost cause due to the thickness of the blood. One of them had been lying in bed for over a month with very little nourishment by either food or drink. Her skin became almost opaque and glossy. There were times when she would stop breathing for three or four minutes and then all of a sudden come back to the world of the living with a quick gasp. Her eyes were covered with a milky film, and it was at first thought that she was going blind. This was finally put to rest when she began to move her eyes, following people as they moved about the room.

At the beginning of the fourth month of having cared for the now four people who had contracted this strange disease, came a wife who for some strange reason became at odds with the entire staff of the hospital. It didn't matter to her that they fought night and day to save the life of her husband, a man who for all intents and purposes should have been pronounced dead two months into his ailment. At each visit she insisted she be left alone for a time with her sickly husband. The charts showed that he never acknowledged her being there. On this particular day one of the nurses passing by to assist another patient who had stopped breathing once again, quickly rang for the physician in charge. She witnessed the woman leaning forward to speak to her husband in a whisper, and seeing the man quickly raise his head, he took a bite out of her cheek.

Marlene Peterson and her team were on the scene in less than thirty seconds. The woman was taken to the emergency room and given a quick but thorough battery of various tests. After an hour and a half had passed, she was cleared to leave and was rewarded for her pain and suffering with several packets of antibiotics to take twice a day.

On the third day she was in a bed next to her husband in critical condition and suffering from excruciating pain in the back of her head and neck. The tests were once again performed, but this time strange little critters were found in her bloodstream. The next day a CAT scan discovered a tiny shadow of something that appeared to be attached to her brain stem. The blood cultures all revealed the other micro-organisms were now dead.

The CDC was advised that another person had become infected with the dreaded disease and, given the circumstances, the CDC decided to entertain the idea that the micro-organisms traveled through the bloodstream and on to the brain in the same fashion sperm traveled toward the unfertilized egg. The first one there was the winner.

At eleven-thirty that evening, Doctor Peterson received a call from the head nurse in charge of the ward. Looking at the caller ID, she groaned and tried not to say aloud the curse words running through her mind.

"Doctor Peterson."

"*Doctor Peterson, we have a problem here. I'm sorry to bother you so late, but one of the patients went into cardiac arrest. It's just strange. I've never....*"

"So what's the problem? This is actually a blessing in disguise. Have the body sent down to the morgue immediately and keep it under wraps until I get there in the morning."

"*The problem is that he's moving. Doctor Peterson, the patient is still moving around.*"

"It's just involuntary movement! It happens sometimes and as a nurse you should be aware...."

This time it was the doctor who was cut short. "*No, ma'am! With all due respect, I'm fully aware of the dead and the dying. This is different, in that, this man is pulling at his restraints. It's the same patient who bit his wife. He has no heartbeat, no blood pressure, and he's not breathing, but he's groaning and pulling at the restraints with every bit of strength he's capable of as a dead man.*"

Marlene closed her eyes and took a deep breath.

"Look, it's late, and I'm really sorry for the sarcasm. I'll be there in about half an hour. Meanwhile, keep far enough away from this fellow. I checked my messages earlier this evening. The CDC left a message that there were now two other outbreaks of the same disease at another hospital."

On the other end of the phone, the nurse smiled. It was always good to win one once in a while.

"*I understand, Doctor Peterson. His restraints are more than enough to hold him in place. He's not going anywhere for the time being.*"

PART ONE: THE ONSET

CHAPTER 1

Agent Christopher Kearns pulled into the Breezy Point Medical Center listening to the ring tone of *The Rolling Stones' Brown Sugar*. When it finally stopped he glanced out the window at the medical building and shook his head. He was detailed from the Secret Service to work closely with the Center for Disease Control. The outbreak of a strange and deadly disease had Homeland Security paranoid that it may be some form of terrorist activity involving chemical or biological warfare.

Kearns waited a few more seconds before checking his cell phone and the number for the missed call. It was his ex-wife's cell number and probably his son. It was Friday and he remembered his son had a basketball game early on Saturday. The boy probably wanted to remind him not to be late getting him to the school. Kearns signed divorce papers a year ago and shared custody of his two children, a boy eight and a girl ten. There were no evil intentions on either party, she got the home and one of the cars, and he got to live wherever he wanted on the east coast.

Kearns was assigned to his last office out of Washington, DC, so there was no threat of being transferred anywhere else. His ex-wife, Jennifer, was an editor for a major publishing house and made more than enough to cover the mortgage and other bills. She was used to doing things on her own and never asked him for a cent. She refused alimony; and he had no problem with those terms whatsoever.

The news on the radio was about a plane crash that happened a week ago in Southern Maryland. He listened to the commentator announce that Pentagon and other military officials were still trying to sort out what had happened to a private jet carrying 34 passengers and two bodies.

Military killed in action no doubt; taking two more kids home for their parents to see for the last time, Kearns thought.

He stepped out of the car and glanced at his watch. This didn't sound like something he actually wanted to see at half past seven in the morning. Whatever the disease, it had a dead man inside who could move around as if severely retarded. It was a scary thought, to just be perfectly normal one day and then have your husband bite you on the cheek the next, making you the cover shot for *Fangoria*. It was also a scary thought not knowing where the hell this shit came from. He could tell there was someone here from CDC, and made sure he took his notepad and a pen. There was suddenly a little voice in the back of his mind. *Eggheads! All scientists seemed to be above normal thinking. You had to have a thesaurus and Webster's newest and most up to date dictionary to figure out what the hell they were talking about.*

The double-glass door opened automatically. He looked around for a moment and then walked directly to the receptionist's desk. It wasn't manned, but there was an envelope with his name on it taped to the back of the computer monitor. A security guard was directly on the other side of the receptionist's kiosk. Kearns hoisted his commission book and flipped it open, exposing his picture and badge. The guard checked the name on the envelope and matched it with the ID.

"Strange shit!" the guard said.

Kearns nodded. "It's not something I would have planned myself if I had anything to do with it." He opened the envelope and read the card that had been signed by Doctor Marlene Peterson. "This shit is right out of the *Masters of Horror*, huh?"

The guard, who was a few inches shorter than Chris' six-four frame turned back around as he walked away. "I'm afraid to eat or drink anything anymore. This is even worse than the sniper shootings around DC."

The elevator started its ascension with a slight jolt. Opening at the sixth floor, Kearns stepped out and made his way toward the nurse's station. A hefty babe with long brunette hair looked up for a second. She had one of those faces where you could actually see the prettier and skinner version wedged inside the roundness of it. She turned away for a moment before he could check her nametag.

"Agent Kearns?"

Kearns turned and met the smiling face of a woman about five-six and pretty as a picture. Her sandy-blonde hair was pulled tightly back on both sides to form a sub-roll of hair in the back of her head.

"I'm agent Kearns. Doctor Peterson?" He held out his hand to take hers and could immediately feel the slight roughness of her palm. A trait usually found in people who spend a good part of their lives washing their hands and slipping them in and out of latex gloves.

"I'm Doctor Marlene Peterson," she said, pointing toward a room off to the side of the elevator. "We have fresh coffee if that's what you drink in the morning. I know it's early and I appreciate you showing up at such short notice. Actually," she shrugged slightly, "I guess I should thank the Secret Service for lending you out."

"I'd love a cup of coffee and please, call me Chris. I rarely go anywhere this early in the morning, even as an agent. Can you believe that?"

"Fine then, we'll agree on calling one another on a first name basis. To answer your question, yes. After what I've seen here these past few months, I can just about believe anything."

Chris poured himself a cup of coffee and asked her his first question. "What exactly have you seen here, Marlene?"

The doctor waited until he took his first sip. "I've never saw anything like this, that's for damn sure. The first patient was brought here several months ago. She went through two days of headaches and then nausea. On the third day she was practically comatose. We ran different tests and tried to pinpoint where the infection may have started, but nothing rang a bell until we did the CAT."

Looking behind him, Chris pointed to one of the chairs. "You mind?"

"Oh! Goodness sakes, no. Go right ahead. Sit and enjoy your coffee. Lord knows what you're about to see isn't pretty. Not even for someone like me who worked on cadavers in my medical studies."

Chris took the pad out and clicked the pen into action. "Now, from what I understand there's something with this illness that attacks the brain?"

Marlene dug her hands deep into her white smock and walked back and forth for a moment. Chris scanned her body without being overly obvious. She looked to be in her mid-thirties. Her legs were toned well, but not heavily muscled. He was a calf and thigh man and decided to make a mental note to find out if she was married.

She stopped and looked up toward the ceiling before letting her eyes fall back on her guest. Chris averted his gaze quickly.

"We had a woman visitor come to the hospital at least three times a week," she said. "She would insist that she be left alone for a short time with her husband, who by the way is the man you are about to see. One day he ended up biting her. It wasn't just a normal bite; this was a chunk taken out of her cheek that he actually swallowed. Evidently, she was leaning in to kiss him, or as the nurse put it, to possibly whisper into his ear. We ran tests on her and everything came up negative. We stitched her up, put her on antibiotics just in case, and three days later she ended up in the bed next to her husband, gravely ill."

Chris stopped writing and looked up. "More tests?"

"She nodded. "Yes, more tests. This time we found antibodies, which are a protein produced by B cells in the body in response to the presence of an antigen, for example, a bacterium or virus. And then we found what the antibodies were trying to fight. They were like nothing anything we've ever seen before. The antibodies just couldn't identify the strain, much like when we don't bother to immunize. The body doesn't know what it's fighting and the disease just takes hold deeper and deeper."

"So, can this strain be transmitted by the exchange of bodily fluids like kissing or sex? You'll have to excuse me I'm not your..."

Marlene raised her hand to halt any further apologies. "I don't expect you to understand, Agent... Chris, sorry. We as doctors and even the CDC can't come up with anything like what was found in the blood. The strange thing is, after this organism found its way to her brain stem, the rest of them died. Just like sperm activity and the human egg."

"Why would they just die off?"

Marlene shook her head. "We really don't know, but the CDC feels that the strain actually lives on the antibodies. When one finally reaches the place where it wants to be, the rest begin a feeding frenzy. When all the antibodies are gone, they starve. That's what we have in theory. It's really not much to go on, but it's a start. Hopefully it's a start in the right direction."

Chris downed the rest of his coffee. "I'm glad I passed on breakfast for the moment. I'm ready if you are."

They walked down the corridor, talking about what might have caused the strain and where it possibly came from. At the intersection they made a left turn and walked through two tightly sealed doors. Chris was given a mask and a small white cap. They then passed through two large swinging doors with metal plates at the bottom and into the ward housing the most dangerous disease since cancer.

"What's with the plane crash and the Army? It's been a week now and it's still on the news," Chris asked.

Marlene shrugged. "I tend to believe it was carrying military personnel. I believe the bodies were KIA's being flown home for burial. From what I understand, fourteen of the passengers were killed and no one has any clue what happened to the rest. The two bodies were never recovered, and I've heard from a reliable source that the dead were badly mutilated; animals more than likely. It was a very remote part of Maryland and it happened in the middle of the night. I heard there was no explosion or fires in the vicinity of the crash."

Upon entering the room, Chris' eyes went wide at the sight of the woman lying on her back with huge black rings under her eyes. Chris was glad Marlene Peterson couldn't see his mouth. It was a grimace. Marlene told him this was the woman she spoke of who was bitten by her husband. In the next bed was a man whose glassy eyes looked like they would pop out of his head. His cheeks and eye sockets were sunken in so far that it looked like a skull draped in dead skin. There were four patients in all and each one was strapped down on a bed.

"This is totally repulsive," Chris gasped. He backed up and turned to face the doctor. "How long can they survive like this?"

Marlene put the chart she'd been reading back on the end of the bed.

"Well, Chris, after you see what I'm going to show you next, you try to answer that question for yourself."

CHAPTER 2

Dale Brant wasn't feeling well when he opened his eyes. He laid there staring at the ceiling for almost ten minutes, knowing he should be taking a shower and heading downstairs to the dining room to devour the breakfast his wife was fixing. Even the thought of placing the food in his mouth made him want to vomit. He tried rolling over for a few minutes, but his head hurt no matter what direction he moved it in. He soon found himself staring at the ceiling again.

Getting up slowly, he made his way to the bathroom for a look into the mirror to see if he looked anything like he felt. His birthday was in three days and he needed a vacation to anyplace away from home for a while. Forty-five was just around the corner and he felt like he was at least thirty years older. Flicking the switch, the light immediately filled the more than adequate bathroom. It was for some reason cooler this morning, but he suddenly realized it was because he had the chills. His reflection almost made him jump back. Just below his eyes, the skin was beginning to darken where deep wells had formed. His skin looked like the vampires he saw in all those horror films. There was redness inside his eyes, mostly at the bottom, and it looked as though blood would start to trickle down his cheek.

"What the hell did I do?" he whispered.

He'd have to call in this morning. They would just have to do without him. There was no way he'd get behind the wheel of a car feeling this bad. Dale began to have the shakes along with the chills, and the pain in his head was worsening. As he left the bathroom, he headed for the bedroom door and the stairway leading to the living room. Maybe some coffee would warm him up. An aspirin or two wouldn't be a bad idea either. At the middle of the staircase, he had to stop for a moment to keep from tumbling down the rest of the way. There was a slight creak in one of the steps and his wife came to the entrance way to the dining room.

"Dale? What's wrong?"

He was holding onto the railing and taking deep breaths. "I...I don't feel well. I'm going to have you call in for me. I don't feel like explaining myself to anyone. I just want some coffee...but no food. I don't think I could hold it down."

She quickly went and fetched him a cup of coffee and placed it at his usual seat. She then went into the living room and waited for him to descend the rest of the way. Another four or five steps found him holding onto the railing again.

"Here, let me help you down. Right after you have your coffee you'd better get back into bed. I'm going to call the doctor's office right after I call work."

He sat down with a dull thud and stared into the cup. The black coffee acted like a mirror, showing his eyes once again. They were skeletal like. His temples had sunk in even more in just that short a time. He raised the cup and put it to his dried lips. The coffee was sweet and strong. Stomach spasms nearly had him regurgitating it back into the cup.

"Helen?"

She turned to him quickly. "Dale, what's...?"

His body shook with the chills that once again overcame him. Helen looked down at his feet. On the floor a puddle had formed and the liquid dripping from the seat soaked his crotch and pajama legs.

"Oh my God! You've peed yourself!"

His work could wait, and the doctor's office could wait. She was on the cordless in a matter of seconds calling 911 for an ambulance. Dale Brant sat with his mouth open, staring at her with blood-red eyelids. The noises started soon after. Helen Brant felt like she was in some kind of exorcist movie. When she finally heard the sirens, it was only then that she breathed a sigh of relief. That was until her husband got up from the chair.

He grasped the back of his head and began to pull his hair out in massive clumps. He screamed as the back of his neck began to bleed. He screamed until he went limp and fell face forward onto the table.

CHAPTER 3

In the elevator, Marlene pressed five before turning to face Chris. As the door closed she pointed downward.

"We're going to five because this is where we keep the patients whom we believe to have mental issues. That would be the suicidal, the ones who hear voices, the schizophrenic type. We have rooms with padded walls, but in this man's case we really don't believe we need them. It doesn't seem like these people are out to hurt themselves, but may be a danger to others."

"I take it you mean because of the biting incident."

"Exactly. But as you'll see in this case, this guy just seems to run amok. He moves around the room and sort of growls. It's like he no longer has a will of his own. Animalistic if you will. We've put food in with him and he's yet to touch it. He's been in there long enough to be quite hungry, but won't even touch a slice of bread. He doesn't seem to want anything to do with normal eating habits."

Chris was smirking when the door opened. "Maybe he just doesn't like hospital food."

Marlene gave him a quick smile. "A stand up comic you're not."

A man Chris recognized as one of the doctors assigned to the CDC came walking up to them just before they entered the main corridor. "Doctor Peterson." He acknowledged Marlene with a smile and held out his hand to Chris. "Doctor Lee Fret. We met earlier at the last meeting. Glad to have you aboard, Agent Kearns."

"Chris," he corrected. "Chris is fine. We're all friends here. At least I hope we are."

Marlene jabbed her thumb at him. "He's trying like hell to be a comedian."

Lee Fret gave him a smile. "That suits me fine. Call me Lee."

Chris nodded as all three of them made their way down the main corridor. There were several people ogling a door to the left of one of the offices. Marlene stood next to the door and held out her hand.

"Here we are. It's not a pleasant view, Chris. This is something I wish we could identify as soon as possible. The sad thing is; this man has already expired."

Chris shook his head. "I don't get it," he said. Putting his face to the 18x18 inch window with a layer of chicken wire imbedded in the center, Chris looked like he missed the opening act of a play. "So where...?" He suddenly jumped back. Marlene and Lee Fret stood their ground since they had seen it all before. The occupant of the room jammed his face onto the glass before Chris could finish the sentence. His lips were curled back into a snarl and dark circles colored the deep wells below eyes that were brightly rimmed in red. The pupils were almost entirely opaque with just a hint of the iris showing.

"Holy shit!" Chris had a hard time taking his eyes away from this man. "Christ! What the hell do you call this?"

Marlene rested her palm against the door. "We don't have a name for his condition yet. This man's wife used to come and visit him a few times a week. He bit her. Well, I already told you the story, there's no sense repeating ourselves."

Chris wrote down the description of the man. His name was Farin Taska. He was thirty-five years old and had no children. His occupation was car salesman with an impressive record number of sales. He was designated an employee and seller of the month many times over. The man, according to what information the Secret Service and FBI had on him, was just about a genius.

"Genomics," Lee said.

"What's that?" Chris already had the pen poised and ready.

"Well, sequencing the human genome has already proved to be helpful in examining the role of genetic variation in a person's health and diseases throughout their life. It was mainly used for clinical diagnosis of, let's say, hereditary disorders. Now, it promises to provide new information regarding not only a person's lifestyle, but environmental health and the causes of disease. Family history is a barrier that crosses over to human genetics and can show us the effects of, well, shared genes, environments, and complex interactions."

Chris shook his head. "In other words, you're an egghead?"

Lee laughed. "Hey, I have a paper I wrote on it for Maryland University. I'll share it with you later on."

Taska stumbled around the room almost blindly. He would wander around slamming his hands into the padded walls before making his way back to the door once again. His teeth were now a brownish-yellow. His eyes were always set on Chris no matter which way he moved. It was as though the man gravitated to his body heat.

"So, what does this...gnome thing have to do with our friend here?" Chris asked.

Lee looked at Chris's notes and poked a finger on the paper. "Put an E between the G and the N and you have it. It's spelled g e n o m e. It just might be a way to crack the code of this disease. If that's what we're dealing with."

Chris scrunched up his face. "What? You think it might not be a disease. It might be something...well, maybe somebody put in the water supply?"

Marlene stepped up to the window. Taska was now staring out at her, drooling and slobbering all over the inside of the glass. When she placed her hand over the outside of the pane, Taska attempted to actually gnaw at her palm. His teeth and lips slammed against the glass, leaving a disgustingly white film to slide downward and out of sight.

Chris made a notation on his pad. "It's as though he wants to eat your hand."

Marlene nodded. "As of right now we're writing him up as clinically dead."

"I'm looking at a dead man?" Chris asked. "You mean as in *Night of the Living Dead*?"

Once again Marlene nodded. "A person that is clinically dead can actually be brought back to life. Drowning and electrical shock victims are prime examples. This is what CPR is all about, and what they do when using the defibrillator paddles. The person is actually clinically dead, but there still is brain function if action is taken immediately. With brain-dead individuals, they have no electrical activity in the brain or no evidence of any brain function. Our friend here has something that is keeping the brain alive." She shook her head and exhaled quickly. "We tend to think it's whatever attaches itself to the brain.

Chris walked to the middle of the corridor and turned to face Lee and Marlene.

"Do you know what the service will do to me if I put the word zombie in this report?" He walked back to the window and smacked the glass with the side of his fist. It didn't faze Taska in the least. "I believe that's what you're telling me, right? We *are* talking about zombies, right?"

Lee stood in front of the door and stared back at Taska. "He has no heartbeat, no respiration, no pulse whatsoever, but he's still moving around. That's the reason why we're calling it clinical death. Although, I think we can all agree that he's not going to come back from this. There's no way. His blood is totally coagulated and corrupted in his veins. As a matter of fact when he was put into this room he was starting to smell from decay."

One of the persons standing at Taska's room when they arrived handed Marlene a manila envelope. She removed its contents and looked over the information. Photos had been taken of each patient with special attention paid to Farin Taska. A compilation of tests and other information was carefully cataloged in the form of a spreadsheet.

Marlene held up the paperwork. "I'll see that you get copies of these, Chris. Anything else we come up with will be added to this and delivered to your office as well."

Before Chris could answer, Marlene's cell phone rang. "Peterson." She moved toward the center of the corridor. "When?" She listened for a moment and then placed her hand on her forehead. "What were his symptoms?" By this time Lee and Chris were standing there looking at her inquisitively. "This is not good. Somebody has to get to the police and form a search. This person is a danger not only to this entire community, but possibly to the entire state. He has to be found." She closed her phone and stared at Chris and Lee as though she saw a ghost.

"What's wrong?" Chris asked.

Marlene started walking down the corridor at a quick step. "A tractor-trailer ran a stop sign and hit one of our ambulances. They're bringing in one of the victims now, but the others didn't make it. The wreck site is a mess and the ambulance was completely destroyed and is now half way into the bay. But it gets worse."

Lee stepped closer to her. "Do I really want to hear the worst?"

Marlene stopped at the elevator. "The 911 dispatcher claims they were heading out to pick up a man who was face down on a table. The call came from a residence, a woman down at the beaches. She's dead, along with the two paramedics and the driver. The paramedic inside the vehicle's unit with the wife and the original patient is the one who's down in the emergency room."

"And?"

"The woman's husband, the man they were dispatched to pick up was displaying the very same symptoms as the woman who was bitten by Farin Taska. They can't find his body."

"Well, I'm sure they're going to form a grappling party, right?" Lee asked.

Chris volunteered the answer. "The Chesapeake Bay is pretty big, Lee. There's no telling where the hell he'll turn up."

CHAPTER 4

At the accident site on Beach Street, an officer was detouring drivers off to one of the side roads. Chris pulled the vehicle to the side and flashed his commission book at the deputy. Lee did the same, announcing they were with CDC, investigating the possibility of an infectious disease. The officer nodded and let them pass without commenting. The ambulance was still in the water with most of the tail end submerged. The driver's side was crushed beyond recognition. Two attendants were sliding a body bag in the back of the coroner's van with another one right behind.

The tractor-trailer was jackknifed with the box on its side resting partially on the road and partially in the cove. The tractor, farther up from where the ambulance was resting, was amazingly still upright, but with the rear wheels sticking out of the water. On the side of the cove was the usual gravy train of reporters talking to several police officials who were encircling a man engulfed in a blanket. Chris and Lee surmised it must have been the driver of the rig.

The cove was dotted with boats, some of them just looking down into the murky water; some of them dragging grappling hooks. Those grappling were emergency rescue boats from contiguous small towns. A contractor from a nearby town lent a hand by using its crane to eventually right the trailer and pull the tractor and ambulance from the water, each placed out of the way on the side of the road. By two that afternoon most of the debris was cleared from the road and the emergency personnel were gone. Chris and Lee examined the structural damage of the ambulance. The left side of the van's wall was crushed in far enough for it to touch the other side. In order to get to the bodies of Helen Brant, the dead paramedic, and the one critically injured, they had to cut a hole in the right side.

What was left of the inside was splattered with blood and debris from the bay. One of the officers on the scene suggested that the body of Dale Brant might have been wedged in the bent metal. The rescue team blow torched another hole but found nothing.

"This isn't good," Lee said.

"What's the worst that can happen?" Chris asked.

Lee walked to where a railing had been bent like a plastic straw. "If those afflicted with this... whatever the hell it is, can survive without oxygen or a heartbeat, then there's no telling what can happen. His body can wash up anywhere around here; the eastern shore for that matter, who knows. He's not going to drown, that's for damn sure. And if this guy ends up anything like Taska...holy Christ! He could infect the populace of this entire area. Maybe even beyond this entire area."

Chris looked up from taking notes. "What exactly does the press know?"

Lee let out an exasperated grunt. "The press? That's exactly what we need right now. They don't know anything with the exception that there was a fatal accident involving an ambulance and an eighteen-wheeler."

Chris motioned toward the water. "The tide was going out when we got here. So, he's probably in the main portion of the bay by now. Maybe the fish will take care of the problem for us." Chris squeezed his nose to stifle a laugh.

"What?" Lee shrugged. "What's so funny?"

"I was just thinking of a bluefish in the oven jumping around when someone tried to bake the damn thing." He looked at Lee and made a gesture with his hands to show he was trying to lighten the mood.

Lee wasn't laughing. "We need to do some experimenting when we get back to the medical center."

"Experimenting? On whom? Farin Taska?"

"Somebody," Lee said. "What you just said could bring extra innings into our little ballgame here. What if...I say, *what if* that's true. What if somebody eats a fish that was feeding on this guy? If this shit can be transmitted by consuming any food it happens to come in contact with, we have an even more serious problem on our hands. Right now we're only looking for one fucking guy."

Chris shook his head. "Lighten up, Lee! I was making...."

"I know, Chris." Lee pointed to the bay. "That's a food source to hundreds, thousands of people. If this shit turns out to be that contagious there's no telling how many people could become infected."

Chris made notes on the pad and gave Lee a more serious look. He shook the small pad in Lee's direction. "Hold the phone! I made notes in here earlier about these parasite things dying off once one of them reaches the brain. So, if they're dead, then there can't be any chance they could cause more problems. Look, I need to get some kind of a report back to my office. We need to get this shit straight long before I do that. I can probably stall for a few days, but they're going to want something soon."

Lee pointed toward the vehicle. "Okay, let's go have a chat with Marlene Peterson and see if we can get something started on this."

CHAPTER 5

Prior to the sixth day of Dale Brant's body not turning up, the CDC had already taken steps toward experimenting with laboratory rats. Small pieces of flesh were taken from several of the patients and fed to the animals in tiny portions. After the fifth day of no reports of a body being found, it appeared none of the animals showed signs of becoming ill. Still, no one's minds were put at total ease. The question that repeatedly crossed their mind was simple, but didn't come with a simple answer. If Farin Taska could bite his wife and cause her to become ill, why was it not possible in reverse?

Inside the Prince Frederick Library, Chris sat looking over the papers that Lee Fret promised to give him. Here, there were no phones ringing and very little disturbances. The photos that accompanied the paperwork he simply flipped over, opting for more of the written material instead. He read over the CDC's report on the lab rats several times over until he felt like his head was going to explode. Highlighted in yellow marker was the question of the month. If Farin Taska was a host to a parasite and all the other parasites were dead, why was it he could infect his wife with a bite, but not the reverse?

"The reverse." Chris looked around realizing he spoke the words aloud.

He needed a break and went over to the window to gaze out over the new shopping center. In his mind he saw his son shooting baskets at the church's gym. It was a complete blowout, with the sideline finally giving up on keeping score at all. There was no need to further embarrass the other team. They were only kids, but pride still found a place to occupy a child's heart. His daughter played as well, and both their final games turned out to be to *their* team's advantage.

The separation was a bit hard on both the kids and a bit harder when the divorce was finalized. He remembered the marriage counselor's words and how he wanted both he and his wife to look at, not only marriage, but life in general. It was a road, and at one time or another there were potholes, some deeper than others. You either navigated around them or you ended up on the side of the road looking for help. And sometimes you simply ran out of road.

The only heated discussion was when they finally got around to discussing jobs. An editor for a major publishing house often came home mentally tired and, at times, a bit grouchy. An agent for the United States Secret Service sometimes came home both physically and mentally tired. There were mandatory workouts and mandatory travel, often taking him away from home for more than thirty days at a time. The toughest part of the job meant packing up and selling a home. This was one thing Jennifer refused to do, leave the Washington, DC area to follow her husband. There was too much at risk, plus she had several best sellers on her list of authors. *Sometimes the road is one big pothole, and maybe this is where I actually run out of road*, he thought.

His cell phone vibrated and he quickly checked the number. It was Lee Fret.

"What's up?" he asked with the phone to his ear.

"Some kids found a body over in Deale. Severe neck wound. According to what the coroner was saying it looked an awful lot like a bite, but it also looked like the flesh had been partially devoured. Anyway, they got the guy over to the hospital to perform an autopsy and just as the mortician slices into the corpse, the guy ups and takes a bite out of his arm. Now the mortician is in the hospital. They're trying like hell to clean and dress the wound and bombard the guy with antibiotics."

Chris looked around to see who might be in earshot. Antibiotics were not going to do shit. The man was as good as...deadish?

"So, Brant's body must have turned up someplace in Deale. Who else is out there with this kind of shit?" Chris asked.

"No one is sure what the hell happened. The press is going to be all over this, and there's no way around it. I'm heading out there now and I think you should take a look yourself so you can see this first hand."

"What about the guy who bit the mortician? What the hell are they saying about a dead man who decides to bite somebody?"

"*This guy just walked out of the hospital completely naked. His chest had the beginnings of an autopsy opening and the guards at the main gate shot the bastard six or seven times a piece. Somebody walking around the streets naked shouldn't be too hard to find. It's the other one I'm worried about.*"

Chris listened carefully as Lee told him where he would be. He quickly packed his gear and headed for the parking area. He put his cell on ring tone, set it for speaker, and stuck it over the visor. Just out on Route 4, Keith Richards' electric guitar once again banged out *Brown Sugar*. He flipped it open on speaker.

Lee's voice filled the vehicle again.

"*Two kids claimed they saw a man come up out of the water and, get this, he had crabs hanging on him. They said it looked like he had on old soggy pajamas. The kids are with their parents at the Deale PD. It looks like our Mr. Brant has made an appearance after all.*"

"Yeah, I'm on my way, just passing the high school now. I should be there in about half an hour. I need to check in with headquarters and give them a briefing. I'll do that while driving out your way. Look, get what you can for me, will you? I need everything I can get on this."

"*Okay, see you there.*"

Chris decided to brief headquarters when he got to Deale. Putting the bubble on the dashboard, he made it there in twenty minutes. The area where the body was found had been cleared of anyone who was there earlier. Chris and Lee talked with the parents of the two children who might have seen the body of Dale Brant. According to the parents, it was on the small beach at the far side of the Harbor Yacht Club. After combing the area, it was found to be void of any clues of who it might have actually been.

Chris contacted headquarters and gave the SAIC a short briefing. Lee called the medical center at Breezy Point and spoke with Marlene Peterson. After speaking with her, he contacted his own agency and gave them whatever he had, which was nothing. The only substantial information they had to go on was a medical examiner with a gaping wound in his left forearm.

His story made even the two surgeons who happened to be in the area cringe in disgust. They still had nothing to go on in the way of transmitting the illness with the exception of being bitten by an actual host. Now there was another infected person somewhere in the area. How hard could it be to find a walking dead man who just happened to be totally naked?

CHAPTER 6

Rose Rasmussen, just shy of her seventy-seventh birthday, stroked her cat as she continued to watch the grisly scene unfold on the television. It was after ten o'clock. Tonight she decided she was going to lock up no matter how safe they said the neighborhood was. On the table to her left was a picture of her daughter, also named Rose. She worked as a tour guide at one of the local attractions, but for the life of her she could never recall where it was exactly; not that it mattered.

Just another part of getting old, she supposed.

"Neighborhood watches my ass. How much of the damned neighborhood can they see from their house? What are people going to do to one another next, Windsor?" she said to the cat as she made her way to the front of the house. "It's getting so I'm afraid to go out anymore. I'm glad you're an inside tabby. Next they'll be looking to bite animals instead of the other way around."

She turned the knob on the brass lock and sent the deadbolt through the double holes. It wasn't until she was halfway to the living room when she remembered there were clothes in the washer that needed drying.

"Oh, shoot! Damn it! Now I have to go downstairs and get the clothes into the dryer. I should have remembered and you were no help." She stroked the cat's ears as she playfully admonished the animal.

The basement door opened with a slight squeak. For a second or two she stared down into the darkness. For some strange reason the cat was having none of it. It leapt from her arms and bolted into the living room.

"Now what in blazes is wrong with you? You've been downstairs with me before. All right, stay up here and be finicky all you want. Two can play at that game, you know."

Flicking the light switch at the top of the stairs, she took hold of the railing, making sure both feet were on each step before taking another. Slowly and carefully, she descended into the semi-darkened room. The walls were made of cinder blocks and covered over with a thick coat of cement. The left side of the room alternated with a rapid display of light and dark as one set of fluorescent bulbs flickered on and off. She hated coming down here at night, but she also hated the thought of something going wrong with the washing machine and having water all over her floor upstairs. Her son told her this was unlikely to happen, but what did he know? He was no handyman like his dad was.

Looking around the room, melancholy thoughts of her husband crept into her mind. All his tools were still hanging over his now dusty and idle workbench. One day he'd converted half the basement into a makeshift workshop. He must have put hundreds of dollars into his tools and other odds and ends.

She thought back to the court proceedings and how she had stared at her husband's killer with utter contempt. It wasn't enough to steal a person's car; to take a person's wallet and his dignity along with it. But to shoot him, too. Not once, but several times, including once in the head, and then leave him lying on the side of the road like a dead animal; like road kill.

She quickly turned away and made her way to the dryer. That was three years ago and nothing was going to bring him back or change anything. She put the thought out of her head and went about the task of putting the wet clothes into the dryer. Pulling the lint collector from its cradle, she tossed the small bit that was there into a plastic pail. Something upstairs made a sound and she yelled up to the cat.

"Don't you go knocking my tea over! And don't come down here wanting to play either! You'll be playing by yourself!"

Once again there was a sound like something was bumped into. There was even a scraping sound as though whatever was bumped into slid across the floor. It seemed like it was much too heavy to be her cat, Windsor.

"Hello? Is anyone up there? I'll be right up in a minute if so."

Rose made her way toward the stairs and stopped for a second to listen. Who would just walk right in? Her old heart began to pump more frequently. It was then that she remembered the back door upstairs was still unlocked. It backed up to two and a half acres of wooded land. Rose grasped the front of her dress and clung to it for a moment. She was being foolish.

She could hear Windsor running from the kitchen to the living room. Rose passed the furnace and moved away from the railing. There was another sound she didn't recognize immediately. At seventy-six, her eyes and ears still hadn't failed her. Opening her mouth slightly, she stood her ground and listened carefully.

There it was again.

This time she recognized the rasping sound. It was the sound of someone trying to take a breath. It was also the sound of someone perhaps choking on something. It was now at the very top of the stairs.

"Who's there? I have a phone down here! I'm going to call the police! I also have a shotgun! My husband showed me how to use it!" she yelled.

Rose did have a phone in the basement, but not a shotgun. Her husband wasn't a hunter and loathed everything about it. She turned and made her way to the workbench where the phone was located. There was a loud moan from behind her and then the sound of someone stumbling on the stairs. Then there was the sound of someone falling down the stairs. Rose turned just as the nude body landed with a dull thud on the cement floor. She screamed, but at her age the vocal cords produced only a gravelly screech that sounded more like she was clearing her throat.

There was no dial tone. Rose banged the receiver on the bench and began to pray with all her soul. All the prayers she once learned in Sunday school came to mind. These were all the prayers on her knees in the pews and confessional booths. The prayers she said every Saturday afternoon as she confessed her sins. They weren't complete prayers, they were half this and half that.

"Oh, my God, I am heartily sorry."

Rose ran to the back door as the man rose from the floor. He was badly hurt but still able to stagger toward her. His arm was now twisted the wrong way, and his neck showed signs of something protruding from the side of his throat. Still he came towards her with his bare feet scraping and making dull thuds on the smooth concrete. The skin on his hairless chest was cut in a Y shape.

The lock on the basement door was old. It was of the old type that needed a key to open on either side. It was a lock that her husband meant to change years ago. It was a lock her son told her was extremely dangerous if the key could not be found and the only way out had to be the basement door. She looked at her attacker carefully before navigating around him and toward the workbench. The key was in a small drawer with the extra keys to all the other doors around the house.

He stopped for a moment, looking up toward the ceiling with an awkward motion of his head. There was something oozing from a gash on his scalp that would have been a terrible bleeder on any other person. His eyes were glazed over; his mouth open and dry. Any normal man would have been drooling all over himself. The television came to mind. A man was pulled from the water with a terrible wound on the side of his throat.

Rose pulled the drawer open and tried to clear the tears of fear from her eyes. There was now someone banging on the basement door. She turned to see a woman on the other side of the glass. Her print dress had what looked like a huge blotch of blood on the front. The woman looked crazed as though she escaped from some asylum.

Moving to the side, it was fairly easy getting around the naked madman and back to the stairs. Her only problem was the pair of legs standing in the center of the staircase; a pair of legs that looked like they were still in a pair of pajamas. Rose ran to the workbench and snatched up the first thing she could find to use as a weapon. The hatchet wasn't all that heavy, but the thought of actually having to use it made her want to vomit.

The woman in the bloody print dress had now broken through the glass in the door. Rose moved to the side and closer to the now shrieking woman, barely able to disguise her disgust at the sight. Shards of glass were now stuck in the woman's forearms and hands. There was blood, but only the coagulated kind that told a person that it was either old or had come from a body that was already dead.

The man in his pajama's was now rounding the staircase and following the racket that was going on behind him. Rose moved away from the door once again and positioned the hatchet over her head with both hands. The man in pajamas was now moving faster. She came down hard on the naked man's head. It made a horrible *cracking* sound as the skull split with the force and weight of the hatchet blade. He went to his knees, but once again regained what footing he still had and was soon standing and staggering, this time in circles, one way and then the other. Screaming, Rose made her way to the stairs and mounted them as fast as her old legs would carry her. Halfway up, she found herself looking into the eyes of her son.

"Oh, my God! Oh, my dear sweet Jesus. They're down in the basement. I think they somehow came back from the dead!"

Her breath was about to give out. Rose felt a pain in the left side of her shoulder. She reached her son with only five steps to go as he came down the steps to meet her. His eyes were strange. Something was terribly wrong with him. It was only after she grasped his arm that she found the torn flesh and the bone protruding.

Rose tried to scream, but half her face was now being bitten away. She lost her balance and drew her son backwards toward the cement floor. On the way down, her neck broke along with one of her arms and an ankle.

Her body was still warm as the walking dead helped themselves to what was left.

CHAPTER 7

Chris parked several houses down the street, keeping well away from the bystanders and emergency vehicles. As he approached the house, he found one of the paramedics leaning over the side of a fence and vomiting whatever it was she'd eaten for lunch. Police and other emergency vehicles were pulled up on the curb and lawn. Another paramedic came out for some air.

"It's the worst I've seen in my five years on the job," he said.

Chris looked at his pasty face, thankful there were people like this kid who were willing to do this kind of job.

"It's that bad, huh? Anything left?"

The paramedic nodded. "They have one bagged. Goddamned hatchet buried right in his head. Damnedest thing though."

"What's that?" Chris asked.

"The guy was naked. It looked like somebody had started an autopsy on him, too. His chest is all cut up." He drew an invisible line from each shoulder to the middle of his chest and then down.

Chris looked over to the female paramedic leaning on the fence. "She's had a busy day even if this is the first call she's been on. This kind of shit isn't pretty."

"I don't get it. What the hell is going on lately? People are killing one another all of a sudden. Now this crap. This guy," he pointed to the body bag coming out the door, "looks like he's been through a freakin' gang war."

"I have a feeling we're all gonna feel that way before this is over. Look, keep this under wraps will you? For right now the press doesn't know anything about whatever it is these people have. I know it's a hell of a story to keep to yourself, you know…a hatchet buried in a guy's skull. But until we know what we're dealing with here, I'd appreciate your cooperation."

The tech agreed and helped guide the stretcher down the front steps. "What do you mean by *what these people have*?"

"The hatchet?" Chris pointed to the bag, ignoring the question.

The tech nodded. "It's still there. Nobody touched anything, the police saw to that."

Doctor Marlene Peterson was coming up the walk as Chris turned to go inside. He pointed once again to the bag.

"We have one. Now we can get a chance at seeing what the hell's inside their heads," he said.

Marlene shook her head in disgust. "The fax came in from your headquarters. Everything is in a manila envelope. They ran checks on the address. The woman, Rose Rasmussen, lived alone. Her son, George, lived in Solomon's Estates, farther south and her daughter, named Rose also, lives the next town over. Her husband was killed on Suitland Parkway three years ago; a car jacking. The police went to the son's residence, but no one was home. They went to his place of employment and were told he hadn't showed up for work after the weekend, and they've been trying to call his home with no luck. The daughter isn't around either, but may have a boyfriend and is shacking up there most of the time."

Chris wrote down the information and looked up to see Marlene staring at him and shaking her head.

"You were a nerd in school, weren't you?" she asked. "You were the one who always kept the meticulous notes, brought home your books even though you didn't even have any homework. Am I right?"

Despite the situation, Chris couldn't help but smile.

"I'm used to running along side limos and staying no more than a few feet behind a protectee. You see, this type of duty is just perfect for making me look like the intellectual type," he said.

Marlene once again shook her head. "I hate to tell you, but it shows."

Chris put the notebook back in his pocket. "The circle seems to be getting bigger. We definitely have a serious problem. Was George Rasmussen a patient of yours? Or do you know who his physician was? We need to get blood samples from the police and see if we can match anything up. Anyone who's missing is suspect in having this condition."

Marlene walked to the front door and turned. "I can get the blood samples from the police and probably without any paperwork. I don't know who Rasmussen's doctor is, but that shouldn't be hard to find out either. If he had any surgeries in the past or saw some kind of specialist, we can check the records at the center. I'll check with Solomon's. We can match what we get here with what is on record at my center, and anywhere else. So, if what you say is right, Rose Rasmussen is gone, her son is nowhere to be found, and I feel more like a cop than I do a doctor."

Chris shrugged. "It's not too late to change careers. The service can use doctors. You'd get, let's see, at least twenty-two years in. That would make you...fifty."

"No thanks!" She cut him short and turned back around. "I'm sworn to save people's lives, Agent Kearns, not shoot them." She yelled to the paramedics as they lifted the stretcher onto the back of the vehicle. "Don't let anyone touch that until I get back."

"All right, Doctor Peterson," one of them acknowledged. He made a motion as though he was jabbing something into his head.

Entering the house and reaching the door leading to the basement, Chris looked down at the top of the basement steps. There was a smear of blood on the wall, and what looked like smudged footprints coming back up the steps. Down at the bottom, it looked as though a crazed tiger had found an easy meal. The blood had already coagulated, and pieces of flesh were found all along the cement floor. The window at the back door was broken with bits of skin mingled in with the blood and glass. Sharp triangular shaped fragments of glass were still wedged in the frame.

Chris used a piece of cloth to pick up the phone receiver. The coiled cord swung back and forth where it had become unattached from the wall unit.

"It looks like somebody was trying to make a call. If you were as scared as whoever it was these things were after, would you have noticed the cord had come loose?"

Marlene made a face that showed doubt. "Maybe it was Rose and she pulled it off the phone with all the excitement. And you mentioned *these things*. Are you saying you *think* there was more than one?" She thought for a moment. "You're right. The man with the hatchet in his skull was still here, but somebody went up the stairs. The footprints were kind of smudged, so I take it there could have been two or more of them."

Chris was opening the dryer as Marlene finished speaking.

"You're getting more and more like a cop every minute," he joked. "I believe there was more than one. It's my guess there was one at the back door and two that came down the stairs. There must have been a damn good reason why she didn't go up the stairs to safety and I think it was because the stairs were blocked."

As Chris walked slowly around the rest of the basement, Marlene spoke with several of the fingerprint people from the sheriff's department. They agreed to get extra samples and turn them over to *her* only. When they were finished, Chris and Marlene were the only two people left in the basement.

Chris' cell phone played its familiar tune. "Kearns."

Marlene stood next to him to openly eavesdrop. Chris held a finger up to avoid a question. "I got it. You'll make me copies as well? Good. Thanks, Lee."

"Good or bad?" she asked.

"They found Rasmussen's car over at Willows Grove. Evidently he was screw...."

Marlene raised an eyebrow.

"He was...seeing someone over there," he corrected. "The woman he was seeing hasn't come back home either. According to the post office, no one has picked up the mail or the paper in about four days. Her car is still in the driveway along with Rasmussen's."

Then it was Marlene's turn to have her cell phone ring.

"Doctor Peterson here. Light? Are you absolutely sure that's it? Right. Well, that explains why they're so aggressive during the daylight hours and in well lit rooms. Their pupils are perpetually dilated. Agent Kerns and I will be back in a short while."

"Good news?" he inquired.

"Maybe. It seems they're sensitive to light in a big way. Think about it. These people are missing and no one's seen them. Where the hell do they go? It's got to be someplace where there is very little light. Someplace where there is also very little people traffic."

"That could be a lot of places around here, Marlene."

"Name one."

Chris thought for a moment. "How about the cliffs just below Willows Grove. There's old caves down there and...."

Marlene held up her hand. "Do you know how many patients I see who come to me with abrasions and cuts from being in those caves? No, they would have been found by now if they were there. Mostly, it's kids looking for Indian relics and shark teeth."

Chris tilted his head to one side. "A long journey begins with a single step. We have a lot of stepping to do...Doctor."

CHAPTER 8

Chris was used to forensics being the types of ink and paper used in counterfeit cases by his own agency's Forensic Services Division. Walking through the doors of the medical center with a cup of strong coffee, he prepared himself for viewing the inside of a human being along with anything else that would fall under the totally unexpected. The elevator doors slid open and he took a deep breath before making his way toward the doors marked **Medical Examiner**.

He figured Marlene Peterson saw him get off the elevator, since she suddenly came pushing through the double doors with a look of surprise on her face.

"I thought you'd pass on this one. No offense, but I've been stood up a few times on these things. Believe me, if you did the same I would have totally understood why."

Chris took another sip of coffee and another deep breath. "None taken. I'm used to inks and hundred dollar bills under magnification. Did I miss anything worth missing?"

Marlene gave him a short smile. "We spared you all the graphics to the inner chambers of the human body. In short, yes, you did. We left the skull open so you could have a look at exactly what's getting inside these people's heads."

Chris raised one corner of his top lip.

"Oh, come on. You're a big boy now."

Chris nodded. "Yeah, my mother used to tell me that when I was a little kid in the tub. I thought I'd go down the drain with the dirty water."

They made their way through the double doors and to the back of the room. The examiner working on the body looked up and gave him a nod. Marlene pointed out to the examiner that Chris was a newbie at this sort of thing. Chris could almost see him give a wicked grin under the mask.

"Chris, this is Doctor Lawrence Lenihan. He's filling in for the medical examiner who got the bite," Marlene said.

"How is that guy by the way?" Chris asked.

"Sick. Just like the others. Larry, this is Special Agent Chris Kearns with the Secret Service. He's working with the CDC as a temp."

Lenihan once again nodded to Chris and placed his fingers on the sheet.

"Okay, let's see what's behind curtain number three, Monty."

Marlene shook her head. "Funny, Larry."

Chris was now looking at a human face that had been pulled down over the front of the skull from a surgical incision just above the back of the neck. The crown had been sawed away, leaving the brain completely exposed and lying on a stainless steel tray. On the top of the organ was a creature that looked like an oversized grub. The thing's head was severed from what Chris figured was due to the hatchet.

"Christ!" Chris gasped.

Lenihan shook his head. "This is something he had nothing to do with. I counted fifteen of these strange looking tentacles." Lenihan used a long pair of tweezers to lift one of them. "As far as I can tell, they all seem to control something on both sides of the brain. Let's start with the sensitivity to light in all these people. When light rays pass through your pupil, the iris makes the size of the pupil change depending on the amount of light that's passing through. If you look at your eyes in a mirror you'll see your pupil shrink to limit the number of light rays that enter. In reverse, if there is very little light to pass through the pupil, it will enlarge to let in more light."

"Sort of like a camera then," Chris said.

"Exactly," Lenihan said. "It's the same principle as the camera. The f-stop is the pupil for the lens on the camera. Just behind the pupil is the lens. This lens focuses the image through a jelly-like substance called the vitreous humor, projecting it to the back of the eye to the retina."

Marlene held up her hand for a second. "So, the pupils in all these afflicted individuals aren't working. Is that what causes the sensitivity?"

"So, then this...whatever the hell it is, is not really controlling the body very effectively," Chris added.

Lenihan shrugged slightly. "Let me try to explain it as in a college lecture. The retina, which is the size of the thumbnail, has about 150 million light-sensitive cells. These cells are known to scientists and doctors as rods and cones. The rods identify shapes and they work in dim light. Cones on the other hand, identify color and work in bright light. They both send information to the brain by way of the optic nerve." Lenihan touched the area with the elongated tweezers. "The amazing thing is that they send the image to the brain upside down instead of the way we actually see things. The brain turns the image right side up and then gives you a show and tell of what you are looking at."

Marlene looked at Chris. "You're not taking notes."

"I only let someone make fun of me once," he said, glancing at her.

"So, these people have no use for the cones? The only thing that's working in the eyes are the rods?" Marlene asked.

Lenihan held up a bloody rubber glove. "In short, these people suffer from what is known to ophthalmologists as photophobia. It's usually accompanied by other underlying health problems. This parasite is controlling certain parts of the body, but as the agent pointed out a moment ago, not very effectively. One thing it is doing well in is the hunger department. I checked on the blood samples that we were given. There's an inordinate amount of a protein called leptin, which controls the appetite. As long as there's living people in the world these people will never run out of a food supply. Where the food goes a day or so after consumption, I have no idea. There is no digestive system. What they swallow just decomposes right along with their own bodies in the natural manner."

"Am I right to assume that if one of these people gets shot in the head and, that thing is hit just like I see there, then we can actually stop one of these things?" Chris asked.

Lenihan scrunched up his mouth. "Maybe George Romero actually knew something we didn't. To answer your question, yes. This thing is dead. Kill the parasite and the body dies along with it."

Chris crossed his arms and grunted. "The sad and ironic thing about the Rasmussen woman is that she actually aided us in determining the way we can truly kill these things. Do you have photos of all this?"

"Everything will be in your manila folder," Marlene said.

"Hungry?" Chris asked her.

Marlene gave him a surprised look. "You're actually hungry after this?"

Chris turned to Lenihan. "Doctor Lenihan, thanks for the briefing and the excellent show and tell. I have one question before I leave. It's probably not something you could actually answer with one hundred percent accuracy, but here goes. Would people who are stricken with this problem look for a dark place during the daylight hours?"

Lenihan tilted his head to one side. "On a cloudy day I would venture to say they'd be more comfortable outside. During full sunlight, yes. I believe and, this is only something I can only infer, but I believe that direct sunlight could actually bring harm to our parasite friend here." Lenihan pointed to a dark spot on the dead creature. "I would say this one got hit with halogen lights. A car maybe."

Chris nodded. "That's good enough to go on right now. Thanks again."

"Well, I know a great place for salads and sandwiches," Marlene suggested.

"Good," Chris agreed. "But, please, no Italian food. Red sauce wouldn't be my thing right now."

CHAPTER 9

Behind his desk at the Secret Service's Intelligence Division, Special Agent in Charge Aidon Richards leaned back in his chair while listening to the voice of the Homeland Security Director tear him a new asshole. He tried to keep his cool. Although it made sense to have different agencies in on whatever was happening, it was infuriating to have certain people believing they could just take over or give orders. Tempers were flaring out in the field and it was less than a pretty scene in some places.

Customs, the FBI, and now the Department of Natural Resources had personnel in the field who were tossing orders like Frisbees. Right now, the Director of Homeland Security wanted answers, and Richards had none. What he had was a fax from one of his agents working with the CDC, and right now it didn't really shed much light on the situation. No one had any idea about what the hell was happening out there, or what the hell was to be done about it.

Richards highlighted the word *parasite* and waited for a break in the phone conversation that never came. As of yet there was no way to explain where the creatures came from and how they ultimately attached themselves to the human brain. There was no evidence of foul play, and that pissed the DHS off more than anything.

They had to have someone, anyone, to pin this on. They needed anything to take the pressure off the U.S., its officials at high ranking offices, and, most of all, the current administration at the White House. Richards knew that eventually someone would be the fall person. There was always a fall person for situations that weren't quickly snuffed out.

Dead people walking had to be put on the back burner. It didn't make much difference to those who came in contact with the parasite. They weren't coming back to the world of the living. They were for all intents and purposes...dead. This was something DHS didn't particularly want to hear. The term they used was ludicrous. It was ludicrous to believe that the dead could come back to life and feed on the living. These people were simply debilitated and nothing more. It wasn't made reality until the pictures of the naked man sporting a hatchet in his skull were faxed to the department's front office. Now, that had them singing a different tune.

Richards hung up the phone with as much pleasantry as he could muster up. He hated cliques and the fucking buddy-buddy system. Some people clawed and scraped their way to the top in their careers, while others played the, *not what you know, but whom.* It was only getting close to retirement that kept him from blowing his top.

He had an office meeting scheduled to get things out in the open, and there were several visits coming up for foreign diplomats. The Dignitary Protective Division was pressed for answers on the where and the hows of this outbreak. It had to be controlled and fast. Richards didn't have the answers and very little suggestions.

Chris Kearns made sure he arrived earlier than most of the other agents, since he had requested Marlene and Lee to be present to help explain the more technical aspects of any questions they had.

Protective details were discussed prior to the two guests taking a seat. When everything involving protection was over, Richards made room for Marlene and Lee to the right of where he sat.

"I'd like to welcome Doctor Marlene Peterson of the Medical Center out of Breezy Point, and Doctor Lee Fret of the Center for Disease Control in DC. They're going to try to explain what's going on with this virus or whatever disease we have going on here, and I'd like you to give them your full attention," Richards said.

Lee Fret was the first to stand and address the group. "Thank you, Agent Richards, and hello to all. I'm afraid we don't have much to go on and I can certainly understand any frustrations felt by anyone who may be involved with this situation. The most recent discovery we've made is that of an unknown parasite...." Lee shook his head and looked down at Marlene briefly. "I don't have any other term for it, but if you'd all be so kind as to look at the photos that are being passed around, you will get a good idea of what we're actually talking about. I'm afraid they aren't very pleasant, but it will give you a better chance to use less of your imagination and to actually see what we're up against."

Several of the agents made faces and passed the photos on quickly. Others stared in disbelief. Several hands went up but were waved off by Richards who told them they would have time for questions when the briefing was over.

Lee continued. "This...parasite, attacks the brain and we believe it actually controls, to a certain extent, motor functions like sight, sound, movement, and speech, which are simply grunts and groans as far as we know. These are all controlled by those small tentacles extending from the upper part of the creature's body. The human body affected by this parasite has no blood pressure, no pulse or heartbeat, no respiration, yet they function as though they were persons suffering from severe mental disorders. These individuals are dangerous to anyone they may come in contact with, in that they will attempt to bite and even devour flesh, thus leaving the victim of such an attack a prime candidate to become one of them." Lee relinquished the floor by nodding to Marlene.

"Thank you Doctor Fret." Marlene nervously cleared her throat and looked around at the faces staring at her from around the table. "I never thought I would be nervous in front of a group, but I guess that shows I'm still on the same level as everyone else." She waited until the quiet round of laughter died down. "The man in the photographs was found with a hatchet buried in his skull. It appears that someone was attempting to fend off this individual before succumbing to the attack. I don't know if you noticed, but in one of the photographs you can clearly see where the creature's front part of the body was severed by the blade. This we believe is what actually caused the body to lose those motor functions and therefore leave it incapacitated." She gestured to the photos.

"We also gave you photos of an accident that took place on the other side of the twin beaches," she continued. "The ambulance you saw in the photos was carrying a man we believe came in contact with one of these parasites. That man, Dale Brant, is missing. His wife was killed in the accident, but where his body went to we have no idea. We do believe he is wandering around somewhere very sick and very dangerous. As mentioned in the report, you will all have a chance to read later, we have no idea as of yet where this parasite comes from and, if not indigenous to the United States, how it got into this country. If there are any questions we can try to answer them as best we can."

One agent in the back raised his hand first. "Are we actually talking about the walking dead here?"

Lee once again gave the floor to Marlene. "I know this sounds incredible and, for lack of a better word...preposterous, but I would have to say yes. These individuals are clinically dead. They lack the vital signs of life and have no mind or will of their own."

An agent beside Lee Fret raised his hand. "We're taught to look for individuals who are the nervous type. That would be those who move around frequently or suspiciously. Then there are others who hold their ground in a crowd no matter how much the crowd moves around them. We look for people who tend to have some sort of strange expressions on their faces; scowls, strange or stupefied smiles. What are we looking out for with these individuals?"

Lee stood up this time. "They tend to look pale in color; grayish type skin. They actually look like a corpse. The skin under their eyes is discolored. They move as though they are suffering from a degenerative disease. I can tell you they would probably be very easily spotted, especially in a crowd. That meaning, they would probably attack anyone close by."

One of the agents held up a photograph. "Doctor Peterson, you mentioned in this photograph that you believe the body actually became incapacitated because the... whatever this thing is, was damaged by the hatchet blade. So, can we assume that a bullet in the brain would put one of these individuals down? Are we actually talking about zombies here? I don't mean to sound condescending here, but this is like something I saw a few years ago in a horror movie."

This time Chris chimed in. "*Night of the Living Dead*, George Romero, 1968. Then there was a remake in the late nineties directed by Tom Savini." Chris ran a hand over his mouth and chin. "I saved this for last and I think this will answer your questions about their looks and movements."

He produced a DVD made by one of the service's camcorders and looked at Richards, who nodded and directed everyone's attention to the TV screen. Chris placed the disc into the reader and picked up the remote. When the screen came to life, Farin Taska's face was pressed up against the window of his holding room. At another angle, a camera inside the room recorded his movements around the enclosure. He staggered and twisted his body in several different directions as he made his way around the room, often smacking the walls with an open hand before coming back to the window. Taska's face and complexion left nothing to the imagination.

Taska was a dead man walking.

CHAPTER 10

After taking a call from his office, Lee Fret went back to the city for a few days. He called Chris several times and gave him the rundown involving the talk on the street. It appeared someone was volunteering information or answering questions that should have been kept under wraps. Washington was now buzzing with talk of the return of some type of plague. The CDC knew it was getting close to the time for coming clean. Someone would have to take to the podium and explain what the hell was happening.

Really happening!

Chris closed his cell phone and sipped his coffee, watching Marlene spill a half of a pouch of sweetener into her cup.

"So, are you married? I never hear you talk about a husband or family," he asked.

Marlene smiled. "I was wondering when that question was going to come up. It always does with people I meet and do business with for more than a few days. That is, the ones I'm not seeing as patients. No, I'm not married. Never have been, and not looking right now either. Why do you ask?"

The waitress brought them their breakfast and refilled their cups.

"Hello, Doctor Peterson. I never see you here. I thought doctors went to the big fancy restaurants." The waitress smiled as she said this.

Marlene laughed. "It's the company I keep."

"Ouch!" Chris placed a hand over his chest.

"Well, if there's anything else I can do, please let me know. It's good to see you."

Chris smiled. "So, you're well known in the community, I see."

Marlene placed her cup down, turning it right and left a few times. It was something to do while she decided on how to ask her own question.

"How about you? I haven't heard anything about your marital status."

Chris looked out the window. "It's not worth repeating."

"Ah! I hit a nerve and I'm sorry. Let's drop the companionship chatter and enjoy our meal, shall we?"

He could see Marlene's reflection in the window and all of a sudden felt like a damned heel.

"I have two kids, a boy and a girl." He shook his head. "It just didn't work out. We tried to do what's right, but nothing seemed to fit. My job is very demanding and entails a lot of travel and long periods of time away from home. I'd be coming home and she'd be just leaving. Sometimes it was the other way around, but mostly me coming home in the middle of the night or the wee hours of the morning. We tried not to air our differences in front of the kids, but given the time and place of both our jobs, well, it just happened a few times too often. We felt it was best for the kids if we separated for a while. Then the separation became, I guess...just the thing. Fit like a damn glove. The divorce papers were signed and we went our own way."

Marlene pushed a piece of ham on her plate with a fork.

"I'm sorry, Chris. Do you see the kids very often?"

Chris nodded. "I had them every other weekend. Then this came up and the whole fucking vicious circle started all over again."

Marlene sat tongue in cheek for a moment.

"I'm sorry, Marlene." His big hand grasped her thumb and shook it softly. "I do see them and we have joint custody. It's just...."

"Enough! I understand. I was almost engaged once."

Chris bit off a piece of sausage. "From around here? Washington?"

Marlene shook her head. "New York. We would set up dates to see one another when the time was right. He worked out of a medical center in Melville. He left and went into his own family practice. From there he went into the specialist field. It was a very platonic relationship that we both decided to agree on for a while. He had it all on the ball. He was a good man, a very good doctor, and a great lover. At least that's what I was told."

Chris swallowed what remained of his toast. "You were told? You actually mean you...."

Marlene's eyes seemed to mist over. "We were going to go away together. We planned a trip to Italy over the Christmas holiday. Then one day I received a letter from a woman who claimed to be his fiancée. How she got my address I have no idea. Come to find out she was actually a stalker and was harassing him for a time, either on the phone or going to his office several times a week until he had a cease and desist order put out on her. He told me she was a part of his life at one time, but broke it off when one day she suddenly appeared at his office totally irrational. Luckily it was before anyone actually got there for their appointments. I never saw him again."

"You broke it off?" Chris could now see tears in her eyes.

"No, Chris. Terrorists did. You see, his office was just on the other side of the World Trade Center."

Chris grabbed both her hands in his. "You're a pretty damn nice lady even after all that. I think so anyway. Anyone else might have it in for society in general. I've seen grief turn into nastiness before."

"It's not the world's fault. There's just too damned much unhappiness. If people would only look around and see what they have going for them. Sure, there's sickness and death all around us, but no one wants to take the time to smell the roses anymore. Everything and everyone seems to gravitate towards the almighty dollar. It's a power play for people who are in high places and intend to stay there no matter what the cost to anyone else."

Chris started to say something but was interrupted by the waitress turning up the volume on the television.

"I'm standing here in front of the home owned by Mrs. Rose Rasmussen, a seventy-six year old woman who has been missing for several days. Area police are putting together information pertaining to what looks like a massacre in the basement of this small Cape Cod style home. Neighbors say they saw what looked like a body being removed and paramedics who looked to be physically ill over what they may have seen."

The reporter put the microphone in front of a woman who was standing next to her. *"Did you know Mrs. Rasmussen?"*

"Oh, heavens yes. We would talk sometimes for hours. She was great company. I hope everything is all right. I don't understand how she could be missing. She really never went anyplace on her own."

The reporter nodded. *"Were you in the area when the police came?"*

The woman nodded quickly. *"Well, I heard sirens and didn't think anything of it. You know, you hear things like that all the time. Then when they got closer, I told my husband that they were coming here. Sure enough, they pull onto the lawn and over the curb. I saw one man in a dark suit park down the road there, and he came up and talked to one of the doctors from the medical center. I don't know what that was all...."*

The reporter interrupted. *"Which doctor?"*

"That would be Doctor Peterson. They talked for a bit and then both she and the man in the suit went inside. I remember they were the last to come out, too. My cousin is a paramedic and he said it was a mess down in that basement. He said it looked like there was some kind of mob hit or something. Said there was blood everywhere and that one man they found dead had a hatchet in his head. I hope nothing happened to Rose. I don't have a good feeling about it though. I don't have a good feeling anymore about this neighborhood either."

The reporter turned back to face the screen. *"Betsy Crowder for Eyewitness News."*

Chris turned back to Marlene and found her looking directly at him.

"You're a man in a suit, whereas I was named. I don't think that's good," she said.

"Damn it! I hate when somebody tells me they're not going to do something and then they turn around and do just the opposite."

Marlene wiped at her lips with the napkin. "Well, they don't have anything to go on yet, but I'm sure with the buzz in DC, the CDC will be scrambling to come up with some quick explanation."

"Let's go for a boat ride."

Marlene looked stricken for a second. "Excuse me!"

"A...boat...ride. I have a friend who wants to get his boat all geared up for fishing season. He charters. We'll take a cruise around the Chesapeake Bay. It's not a date. Call it professional relaxation."

Marlene grinned. "Agent Kearns, I...."

"Chris."

"Chris, I have patients and work to attend to. And you have, well, whatever it is an agent attends to. I just can't...."

"Bullshit. You can get someone to fill in for you for a few hours. Doctors do that kind of thing all the time. A few holes at The Shields, a few casts of the fly rod. Look, I promise I won't be a typical male. No hitting up on the good doctor. Deal?"

She drew a deep breath and let it out slowly. "All right. But just for a few hours."

"Good. Go get straight with the office and I'll meet you at the Waterfront Hotel's dock in about an hour."

CHAPTER 11

In the parking lot of the Waterfront Hotel, an older man sat and watched Marlene and Chris as they waited for the captain of the Yankee Dollar to make preparations for getting underway. He watched them climb onto the boat. The Secret Service agent and the two doctors were getting closer to what was happening, but they were still too far away for the CDC to actually call their findings fact.

As the boat pulled out of the slip, he sat for almost ten minutes watching the craft get smaller and smaller as it moved farther away from land. Although it was overcast, the bay was dotted with trawlers and pleasure boats, most of them probably fishing since they either sat dead in the water or were moving at trolling speeds. He thought about the many fish in the bay and the many tiny parasites that may now inhabit the waters. The parasite laid dormant in fish, but not in warm blooded animals.

If they could find him, an autopsy of the missing Dale Brant would show that he had more than likely eaten some kind of seafood. It would've been something that was cold blooded. Once again, it wasn't cemented in stone that this was true. More experiments were necessary.

He drove through the parking lot and out onto the main street of Twin Beaches. He took a right this time and made his way toward the outskirts of town, driving until he passed a small town called Friendly. There, he took another right that would take him to the dirt road that followed a cove to Old Solomon's Creek, a quarter mile from Route 2. It was entirely secluded. A place where the government had small cabins built for his research. On the property was a great pond filled with various species of fish. His library was filled with many video cassettes and DVD's regarding bass fishing, lure tying, and every other thing there was to know about the sport. It was his most fond desire at times to go out on the pond and practice catch and release. This was especially true with the bass.

Clicking the imbedded remote attached to the vehicle's roof, the gate opened inward and he pulled his vehicle between two of the cabins. One was his library and living quarters, while the other was his garage. In the back and standing alone, was his research lab. It started out as a very plausible enterprise that had the Pentagon buzzing with promising words of riches and fame for his research. It would be the next best thing to having cyborgs posing as humans in wars that required fighting in the most dangerous of battle zones. What enemy was actually shooting for the head?

He walked slowly toward the pond. Standing at the edge of the water, he could see his reflection staring up at him. How long would it take the military and the politicians looking to cover their own asses to point fingers his way? The smile that was once on his face was now replaced with doubt and regret. Even his hair seemed to have turned to salt and pepper almost overnight. Every so often he thought he saw the fish in question. The Grand Poobah of them all. In his mind he could still remember his recorded notes.

The fish was none other than the Spotted Rosesnapper. Upon purchasing a Red Snapper at a local fish market, he found something odd inside the fish's mouth. It turned out to be a distant relative of the human head louse, the Cymothoa Exigua, a parasitic crustacean of the family Cymothoidae. This parasite, he found, attaches itself at the base of the fish's tongue with the claws on its front legs while it extracts blood from the tongue. As the parasite grows, less and less blood is delivered to the tongue. The fish goes on about its business unharmed and seemingly unaware.

Eventually the organ atrophies from the lack of blood and the parasite replaces the fish's tongue with its own body. It does this by attaching itself to the stub. The fish is actually able to use the parasite as though it had its own tongue. The only drawback was that the fish now had to share its food with the creature.

Several years of research went into his program. Several years of attempting to morph the parasite into something that would replace those soldiers who were severely wounded in battle. A parasite that would think the brain was nothing more than a human tongue. It was in the fall of '06 that he accidentally fed a fish to one of his cats. Although the cat appeared to be ill, it managed to take care of itself rather than wait for its master to feed it. He kept the cat under constant surveillance for several months. It was again by accident that he found the cat would not die. This he found out by chasing kids away from his fence who were hunting in the nearby woods. He had it posted as big as life. **No Hunting or Fishing. Private Property, No Trespassing**.

They shot his cat out of a tree. The animal tumbled through the air like a rag doll and landed with an almost silent thud. In a matter of seconds it regained its footing and ran to the main cabin. The next afternoon he actually saw the cat attack a medium sized dog just beyond the fenced in area. Within a week the dog appeared at his doorstep. It was the most god-awful being he had ever laid eyes on. The animal had been shot with an arrow that protruded from its side. He finished it off when it attacked his door with a fury straight out of Hell. One shot to the head and it fell to the ground in silence. The dormant parasite in the cold blood of the fish was activated by the warm blood of a mammal. This he put in his notes, and made a mental note to experiment more on the subject.

His research was brought to the table of several high ranking Pentagon officials. Once again, he went through the motions of producing a snapper with the parasite within its circulatory system. Once again he fed the fish to a different cat. Several days later the cat displayed signs of being ill, however, it quickly regained its strength, but with a lust for blood that seemed insatiable.

It was only weeks later that things began to go terribly wrong. One of the assistants assigned to the project was bitten by the cat while not wearing protective gear. By surveying the animal carefully during feeding time, it was a proven fact that it refused to eat regular food and was fed either raw fish or meat with certain amounts of blood still intact. The assistant said nothing and went on about his business. Over a weekend he became ill and had his wife call in sick for him. The government became inquisitive and asked about the type of symptoms he was having. After the fourth day of no other phone calls from the man, he went out to check on his assistant with a security detail at the military's orders.

The couple lived in a remote area of Northern Maryland and, by the time they arrived at the residence, the husband and wife were gone. Upon entering the home, they found several pools of blood on the floor and coppery stained handprints on the walls. The trail of blood led to the master bedroom where they found the unmade bed soaked with dry blood. Only one of them was ever found. His name was Ike Surry and his last known whereabouts was once again on an autopsy table at the Breezy Point Medical Center with a hatchet buried in his head.

Sitting in his study at the research lab, he picked up his credentials and couldn't help but laugh at himself. He poured himself a generous snifter of brandy and sipped at it while still staring at his image encased in thick plastic. The words **MILITARY OPERATIONS DIVISION** were sprawled across the top, with an impressive shield handsomely sitting next to his relaxed but serious facial expression. Once again he poured himself a drink. This time he put it to his lips and quickly turned the glass upside down. Opening a drawer in the desk, he reached in and pulled out the gun he kept fully loaded in case of emergencies. He poured another half glass of brandy and studied the weapon as he sipped the drink. Scientists worked with animals that were caged. If that scientist fucked up and didn't want to end up like the animals in the cages, well....

He abandoned the thought and pressed the release at the upper left side of the grip, letting the clip slide onto the desk top.

He lifted each bullet out of the clip and stood them up in a straight line. Maybe each of them had a name on it. He sipped his drink and started giving them names, smiling and laughing under his breath. He knew they were already whispering to one another in great detail about F U B A R. That was it, wasn't it? Fucked Up Beyond All Recognition.

Next he went to the safe and pulled out the notes on all the experiments ever done on this particular project. He brought them back to the desk and sat down. If he burned them then they had nothing. They had no one to point fingers at, and no one could point fingers at them as well. He slowly walked back to the safe and threw the binder carelessly into one of the compartments, pushing the door closed and not bothering to spin the tumblers to relock the safe's drawer. Something made a noise. Looking behind him before turning all the way around, he made his way back to the desk and reloaded the weapon. His fingers were fighting to find coordination with his brain, and several bullets fell back onto the desk.

There was a noise from the front of the cabin. He couldn't remember if he locked the door upon entering, but the sound of the front door slamming against the wall gave him his answer. Lightheadedness had drifted in now. The brandy was doing its job even though it would only be on a temporary basis. He weaved slightly in the chair as he pushed the rest of the bullets back into the clip and slid it into the weapons grip.

Wandering out in the main area on slightly unsteady legs, he stopped just after passing through the door and let his eyes scan whatever part of the room he could actually see. The blinds were opened enough for him to see that the sun was still being filtered through grayish clouds. Another noise had him snapping his head to the left of the room. A clinking of glass and a thump coming from the adjoining area had him moving carefully to the center of the room. He called out, but there was silence and nothing more.

He closed the main door and locked only the deadbolt. As he turned and mustered up the courage the brandy had instilled in his psyche, he came face to face with his visitor. Even as a scientist he was not prepared for what the parasite could do to a dead body. The woman's eyes were glazed over and staring. Her mouth formed a war cry displaying brownish teeth, blood-red gums, and a grayish discoloring under her eyes. Her whole being was ghoulish in nature. An abomination as to what God had intended life and death to be. As she rushed forward, her groans and growls sent nightmarish chills through his entire body. He raised the weapon to take a bead on her forehead and cursed her lifeless soul. He cursed himself for ever entertaining such thoughts as he squeezed the trigger.

The gun refused to fire because there was no bullet in the chamber. She was on him and pushing his semi-drunken body against the closed door. He came across with a roundhouse right, slamming the weapon into her temple. It pushed her back far enough for him to kick her in the chest. Once again it put some distance between the both of them. This time he worked the lever on the weapon back and forth, sending a bullet into the chamber. Her open mouth was the passageway to her brain. The bullet ripped the top of her head off with a disgustingly wet muffled thud.

Two young boys standing outside the fenced area ran home without looking back, as the window facing them exploded outward in a spray of red gore.

CHAPTER 12

Dave Mace's Yankee Dollar was a thing of beauty. The outside deck was big enough to accompany at least twenty people. Toward the front was a spacious glass enclosure with the luxury of both heat and air conditioning. Below the decking, the twin 450-hp Cummings Marine engines vibrated only slightly.

Though the sky was overcast, the cool breeze felt good as the craft made its way through the Waterfront's channel.

Chris brought Marlene up to the flying bridge. "Marlene, this is Dave. Dave this is Doctor...."

"Marlene Peterson," Dave said, interrupting. "We've met before. Nice to see you again, Doctor Peterson."

Marlene smiled. "Nice to see you again, Mr. Mace."

Dave looked down at her with a huge smile. "If you say that the next time I make an office visit I'm liable to blush."

She laughed, shaking her head.

Chris gave her a puzzled look. "You two know one another I see. I guess I'm a day late and a dollar short with the introductions."

"Up close and personal I might add, and she didn't even buy me dinner." Dave gave off a satisfied laugh as he turned back to the helm.

Marlene's face was now tinted with a bit of pink.

Chris thought for a moment before opening his mouth and tilting his head back. "Okay, now I get it, and that's probably more information than I really needed."

Dave nudged Chris. "There's fresh coffee down in the cabin. I'll get us a bit farther out and then head south. We'll head on down past the beaches and then on out and around the lighthouse. That's a pretty good trip to get these babies ready for the season." He pointed down to where the two engines were purring steadily beneath the outside deck.

Marlene and Chris went below and sat at a small square table looking aft and through the glass. Dave kept the boat at a slow and steady pace as he navigated it toward more open and deeper water. Chris suddenly felt like he was fifteen again and on his first date. Things that he wanted to say went steadily through his mind, but he found it hard to actually verbalize his thoughts. Catching quick glances at her, he couldn't help but see what a remarkably beautiful woman Marlene was.

Marlene was the first to break the silence.

"I was preaching before when I mentioned smelling the roses and all the unhappiness in the world. I apologize for that. Now that I see the world this way, from the back of a boat looking into the open water, I just want to take all of it home with me. I wish I could find a place to put all this beauty into my rooms so I can look at it any time I like."

Chris leaned back in his chair. "No need to apologize. I agree. So, why don't you just buy yourself a boat and live it up? Lord knows you've been practicing for a while and, at the risk of sounding disingenuous, I can't afford something like this, but you can."

Marlene simply smiled. "What would I do with a monster like this? I'd have to take lessons and tests to become a captain. Then I'd make you salute me and the flag every time you came aboard."

Chris gave off a hardy laugh. "Very funny, Captain Doc Peterson. Maybe we could put a patch over one eye while we're at it, huh?"

Marlene got up and stood next to the glass. It was the tinted type so that a person could see outside very clearly, but could also see their reflection when standing next to it with an unabridged clarity. Chris let his eyes roam over her reflection. She wore tennis shoes and a pair of long white pants. This time she let her hair hang down over her shoulders, giving off a sparkle every time she moved her head. There was a slight smile on her lips, but also a touch of sadness in her eyes.

Chris got up and went to stand behind her. Their eyes met in the glass and he let his hands rest on the sides of her shoulders for a moment.

"There's a subtle hint of sadness in your smile, Doctor Peterson." He turned her around to actually look down into her eyes. "If you ever want to talk...well, I want you to know that I'm a good listener. I also want you to know that I'd like to get to know you a whole lot better. I know with everything that's happening this might not be the best time to bring it up, but there are some that say there's no time like the present."

Taken by surprise, Marlene looked away for a moment, wetting her lips and trying to come up with something to say. Her lips moved, but the words never came.

Chris moved his face slowly towards hers and tilted his head to one side. When he could feel her warm breath on his lips she turned her head away.

"I'm sorry. I...," he began.

"No, it's nothing you did, Chris. I just can't right now. Please understand that I really enjoy your company, but I'm just not ready for a relationship with you or anyone else. I've already been through this before with someone. I just want you to know that it's not you. It's me. In time I'll get this all sorted out, but it's time that I need right now."

Chris nodded. "Being a doctor I know you must have a few friends on a professional level that would be more than willing to lend you an ear. Sometimes it's nice to talk to a friend and share problems. Consider me a good friend, Marlene, and think about my offer."

She leaned forward and gave him a little peck on the cheek.

"It's already been considered, Chris."

Dave took them several miles down the bay before making a wide arc to the left and positioning the eastern shore on the starboard side. On the outside deck, Chris and Marlene let the wind blow over their faces and through their hair, the cool air leaving a salty residue on their lips.

The *Stones* went into a familiar tune. Chris flipped his phone open.

"Kearns," he said.

Marlene listened carefully, making a mental note of how handsome a man he was and to try to get her social life back on track.

"I never heard of him. Did anyone go in and check things out?" Chris listened for a moment. "I could be...." He glanced at Marlene. "We could be over there in about half an hour. I'm sure the good doctor knows where it is." He turned to Marlene again. "A town called Friendly?" She nodded and Chris went back to his conversation. "Yeah, she does. The dirt road to Old Solomon's Creek. Got it."

"What is it?" Marlene asked.

"Remember the old woman's place where we found hatchet head?"

"Yes."

"Well, this one isn't much better from what Lee just told me."

CHAPTER 13

When Chris and Marlene pulled up to the gate, sheriff's deputies and state police already had yellow police-line tape in place. The gate was open and Lee Fret made sure they were allowed to enter and park in a neutral area. A generous crowd of people from the surrounding areas had already claimed squatter's rights, pointing and mumbling to one another from the other side of the fence. From the outside of the cabins there didn't seem to be anything wrong. It was the sight of the broken window that changed everything. Thick globs of blood covered the remaining shards of glass, sliding down the outer wall and onto the ground. It looked as though someone had been thrown through it.

Lee walked up to the car and waited until Chris and Marlene got out. "They're in there taking pictures and marking things off as evidence. The fingerprint team is still working and probably will be for the next few hours. We have two bodies, a woman and a man. The woman they haven't ID'd yet, but the man was wearing a security badge from the Pentagon."

Chris leaned on the side of the vehicle with Marlene standing between the two men. "I take it the man is the same one you mentioned on the phone then?"

Lee flipped open his own notes and nodded. "Professor Delmar Oberbraun. We're expecting Army Intelligence to be rolling in here any minute. While the fingerprint team was working on the cabin in the back, which by the way is some kind of a laboratory, the phone picked up a voice message from what sounded like a military installation. I'm betting it was the Pentagon. The last part of the message said that if he didn't respond within two hours they would send an advance team out to check on certain matters. This voice message wasn't scrambled, although it did come into a scrambled line known as an Advanced Voice Scrambler or AVS.

Some kind of new secure phone the military is working on to waste more money.

"Professor? He's some kind of doctor?" Marlene asked.

"We don't know who the hell he is right now, but there's a safe back in the laboratory cabin that looks like it might weigh a ton easily. There are red magnetic signs on it that read secure and classified," Lee said.

"What about the dead woman?" Chris asked.

"Lee cocked his head to one side and raised his eyebrows. "She was dead before he shot her in the head. She just didn't know it."

Chris stood straight up. "One of our zombies?"

Lee poked at the air with his thumb. "The two kids over there with the police said they heard some screaming and other strange sounds coming from the cabin with the gory window." Lee used a head motion to point out the shattered glass. "It looks to me like the professor did her and then himself. Christ! Not only is the brain matter all over what's left of the window, but on the ground, too. The kids went back home and evidently someone called 911."

Chris shook his head. "We don't have any authority in this investigation. If the military wants to keep things under wraps, they could keep it bottled up for years. Our guy shot a zombie in his home and then shot himself. Why?"

Lee pointed to the gate. "That's not our only problem."

Marlene and Chris turned to see Eyewitness News reporters standing by the gate, trying to gain access through the officers standing guard. Behind them was Dateline News and behind them was another vehicle that was soon hustled around the reporters and quickly parked just behind Chris and Marlene. Two MP's, man in a suit, and an impressive gentleman in an Army dress uniform with two gold stars on each shoulder stepped out. The general had eyes that from a distance looked coal black. They reminded Chris of a deadly bushmaster, staring out and not blinking.

"Shit!" Lee turned away and moved closer to Chris and Marlene. "That's General Hamlin. He's responsible for more dead in the water investigations than you can shake a goddamned AK-47 at."

The reporters were now standing in front of their cameramen and making some kind of offbeat reports that no one could make out. Chris now realized the shit had finally hit the fan and the reporters were going to dig until someone gave them the scoop they wanted.

"We need to get this out to the people, Lee. This is no longer something to keep to ourselves no matter what the fucking military says. God knows how many of those things are out there as of right now."

Marlene nodded, quickly adding her two cents. "This whole thing can turn into epidemic proportions…if it hasn't already."

The general was now talking to several of the police officers and not looking the least bit happy about the conversation. He pointed several times to the house and then thumped his finger against his stars. Evidently it had something to do with who was better then whom in this investigation. One of the police officers pointed to where Marlene, Chris and Lee were standing. The general and the two MP's made their way toward them, while the man in the suit stayed behind and continued talking with the officer.

"You're Lee Fret with the CDC?" the general asked.

Lee nodded. "Yes, sir. We've been working on this matter ever since we were informed that six or seven people had come down with this type of sickness." Lee pointed to Chris and Marlene. "This is…."

"What have you come up with?" the general asked, ignoring the attempt at introductions.

Lee took a deep breath. "We've got a parasite that attacks the human brain, but not sure where it comes from, General. I have a sneaky suspicion that whatever went on in this place could possibly be linked to this problem."

The general pointed toward the gate. "And the press? What do they know about this parasite? Have you or anyone else been leaking information to the press?"

"Leaking, sir?" Chris stepped in quickly.

Lee made an attempt at introductions again. "This is Chris Kearns and Doctor Marlene Peterson. Chris is assigned to CDC on a temp from the Secret Service at the Department of Homeland Security's orders."

"You say leaking like perhaps the Army knows something about this, General. No one actually leaks anything out unless another party or parties know something about it. The deceased is wearing a plastic badge issued by the Pentagon."

Lee tried to step in but failed. The general was already countering. "And your point is, Agent Kearns?"

"My point is, sir, he worked for the Pentagon. The woman he shot was more than likely carrying one of those parasites in her head. I've seen first hand, General, what the result is in being a host to one of those things. The people who are infected by this have no vital signs whatsoever. They're actually dead people who are somehow reanimated by being host to this parasite. They have no will of their own, and their only purpose is to feed on the living. This isn't the first residence we've been called to, General. The question is: why did Professor Oberbraun kill himself after he shot the woman?"

The general shook his head. "I don't know. Why don't you tell me, Kearns. You seem to have all the inferred answers."

Marlene could see that Chris was getting aggravated. It was Marlene who gave him the answer. "He was afraid of something or someone, General."

Chris nodded. "Exactly! There was a message on his secure line that wasn't scrambled when it was recorded. The fingerprint specialists heard the message and believed it was from a military installation; probably the Pentagon. They were going to pay the professor a visit in two hours. On another inferential note, General, I take it that it's been two hours between the time the call came and the time you arrived here."

"Yes, Oberbraun was working on something that was military confidential, and we did call him several times, receiving no answer. If there was anything going on that was underhanded, Agent Kearns, you can bet the Pentagon knew nothing about it. If there's anything in his files that pertains to the work he was doing for us, then it will become part of the Pentagon's property."

"Not exactly, General." A huge deputy walked up to the men with a folded piece of paper in hand. "We have a warrant to check through the entire house. Anything we find will become the property of this investigation. Anything that pertains to whatever is happening to these people will be forwarded to Doctor Peterson and Doctor Fret."

The general was now fuming. "Do you see that man over there, officer? He happens to be an Assistant U.S. Attorney. We will not let...."

"General Hamlin?"

The general turned to see the AUSA standing behind him. "What is it? We have jurisdiction over any documents pertaining to military matters, right?"

The AUSA shook his head. "I'm afraid not. I just received a call from the FBI. The files found on this property belong to the investigation and they will be adding an agent to the team of investigators, until someone can figure out how they relate to any of this. By the way, the President also knows about this. I'm not about to lose my job the way the others have, General."

Chris turned to the attorney. "Chris Kearns, Secret Service."

The attorney shook his hand with a firm grip. "Darin Ginsberg."

"So, DHS already briefed the President on all of this? I thought we were going to wait until we knew exactly where these parasites came from."

"The White House Press Secretary caught wind of the situation and spoke with the President before he had his press conference. It was to ensure that the right answers were given in case the press had any questions about this mess. As a Secret Service agent, I'm sure you can understand that the President needs to be protected in a crowd. We don't know what these things are capable of doing. The public needs to be told about this as soon as somebody can come up with something to tell them. They need to be able to protect themselves and their families. This could get really big, really fast."

"I agree," Chris said. "Who's going to break the news?"

"Well, I say we notify the FBI. I can do that, and you work it out with your agency. I think the best thing to do is have those two agencies deal with DHS. If the department wants to release the information to the public, then you and your colleagues here can work out a public announcement plan with the police," Lee said.

"You just don't declassify information in that manner," the general jumped in before anything else was said. "What's the sense of having classified information if it's going to be released to the public? Anything in there that's classified belongs to the military. You *know* I'm right!"

"Look, people are dying, General." Chris pointed toward the body bags going into the back of the vehicle. "No one is going to get into a pissing match with you or the rest of the military."

The big deputy pointed toward the cabin as he spoke to the attorney. "We're taking the file cabinet or safe, whichever, back to the office. Doctor Peterson, you and the rest of the investigating team are invited to go over the contents with us. Perhaps you and Doctor Fret can shed some light on whatever we find that involves this...whatever it is. Agent Kearns, I know you're working with the CDC and the sheriff extends the same invitation to you."

Chris gave him a quick smile. "I appreciate it."

The general stormed off toward the vehicle. "This is total bullshit. They tie somebody's hands and expect them to do a fucking job."

The coroner's people drove off and were met with reporters at the gate. They turned on the siren and continued without stopping. At the cabin that substituted for a laboratory, men and women with vests marked **P O L I C E** were putting thick cardboard boxes in the back of a van.

Marlene, Chris and Lee went into the main cabin. The floor was a mess of dried and coagulated blood. The rest of the place was untouched and basically clean. In the room where the safe was, a bottle of brandy sat on a desk with a glass next to it.

"The professor was drinking before this happened?" Marlene asked.

The specialist nodded. "It appears so, ma'am. His fingerprints and, I take it, his lip prints are on the glass and the bottle. Usually we swab the mouth for traces of alcohol, but in this case he put the gun in his mouth and pointed it upward."

One of the computer specialists came into the room waving a floppy disk. "This file has a password on it."

The specialist who had been talking with Marlene nodded. "I figured that. No one working on classified information is going to leave word documents open. What's the name of the file?"

The computer specialist checked the marking on the disk.

"The Lazarus Culture."

CHAPTER 14

Two teens walked the beach, playfully poking and pushing one another toward the water's edge. Every so often one of them would bend over and pick up a handful of small pebbles to sift through for shark teeth. The girl's name was Becky, a fair-skin blonde with a smile that could melt even the polar ice caps. The boy was Andrew. He was tall and ruggedly built without being overly muscular.

Becky and Andrew had a friendship that started since the second grade. They grew up together, practically in the same home. Their parents had been friends ever since high school and were just as close. Andrew was sure that he would end up asking Becky to marry him when the time came. They were almost inseparable according to Becky's mother.

At the caves they stopped and took out two flashlights from a small satchel Andrew was carrying. He checked to make sure both were working before looking into the sky. The light was beginning to fade more and more and, due not only to the hour, but because of the continuous stretch of clouds that perpetually covered the sun all day. They knew the caves were off limits to all pedestrian traffic, and knew why that was when they first started walking the beach. The county said it was because of the unstable structure of clay and tree roots that formed the walls and ceilings, but to two energetic teenagers, it meant excitement in doing something daring.

"Okay, we stick together and make sure we flash the light around the walls and ceiling just in case," Andrew instructed.

"My cousin, the paramedic, got money for tipping off the news about something that happened the other day. Did you hear on the news about the murder?" Becky asked.

Andrew gave off a laugh that sounded more like a snort. "Yeah, which one? This place is rapidly becoming as bad as New York City or Detroit. All you hear are sirens anymore."

Becky stared at him for a moment. "I mean, the guy they found naked with an axe in his head. Someone actually broke into his house and killed him with an axe. Can you imagine being in your basement and...."

Andrew turned to Becky, shining the light into her face. "Okay, for one thing, it wasn't the dead guy's house and, for another thing, they said it was a hatchet not an axe."

"Yes, but don't you think that's horrible? I mean, it was so close to home. I heard a lot of sirens a while ago, too. They seemed to be heading for the other side of the beaches." For a moment Becky stopped before entering the mouth of the biggest cave. She scanned the light into the darkness and looked at Andrew. "I really don't know if we should do this. We don't know if they caught whoever's responsible for those killings, Andy."

He raised his hands in defeat. "Okay, so stay here and let me have a look around in this one. I'll just go in a little ways. There are *no* killers here, Becky. They wouldn't be hiding here of all places. What if the police came to investigate? What kind of excuse would the killer or killers have if they were caught here? What exactly would they say? 'Oh, I was just looking for shark teeth'."

Becky nodded. "Yeah, that's another thing. What if the police do investigate and catch *us* here? What excuse are *we* going to use?"

"We're stupid teenagers," Andrew said laughing. "We get away with all kinds of shit with that excuse."

Becky shook her head and laughed herself. "Okay, but don't go off by yourself. I'm not going in all the way either."

The smell of mold and rotting vegetation filled their noses. On the walls and ceiling were huge roots from the trees that overhung the cliffs at Willows Grove. The floor of the cave was comprised of several different things. Some of it was sand and gravel, while patches of clay and slippery muck were spaced here and there. The huge opening narrowed down after about thirty feet. A wall directly in front veered off to the right and opened up into another smaller tunnel. Andrew directed his light into the opening and immediately stopped walking.

"What?" Becky grabbed his arm. "What did you see?"

Andrew shook his head. "Nothing. Look at the ground. Someone was in here before us. I can see their footprints from here. The water filled them in though, so it must have been a while ago. See?" Andrew once again broke out in laughter. "We're not the only ones breaking the law."

"I don't want to go back there, Andy."

"Let's just look into the entrance. I'm just curious where it goes. It looks like it goes in toward the other side of the cave next to it."

Becky followed Andrew to the opening of the smaller tunnel, keeping her body turned sideways and sweeping the light back and forth in front of her and behind. Andrew picked up a chunk of clay and heaved it into the entrance. It made a wet thud as it hit the ground and rolled into the tunnel. At the mouth, they could see that it went in at least ten feet before making an arc to the left. Andrew took Becky's hand and led her into the smaller entrance. The smell of rot and stagnant water was almost unbearable. As they rounded the turn, a small gleam of light flickered in the distance. The cave next to where they now stood was much smaller, with a huge hole in the ceiling that came out into the woods just before Willows Road.

"It goes to the other cave, and that's the light coming in from the hole just before you get to the road," Andrew said.

"Okay, we know what's way back here now. Let's get going. It's going to be dark pretty soon and I'm starving."

Andrew nodded. "Okay, come on. We'll go back out the way we came in. I don't feel like climbing up that sloppy mud slide out there. It stinks like hell in here, too. Man, it all of a sudden smells like somebody died in here."

They made it as far as the opening to the small tunnel when they realized it just so happened that someone did die in there. When the walking cadaver greeted them with a groan and glottal scowl, Becky screamed and grabbed Andrew. The zombie quickly made its way toward the two of them, stretching its arms out as if it had no eyes.

Under any other circumstances, they would have made some kind of comment, but the look on the dead man's face told the story plain and simple. The whites of his eyes were bloodshot, the sockets discolored and rimmed with deep grooves. The wind coming through the tunnel carried with it another stench, telling them he had more than likely defecated in his pants.

Andrew grabbed Becky by the arm and hauled her toward the hole. The walls surrounding it were encased with thick gobs of mud and snake-like vines. Andrew jumped up and grabbed one that looked to be fairly dry or at least dryer than the rest. It looped out and then wound its way back into the wall again. It came down far enough to where he could jump back down and have Becky grab it and pull herself upward. She was halfway to the exit of the hole when the dead man reached Andrew. The tunnel at this point was too narrow to attempt any evasive action at either side of the zombie. Andrew ran into him with his shoulder planted deep into the thing's stomach. It lurched backward but didn't lose its footing. It once again opened its arms and closed in.

This time Andrew slammed the flashlight across the dead man's face. The blow forced its head to turn away, but came back into place with a huge skin abrasion that oozed thick, light-green pus from the wound. Becky crawled out of the hole and screamed down to her boyfriend. He backed up to the exit and returned the favor. "Get help, Becky!"

"I'm not leaving you, Andy. Push him away and grab the vine like I did. I can't live with myself knowing you did this for me. I'm not...."

"Becky, please!" Andrew planted a foot into the zombie's chest and kicked hard. This time his other foot went out from under him on the slippery muck and clay. He lost his balance and hit the floor with a resounding thud. The dead man was on him before he could regain his footing, the dead weight pinning him to the muddy floor.

"Andyyyy!" Becky gave off one last scream as the zombie tore a gapping hole in the side of the boy's throat, the blood spurting in tune with his excited heart rate.

The zombie looked up at her as it clamped down on the fresh young flesh between its teeth and then swallowed. As Becky ran from the hole, it went for seconds.

At fifty feet from Willows Road, Becky screamed for help to a group of people who were walking down the road and into the woods. As she neared them, she noticed that they seemed to be in some kind of daze. They wandered around nonchalant until their eyes actually focused on the warm-blooded girl who addressed them.

Once again she looked into the eyes of horror. There were at least twelve of them, all looking like the madman that had just killed her long time boyfriend and soul mate. Some of them moved faster than others, chasing her as she made a wide circle around them and finally onto the road. Running for her life, Becky never looked back. Her house was only several blocks away, but it might as well have been a mile. Behind her, she could hear their moans and groans as they continued to pursue her at fifteen to twenty feet behind.

A police cruiser carrying sheriff's deputies crossed one of the roads and continued on toward Ponds Wood. Becky was now out of breath, but able to get behind the cruiser and frantically wave her hands. The vehicle's tail lights gleamed in the semi-darkness and finally turned out of sight.

Becky screamed at the top of her lungs, once again running across a lawn towards her home. A door opened in one of the houses to her right, revealing a woman in a bathrobe. She called to Becky in a chastising voice as to what the hell was going on.

"Get in your house and lock the doors!" Becky screamed.

The small band of zombies headed toward the woman's door with eyes that glared at her in murderous fury. She slammed the door. They pounded on the door and against the siding of the house. Others attempted to reach up and smack their hands against windows that were just high enough to keep them from breaking and crawling through.

Becky looked back momentarily as she crossed another lawn. As she turned her head back around, a loud cracking sound filled her ears along with a piercing pain that ripped through her forehead. The rake she stepped on had been thrown down with the tongs facing upward. Her knees hit the ground first before her head came to rest quite hard on an ornamental deer made of cement.

The cruiser flashed its lights and pulled to the side. The officer riding shotgun got out and ran quickly to Becky's side. Her head was bleeding from colliding with the cement deer, and an elongated bump stood out vertically on her forehead.

The group of dead men and women now smelled blood. They made their way toward the teenager and the deputy. The driver exited the vehicle and ran forward, drawing his gun as he neared Becky and his partner.

"What the fuck is this?" he yelled.

One of the deputies picked up Becky and made his way toward the cruiser. The other stood his ground, trying to make sense of the oncoming rush of men and women. Some of them had something that looked an awful lot like blood smeared over their mouths, running down their chin and onto their chests.

The officer drew his weapon. "Halt! Goddamn it, halt or I'll shoot."

He fired several rounds into one of their chests. The zombie twisted and looked like it would lose its footing but kept coming. The officer at the cruiser fired simultaneously but got the same results.

The zombies were on the first officer before he could turn. He threw several of them to the ground but couldn't avoid one of them sinking its rotting teeth into his shoulder.

One of the zombies' heads exploded in a gush of brain matter and bone. Several officers stood behind the crowd of walking dead and made carefully aimed head shots. Just coming back from investigating a murder- suicide at Old Solomon's, they knew what the target was.

"The head. You have to shoot for the head!" one of them yelled.

Agent Chris Kearns stepped to the side and leveled the .357 and fired. Another one's head exploded, and then another. In less than five minutes, all the bodies lay on the road in actual death.

Chris raised his credentials for all the deputies to see.

"Chris Kearns, Secret Service. I've been detailed to CDC to investigate the horror you're now witnessing. It's a parasite of some kind that gets into a person's brain. As you can see, even though they're dead, they won't stay down unless you shoot for the head. I heard a 911 call on the scanner about a possible breaking and entering. I heard the address and headed for Willows Grove."

CHAPTER 15

Dr. Marlene Peterson finished up with her twenty-first patient of the day and was called to the phone on business. Chris gave her the scoop on the shooting the previous evening, making it clear they had not started going through the evidence confiscated from Oberbraun's office because of that incident and the one at the caves. The boy's autopsy report was her next call. The coroner quickly made it clear to her that the boy was going nowhere. His brain was removed and kept that way. Marlene made her way to the county sheriff's office and waited outside until Chris's car pulled up next to hers. She could tell the look on his face was more of fatigue than anything else.

Once again a weekend in which he was to have the kids went sour. Winning an argument about it due to his line of work became nonexistent. He wondered sometimes if he should have listened to his sister when she told him he and Jennifer would be headed for divorce court before their tenth anniversary. His sister, Kaitlyn, was married to the owner of a lucrative construction company, Lambert Construction Inc., working out of both Virginia and Maryland. Kaitlyn had the privilege of staying home and taking care of her children, their home, and, most of all, their marriage. Chris couldn't ask Jennifer to give up her career. She wouldn't anyway. What would he do if she had to be the sole support of the family?

Marlene's body covered the driver's side window and woke him out of his stupor. For a moment he actually thought he could feel his eyes mist up thinking about his sister taking the kids in one more time. He opened the door and looked up over the top of it at Marlene.

"I know that look, Chris. It's either work related or family. If it's a work related problem I have a free ear if you want to share." She waited until Chris got out and closed the door. "Family problems are none of my business, but I use the same ears."

Chris shook his head. "The kids. I'm supposed to have them this weekend and they're over at my sister's place as we speak. I can't keep them at my place and do this job at the same time, Marlene. It just doesn't work that way. I'm afraid I may lose the shared custody to a frigging nanny if this keeps up."

Marlene folded her arms over her chest. "If you were working in the office right now instead of on temporary assignment with the CDC, would you be off?"

Chris nodded.

"Then get the hell out of Dodge. Call your supervisor and tell him or her that you need to speak to a counselor about your pre-dicament—namely your children. Is Lee Fret working?"

Chris nodded again. "He's going to be here today. What we find in those files may be crucial to this case. I need this information. I also need my kids." He turned away and folded his hands on the roof of the car. "I remember talking to you about changing careers the other day. Maybe I should become a male nurse."

Marlene gave a lopsided smile he of course didn't see. "You're too good looking. The female staff would never get anything done." She could see his shoulders moving vigorously up and down. He turned back around shaking his head. "Ah, I see a smile. Good thing you don't wear a hat, Agent Kearns, you'd never be able to get it on." She took his hand in hers and rubbed the back of it. "Get what you can out of this meeting and then get your fanny out of here. Go get your children. If the SS gives you any crap, you tell them it was doctor's orders."

Chris was about to start another conversation but decided to store the thought for another time and place. Lee Fret had pulled up alongside their vehicles. He got out of the car and waved a recorder at them. "This is high tech, Chris. No note taking in your little pad this time around."

"You're just too good to me, Lee," Chris said.

"I'm also an egghead, remember?"

Several officers from the state police and the sheriff's depart-ment attended the meeting along with Marlene, Chris, and Lee. Darin Ginsberg and General Hamlin sat in the back. The sheriff,

Zachery Evans, made sure he had everything that would aid his presentation in front of him. Within twenty minutes they had everything they would need brought in from the professor's cabins. Another half hour passed while they sorted through what the investigators had brought in. Within another hour they were down to the desktop computer and a new piece of evidence found in a secret compartment that was located in the professor's main residence. This was a CD found next to a mainframe computer containing information on the file known as The Lazarus Culture.

Lee Fret checked the recorder to make sure it was recording live data and, at the same time, making a backup in the other tape compartment. The general stood up quickly. "That's classified information. Anything you tell these people about that file will result in your being held in contempt of congress." The general looked down quickly at the AUSA. "What the hell are you just sitting there for?"

Darin Ginsberg shook his head. "General, they have warrants and permission from Homeland Security to go through the files. Right now this is out of the military's hands and there is nothing to be gained by getting into a shouting match. Please, let's just try to get through this and see if these people can make any sense of what the hell is going on."

Chris took advantage of the moment. "Unless you already know what's going on, General. And I'll wager my whole paycheck for the next two weeks that you have a damn good idea and that there's something in this file that you don't want out in the open. That's it, isn't it?" Chris picked up the notebook the professor had thrown nonchalantly back into the file cabinet. "I've already had a peek at this. It's pretty interesting stuff, but I'd also bet that in that CD there's a lot more to be gained. The Lazarus Culture is a great name. Lazarus, meaning the man Jesus raised from the dead."

"Goddamn it, Kearns. I'm a two star general. How dare you sit there and speak to me like I was one of your fucking low-level civil servants?"

"How dare you attempt to cover up information that's vital to finding what caused the loss of human lives? Of course you ass-holes are all used to that, aren't you? We have authorization from DHS via the President's desk. If you want to be the cause of putting egg all over the face of the person holding the highest government office in the country, then be my guest. Now, if you're all through playing war games, I'd like to get this over with so I can collect my children and show them they still have a father who loves them."

Hamlin's face was beet red. "You arrogant son...."

The sheriff slapped his hand onto the table. "Gentlemen! We understand that this has been time consuming for a lot of people. The bottom line is that we have the authorization from the courts, Homeland Security, and the President himself. I won't stand for any elementary school shouting matches in my office." He wiped his brow and looked toward the back of the room. "General, if you know anything, anything at all that can shed some light on this information, I would be obliged to hear it. If not, like Agent Kearns just said, I'd like to get this over with and get on with the rest of the day."

A computer tech came in from the dispatch office and made ready the data disk for the department's mainframe. Several minutes later an access file was displayed with no password protection. On it were media files as well as text and sound bytes. The tech set up the data player to start from the beginning and step through each file as it was recorded from a live source. The first section was data describing a parasite found in a Red Snapper purchased at a local fish market. A media player quickly engaged and displayed two hands holding a fish with its mouth opened wide. Inside the fish's mouth was a strange looking creature that resembled a grub attached to the fish's tongue.

Lee Fret made sure the microphone on the recorder was close enough to capture what sound there was attached to the media file. As the files progressed they eventually displayed several cats showing nothing abnormal. Further into the session two of the animals began displaying strange behavior patterns. The next data file explained the procedures taken to introduce the specimen into the bloodstream, ultimately making the cats a host to the parasite. The media file showed what must have been the same two cats attacking a rabbit and killing it savagely. Although the two animals were kept isolated from the other animals, the two were kept together in the same cage. Neither one of them had any interest in the other. Another data file explained the incubation period of the rabbit from sickness to its untimely death. The next media file showed the rabbit fully recovered and savagely attacking the thickly gloved hands of a handler.

Data files slowly appeared describing the transformation of the parasite from a carnivore involving a fish, to that of attacking the human brain stem and finally the brain itself. In several still shots of x-rays, there were clearly several of the creatures inhabiting the brains of what must have been medical cadavers. Several minutes later it was confirmed that the recently deceased individuals, two men and one woman, were that of homeless people who had been living on the streets of DC. Another five minutes passed before the actual media files came into play showing the three cadavers lying face down on an examining table.

In the back of the room, General Hamlin was holding his head in his hands. Chris flagged Lee and Marlene to bring their attention to him. The next media file was made several days later according to a time frame displayed at the lower right hand corner of the screen. In this file, the cadavers were in what looked like prison jumpers and clumsily moving around on their own. Any attempt to approach either one would result in their making a violent effort to grab and bite the arm that was reaching through the slot of the steel door.

The final outcome of the experiment was to introduce the zombie killers to the foreign country in which the United States was at war with. Soldiers would somehow penetrate the area in the dead of night and release the creatures on the enemy. It was noted in several other classified documents that the United States Government knew exactly what the consequence of their actions were. The zombies would violently attack any living person regardless of their patriotism to either side, including women and children. This, the final media file, was presented by Professor Delmar Oberbraun, standing at a podium with a clear picture of General Hamlin in the background sitting amongst several other high ranking officials believed to be the members of the Joint Chiefs of Staff. On the instruction of the sheriff, the tech froze the frame and left it there momentarily.

Looking up, Hamlin suddenly realized that all eyes were focused on him. "It was supposed to be an experiment; that's it, an experiment." He slowly ran his hand through his hair. "We weren't going to use it unless there was a way to get the troops in and out of an occupied zone safely and effectively. The idea was to have *these things* go after anything that was living and breathing. The press was of course kept out of it because of the possible threat of allies to the enemy already living in the United States. As time went on, their entire nation would be populated with these creatures. They not only would attack humans, but animals as well. People handling the animals would no doubt be bitten and then, they too, would become hosts to the parasite. When the threat was over, the object of the whole scheme was to round up and kill what was left of them. It wouldn't be hard. They can't stand daylight, so they would more than likely become huddled masses in the darkness of some buildings."

Chris leaned back in his chair. "You people actually thought this would work? This has to be one of the most insane pieces of work I've heard yet. What about the biting? Why was it that we originally thought it didn't work the other way around? I have notes here that say there were laboratory rats that were exposed to this parasite and they never infected one another."

"That was false information, wasn't it, General?" Lee was next to speak up. "People involved with this program were told that the animals were introduced to this parasite, when in fact that wasn't the case at all. The government knew all along that a human bite as well as someone eating animal flesh, such as fish, would transform a living person into one of those things. The other parasites don't die at all, but just lay dormant until they somehow come in contact with another host."

Hamlin walked to the other side of the room. "You have assholes taping bombs to their bodies and blowing up innocent people. We didn't see what was wrong with playing their game, except just a bit differently. Yes, there were innocent people who would be at risk, but did you ever hear of a suicide bomber being sorry? As far as the rats were concerned...no, some of those involved didn't know. They couldn't know because it would never have gotten off the ground. Our whole government *did not know* the consequence of our actions."

"Well, then it was just the ones who were in favor, right, General?" Marlene stood up and pointed at the screen. "Do you realize what all of you have done? Do you realize how many medical personnel we had working on these people who were infected? A young boy was killed in the caves at Willows just a short time ago. Are you willing to tell his family what you've told us here?"

Hamlin turned from the window to face them. "I'm willing to take the fall if need be. My career is finished as of this day, Doctor Peterson. What else do I have to fear with the exception of going to prison and losing my pension? The man who is responsible for this terrible outbreak is dead. An ironic fate wouldn't you say? I'm sorry for trying to fix something that can't be fixed. We don't know who our enemy is. We can't find the sons of bitches."

Sheriff Evans had the tech turn off the equipment before addressing his own question to Hamlin. "So, what law enforcement officials have to do to stop these things is to shoot them in the head. Is that how you stop them, General?"

Hamlin nodded. "Once the brain has been destroyed, the creatures no longer have a hold on the host. In shooting the brain, the electrical impulses are broken. These creatures keep those impulses thriving and alive. According to Oberbraun, the parasite only controls certain parts of the brain. When those parts are disturbed or better yet, destroyed, the parasite will die along with the brain. The body of these people only lasts as long as a normal deceased person would. There's absolutely nothing keeping the body nourished. Since rigor mortis starts in the brain, the parasite controls this function. The body never truly becomes rigor, but parts of it do stiffen. The legs, arms, hands, and the neck to a certain extent become slightly hard to move, but not like a true dead body."

"One man didn't contaminate all those people last night." Chris leaned on his forearms as he addressed the meeting. "Those people were subjected to that parasite from some other source. The area they were in is dotted with various bars and restaurants. Several of them have sushi bars. Remembering we live on or near the Chesapeake Bay, we have to consider that these places could be selling raw fish that's been contaminated."

Lee shook his head. "It's a good idea, Chris, but I doubt that one man could fall into the bay and contaminate all those fish."

"The Red Snapper." Chris looked over at Lee. "How did the fish actually get contaminated, Lee? Fish live all their lives under the water. If there's that many of them in the bloodstream of a human being...."

"The parasites live in the water as well," Marlene said. "That has to be it. They live in the water because of all the algae and other microscopic organisms that thrive there. They attach themselves to an unwary fish; the fish is eaten by another fish, and so on and so on."

The door opened and a deputy came in to motion the sheriff to step outside. Marlene, Lee and Chris discussed the contamination ideas for several minutes until the sheriff returned to the front of the room.

"General Hamlin, I have a question that needs your undivided attention and an answer that's believable. I appreciate your honesty up to this point, so I'll just spit it out and hope for the best," the sheriff said.

Hamlin walked up to the table followed by Ginsberg. "I just told you, Sheriff, I no longer have anything to fear, and like someone else once said, 'but fear itself'."

Evans nodded. "I'd like to know what happened to those cadavers that were being used as test subjects. You want to tell us about the plane crash that the military was so interested in last week and, in fact, still are? I ask this because one of my deputies just informed me that some of your military personnel; just last night, shot and killed six of the survivors in California, Maryland. Although, I believe the word killed would be the wrong choice of words. Those bodies they shot were already dead, weren't they?"

Hamlin looked long and hard at Darin Ginsberg before answering. "Two hikers found the plane the following afternoon. They made their way to the road and phoned 911 and gave them the details of what they saw and the location. The 911 dispatcher contacted Army Pentagon since most of the personnel were in military fatigues. The...cadavers, as you call them, were aboard the plane. Someone evidently opened the coffins. It's my guess that the bodies were kicking and screaming and...."

"Nobody was told what they were, right?" Chris finished for him.

One of the troopers held up his hand. "Hold on a second. Are we talking about more of these things running around in Maryland? Are you saying that eating fish out of the Chesapeake Bay could cause us to become one of these things?"

Lee Fret was the first to answer. "There's a potential threat only if the fish is eaten raw or undercooked. It's safe to eat when it reaches an internal temperature of 145 degrees for at least five minutes. Similarly, the smoking of fish provides an effective method of eliminating the parasites as well, providing the fish is smoked at 150 degrees and until the internal temperature of the fish is at 140 or so for at least thirty minutes. Since smoking is a bit different from cooking with an oven or microwave, it may take a few hours."

Chris clapped Lee on the shoulder lightly. "This Food Network thing is very nice, but what about the major food chains who are selling fish as we speak? How do we know how long they've had the stuff? Then, of course, we have the already infected who have turned into one of those things and are now running around attacking people?"

Sheriff Evans nodded. "From what I'm told, we currently have people patrolling the borders between Maryland, Virginia, Delaware and Pennsylvania. Tonight we go on live with several of the major networks and pass the word to the public. This isn't going to be either easy or pretty. There's going to be some really pissed off individuals looking for law suits and calling for resignations and arrests. When we finally break this news to the public the shit is going to hit the fan at full force, and we're all going to be wiping it from our faces before it's over."

A young deputy entered the room before Evans could continue. "Sheriff, we have a major problem. A 911 dispatcher says there's a call from Grady's out there in Lexington Park. They started to say something to the dispatcher about a disturbance, and all of a sudden the phone went dead. The dispatcher said there were, I know this sounds really crazy, but she said it sounded like human growling noises."

"Who's Grady?" Chris asked.

Evans stopped at the doorway. "It's an old tobacco storage area that was later used as part of the Maryland Underground Railroad during the Civil War. There are tunnels all over the place. They bring people on tours during the spring and summer months."

Chris motioned for Lee to follow. Marlene followed with the rest of the group directly behind her. She quickly made her way up to Chris, grabbing his elbow and pulling him quickly off to the side. "You're going to go get your children, Chris. This crew can take care of whatever's happening over there."

CHAPTER 16

Three of the zombies wore military uniforms.

Two floors under the ground were storage rooms that once held reaped tobacco leaves. Each room was secured by a swinging gate, much like a horse stall. Several of the eighteen people, one of them a tour guide named Rose, pushed their backs against the old wood. Before long there were two more zombies trying to push their way in. Through the slits in the wood, those inside could see there was something terribly wrong with those individuals outside the gate, other than being totally insane. Three people lay dead on the old dirt flooring just outside. Their blood began to coagulate around the gaping wounds in various parts of their bodies. Two of the cannibalistic creatures were tearing at the intestines of an old woman while several others continued to bite huge chunks of flesh from the already ravaged skin of the two others.

A small door to the right led to the next room. It was checked out by one of the men and found to have a much heavier gate than a normal entranceway. Inside the adjoining room was a barrel full of water. The sliding bolt was rusted, but after the last person was inside, they secured it none-the-less. Several of the men spun the heavy barrel in circles toward the smaller door until it was braced heavily against it. The things had already busted through the old gate and entered, slamming their arms and hands against the small door in an attempt to get to the living. The same type of door to the right of this room was being secured in place with several of the people sitting and placing their backs against it.

The muffled sound of sirens from emergency vehicles whistled through the tunnels and into the ears of those who fought to remain among the living. There were at least twenty of the beings in the next room trying desperately to break in. The gate leading to the passageway outside was indeed much sturdier than the latter, but the groaning and growling of the walking dead left those on the inside with less than any logical reason to breathe any easier. Most of the things had a sickening red mass of blood and other bodily fluids running from their mouths. In the corner, one of the men found an old pitchfork with its tines bent in different directions. Placing it on the floor and stomping down solidly bent them back into a fairly straight row.

"What the hell is happening?" one of the women screamed as a zombie smashed a fist through one of the wider slats.

"They're crazy. They've all gone crazy. Maybe it's like what dogs get. Maybe it's like rabies or something," another man said. When the pallid face of the dead man came through the slats to stare at him, he buried the pitchfork deep into the eyes. A spew of milky white fluids mixed with old blood splattered over the floor and dribbled down the slats. The zombie gave off a loud groan before falling still and silent on the earthen floor.

"I'm afraid, Aunt Kate. Why is this happening to us?" The young girl clung to her aunt with a younger boy pressing his body close to both of them.

The woman huddled against the back wall and held the boy and girl against her. The boy was now shivering as though the room suddenly turned to an icebox.

Kaitlyn Lambert had decided to take her niece and nephew on an outing. It was obvious they were going to be stood up once again by her brother, the Secret Service agent. Now she wondered if they would ever get to see either one of their parents again.

"I don't know, honey. We'll be okay, though. I don't think they can get in here, and I can hear sirens. Someone is coming to get us and we'll be all right."

CHAPTER 17

Chris pulled in the driveway of his sister's home with plenty of room to spare. There were no other vehicles. His heart sank as he noticed a piece of folded paper in the storm door with his name on it. He pulled it from the door and opened it. Kaitlyn decided to take the kids on a field trip, thinking that they were once again stood up by their father. It wasn't a condescending note, but one that hit home, immediately stirring up a slight bit of anger. A thought quickly entered his mind. Why the hell didn't he call his sister right after he spoke with Marlene today?

Chris dialed his sister's cell phone and received no answer. It was just like her to have a damn phone and not turn it on, he thought. It was the only flaw she had that related to his children when they were with her. He no sooner put it back in the holder than it was playing a familiar tune. He checked the incoming number and groaned. Not particularly wanting to, he answered it.

Aidon Richards' voice didn't sound all that pleasant. *"Chris, what the hell is going on? I've been hashing it out with those fuckheads at DHS for the past two days and I haven't heard from you since our meeting."*

Chris closed his eyes and shook his head. "I know, Aidon. Look, I just got word that there's some kind of a disturbance over at the old Maryland tobacco barns out there in the Lexington Park area. I was on my way and just thought I'd stop and see the kids. I'm burned out, Aidon. What I'm afraid of is the thought of losing what rights I have if things don't slow down. I can handle this assignment, so don't think that this is what this conversation is all about; it isn't. I just need some time with my kids. They're off someplace on an outing with my sister. I'm going to get something to eat and then contact Lee Fret and see what's happening. I'll get something to you as soon as I have the information myself."

"Didn't she tell you where she was taking them?"

It was a question that sent a spark of fear through his body. He stared at the phone like an idiot for a moment. It was as if the man had asked the question in Chinese. "Ah, no. Sorry. I had a fucking brain fart for a moment there. No, I don't know where they went, but if I know Kaitlyn, she took them to a mall and they'll end up in an ice cream shop."

"*Chris?*"

Chris bit his lower lip for a second. "Yeah."

"*Take off a few days. You're not on this schedule and there's no other trips planned by the White House. I have enough people to cover as post standers. Just keep your eyes and ears open for anything that I might be able to use.*"

"Thanks. I need a few days to get my head straight. I'll tell you this. The whole situation just got worse. I have enough information to send you that will raise the roof at DHS. It involves a general over at the Pentagon and a scientist who just blew his brains out the other day. As soon as I find out what the hell is going on over there at the barns, I'll get everything I have to you."

Chris heard the rustling of paper before Richards spoke again. "*I saw some of that on the news already, but they didn't get into details. Just put what you have into your report. Before you go, Chris, I want to know what the hell we're actually dealing with here. Walking dead?*"

"It all points to what we all thought to be something right out of the minds of horror writers. We mentioned something about that in our meeting. We hemmed and hawed about it, but now we all know that it's the real thing."

"*You might want to check out the evening news if you get the chance. It looks like those who are supposed to be in charge are taking steps to cover their asses. I saw the last report and I know it was you they were talking about with that doctor. I just want you to know I appreciate you staying on top of it.*"

"I'll see it through and I'll talk to you in a while. Thanks again, Aidon."

Chris ended the call and decided to leave. His kids weren't here and waiting for them would only drive him crazy.

Chris drove across town to an out of the way small diner just outside of a tiny town called Littleton. The place was practically dead, which suited him just fine. People were talking over one another to be heard and juke boxes blaring were the last things he needed right now. He sat in the corner of the room next to the back window and flipped through one of the menus being held up by a sugar container and a plastic bottle of ketchup. A heavy set woman with a broad smile came up to him and asked what he'd like to drink. He ordered a Coke and quickly gave her a cheeseburger order with extra crispy fries.

He once again tried his sister's cell phone with the same results. He could feel his blood pressure going up and decided to give the calls a rest. Kaitlyn and her husband were people who used a cell phone to give one another pick up orders. "Can you pick up some milk on the way home?"

"What was that?" The waitress brought his drink and stared at him for a moment.

"Nothing." Chris gave her a short smile and sipped it slowly. The coolness of the liquid was more than adequate to sooth his dry throat.

"Agitated," the waitress replied, "I know the feeling."

Ten minutes later his food was brought to the table. Hungrier than he thought, Chris devoured the contents of the plate with a steady alternating mixture of bread, meat and potatoes.

The waitress picked up the meal ticket and the money. "Aren't you the guy I saw on the news the other day with that doctor?"

Chris put down his drink and nodded. "Yes, as a matter of fact I am. And you are?"

"Betty Blout. A strange thing happened the other night when I was closing up. Well, not only me...me and Carol Selina, the manager."

Chris leaned back and listened. "In what way?"

"Well, we were just about through when Carol calls me over to the window. There was this guy coming across the driveway. He looked like he was drunk or on something, I don't know which. Carol quickly turned off the rest of the lights and we just stared at him for a moment. Anyway, as he got into the light, he looked kind of sick. His skin looked all pasty and stuff. He stopped and just stood there looking at the place. God! My heart was in my throat when he actually got about ten feet from the big window there." She pointed behind Chris.

"Can you spell the last names of you and Carol? Did he try to get in or do anything?"

"Sure." She gave Chris the proper spelling and continued. "Well, he just stood there for a moment and then he banged on the door a few times. He never said a word, but I could have sworn I heard him grunting or something. He just left after that."

"Did you see which way he went?" Chris continued writing down the information.

"I think he headed toward Solomon's. He must have been home on leave I guess."

Chris looked up from his notes. "Why?"

"He was in a military uniform. No hat, but he had on all the rest."

CHAPTER 18

Rose, the tour guide, unfolded a section of paper and spread it out on the wall. "This is the layout of the underground exit." She pointed to a line that ran behind the bins they were currently occupying. "We can get three doors over and the next one has a trapdoor that goes one more floor down. It's an old passageway that leads out to the field just off the back road."

The crowd of living dead had now gained momentum and strength. They were pushing harder on the gate and attempting to climb over the top. Luckily it was the type that went up close to three inches from the ceiling. The wood was giving way to stress fractures in some places and other places began to show signs of loose nails.

"Let's give it a try," one man said. "But what if they're in the passageway, too? What if we get down there and can't get out on the other side? We'll be trapped with no place to run."

The guide shook her head. "You can't gain access from the outside. There's no other way into the tunnel that I know of. I think there might be a few side rooms that they used for sleeping in, but that's about it. This place isn't going to hold much longer. My God, there must be at least fifty of them out there right now."

Kaitlyn clutched the two kids close to her and went to the other side of the room, where several people were already going through the small door next to the floor. On the other side of the gate, the zombies pounded heavily on the wood.

Three of the men made sure the wood would hold long enough for them to get through the next door and then the next. When everyone had passed through the last door, they pulled the latch and locked it from the inside.

In the dark, they formed one line and headed toward the southern part of the building. A few in the group had small flashlights attached to their key chains. The guide pulled one from her belt and took the lead. The walls were shored with old timber that looked to be at least two hundred years old. Four by four posts pressed two by eight planks up against the old earthen walls, and in some places they buckled outward from age and dampness. The sound of dripping water came from somewhere ahead while stale air rushed up the nostrils of the group.

"This isn't part of the tour, so don't lean on or even touch any of the lumber," the guide said.

Twenty feet ahead there was a room on the right. Old wooden frames and dilapidated buckets were strewn about the space. Several of the men broke off pieces of the frames to use as a sort of weaponry in a 'just in case' fashion. At another fifty feet of the passageway a strange sound came from behind them.

CHAPTER 19

With the sky now turning a purplish color, Chris made his way around the grounds surrounding the diner. Most of it was a wooded area with a small clearing containing a rusty iron grill and an old, weather beaten picnic table. Leaves were still layering the ground, making it hard to see any footprints that otherwise might have been visible. Betty Blout and another woman stepped out on the back porch to see what he was up to.

Chris spied them at the corner of his eye. "What's in the shed? And how far is the road that comes out on the other side of the woods?"

"Some tools for landscaping the grounds, and I would guess the road is about three or four hundred feet. I'm Carol Selina, the manager. I just saw on TV that they've arrested some people regarding the Pentagon and they were mentioning the Secret Service, too. I thought you might want to sit in on it. Betty here says you're an agent?"

Chris came quickly to the porch steps and climbed them in two strides. "Thanks, I was waiting for the news," he said, not bothering to offer any information about his job.

Carol shrugged her shoulders, sensing that it was probably a polite way to be told to mind her own business. "I don't understand what the Secret Service has to do with all that's going on lately." She pointed to the office in the back, suddenly realizing she once again stuck her nose where it didn't belong. "Here, you can sit in my office if you like."

Thanking her, he looked back at Carol as he entered. "I guess you're about to know as much as we do. Just in case there are more of those characters traipsing around here at night, you should keep the doors locked exactly at closing time. You're about to find out why."

Eyewitness news flashed on the screen and then went straight to the commentator. A pretty brunette sat next to a gentleman with white hair and attempted a smile.

"Good evening. Today's top story is more like something out of a horror movie. A top general at the Pentagon was arrested today by county officials. General Norwood Hamlin was arrested on charges of reckless endangerment, conspiring to use chemical and biological warfare, and negligent homicide. We take you live to Wes Tinzel at the courthouse."

"Thank you, Karen," Tinzel said. *"I'm standing here at the main entrance where an hour ago a two star general was led into this building escorted by U.S. Marshals. We learned a day or two ago that another accomplice, Professor Delmar Oberbraun, shot and killed himself after being attacked by what law enforcement officials are calling, zombies. I know it sounds like something you might see in a drive-in movie, but in this case it's all too real.*

"It started with a harmless parasite that attacks a fish called the Red Snapper. The parasite attaches itself to the tongue of the fish and eventually becomes the fish's tongue. Now, this doesn't mean that fish are a danger to consume as food, but according to officials at the Center for Disease Control, the waterways may be contaminated with what these same officials are calling a genetically engineered or mutated strain of the parasite; a strain that Professor Oberbraun had been secretly working on that attaches itself, not to the tongue, but to the human brain. What many people may not know or have forgotten, is that a convention on the prohibition of bacteriological or biological stockpiling for germ warfare was signed at Washington, London, and Moscow on April 10, 1972 and enforced on March 26, 1975.

With me is Doctor Lee Fret of the CDC. Doctor Fret, can you tell us the nature of this research and what exactly happens to those exposed?"

Lee Fret took a deep breath and then leaned into the hand-held microphone. *"We've learned that research with this particular parasite has been going on for almost two years, and conducted by several leading scientists of the federal government. One of them who was recruited and eventually took over the project was a research scientist, Professor Delmar Oberbraun. What we found in both audio and video tapes, journals, and other sources, was that something went terribly wrong.*

"*To answer your question in this particular case, the body actually dies, but the brain keeps functioning in certain areas; this being the motor reflexes and certain parts of the speech, hearing and sight. It's also been found that the part of the brain controlling hunger is also affected. The very bottom line here is that these individuals are dangerous. Citizens should know what to look for in this instance. That being, they act as though they may be in a drunken state, their flesh appears sickly and pasty, and are capable of moving at various speeds.*"

Wes Tinzel moved the mic to his own lips. "*What exactly are these things?*"

Fret shook his head. "*I know it's hard to believe such things exist, but for now the only term we can come up with is a zombie-like being. The Secret Service is also working closely with us regarding this investigation, and unfortunately the agent on this case isn't available for comment. We've found that these things are actually dead people who have come back to life due to this parasite. Incidentally, when we began looking into this situation, there was an unfortunate individual who had fallen victim to the parasite after eating seafood that was not thoroughly or fully cooked. This individual was lost in transit to the hospital when the ambulance was involved in an accident. The patient was lost and believed to have been drowned in the bay. It's highly likely that this strain can be contracted through bodily fluids of any kind. Any seafood consumed at this point should be fully cooked and all raw seafood should be avoided. Period.*"

Once again Tinzel took the mic. "*So we're up against a parasite that can attack humans through any seafood taken from the bay? What about those items currently in stores?*"

"*Those currently being sold to consumers in any of the various markets have been warned about the problem and are labeling their seafood accordingly*" Lee said. "*Seafood departments are asking consumers to thoroughly cook their fish, preferably deep frying if at all possible to be sure to maintain the proper degree of heat. Crabs should be thoroughly steamed before using any of the meat in various dishes, including picking them from the shell.*"

His face grew solemn. *"I'll say this again to make sure all the listeners have heard it right. These individuals are highly dangerous and, due to being highly susceptible to light, they keep mostly in darkened areas and move around at night. One bite or scratch from one of these people can cause serious damage to the body. In essence, the victim will become one of them in a matter of days. As far as the use of weaponry, a shot to the head will kill the brain. Kill the brain and the body will follow."*

Chris took down what he could and made a call to Marlene Peterson's cell. He let it ring a number of times before giving up. The interview ended with Wes Tinzel announcing they would be going to the county offices and talking with the police. Chris smiled for a moment, congratulating Lee Fret in his mind for a job well done. "Thanks for the front row seating," he said, nodding to the manager as he got up. "I'll pass the information on to other sources in regards to whoever it was you saw wandering around here. I checked around the grounds but didn't come up with anything to go on. If I were you, I'd make sure I had some kind of weapon handy. I'd also try to keep a few guys around at night while you're closing up."

The manager nodded. "It's a small family business. I'm going to talk to the owner tonight and see what I can come up with. I don't want to stay here by myself any more than I have to. After seeing that news report, I'm scared out of my gourd. Are those people really serious? Zombies?"

Chris smiled. "You sell one hell of a cheeseburger by the way."

She shook her head. "You guys aren't very good at answering questions as you are at asking them, are you?"

He stood in the doorway for a moment. "You heard what the man said. Get your boss to have someone with you girls at closing time. At all times. I've seen these things first hand and they *are* dangerous."

Carol watched Chris walk toward his vehicle. The shed, she thought. "Betty, do you know if the shed is locked?"

Betty came out of the kitchen and shook her head. "No. I thought Harvey always locked it when he did the lawn and stuff."

"I don't think our friend here checked the shed," Carol said.

"Well, I'm not going out there by myself. No way."

Carol gave her a lopsided grin. "I'll go with you, scaredy cat."

*   *   *

Chris backed up and turned his car toward the road. Once again he tried his sister's cell and got nothing.

If an ass chewing was ever in order... He stopped the thought. If it weren't for Kaitlyn he'd be up shit's creek without a boat, never mind the paddle. He looked back at the diner before actually pulling out onto the road. The two women were walking toward the storage shed. He stopped for a moment and waited several seconds, wondering who the hell would be waiting on people when they walked in.

IIe had to laugh. Betty and Carol were two peas in a pod.

*   *   *

The door on the shed was not only unlocked, but had no padlock on it. Carol pointed the unlit flashlight at the door. "What the hell is Harvey thinking lately?"

Betty shrugged. "I'll consider that a hypothetical question since he tends to think with his little head half the time."

"We didn't even bring anything to protect ourselves with," Carol said.

"From what?"

"Oh, that's right; you didn't hear the great news. We have zombies running around the goddamn neighborhood now. It's not bad enough that we have muggers and murderers, now we have to be eaten alive by dead people."

Betty grabbed a thick piece of wood that was lying at the side of the shed. "Open it and let's find out."

Carol pulled the door to one side and let it swing by itself. She quickly put the light on, directing the beam to the center of the shed. A tractor sat in the middle of the dirt floor and on both sides were several different kinds of lawn equipment, including two gas operated push mowers. She slowly walked into the structure and swept the light back and forth. "Everything looks like it always does."

Betty moved up behind her and stepped to one side of the tractor. There was something different about the place. Something didn't smell right. "Jesus, this place reeks."

Carol sniffed the air. "It kind of smells like something's dead and rotting in here. A dead raccoon maybe?"

Betty turned toward the door. "I gotta get out of here. That freaking Harvey probably uses this place as his own personal shithouse. There's no one in the diner to take orders either, and the cook's gonna get pissed again."

"Again?" Carol looked at her.

"Yeah, well...you know I had to...I had a problem the other day. Okay? Gloria was there anyway. My cramps...."

It was wearing a military uniform when it pushed over the several sheets of plywood that rested on the wall behind one of the mowers. Betty was the first to scream. Carol followed suit, but swung the flashlight toward its face.

The nametag read, **Lawrence**.

* * *

Chris smacked the steering wheel and pulled over to the shoulder of the road. Things on his mind were keeping him from thinking clearly. He left the diner without getting any telephone numbers in case he needed the two women to corroborate what he had written down. This kind of shit had to stop. He thought of Marlene and wished she was with him at this very moment.

He was hooked and he knew it.

* * *

"Get out of there, Carol!" Betty screamed again as she made her way out the door. It was Carol's luck to catch her foot on one of the loose, wooden planks that the tractor tires rested on and fall to the ground. Betty ran forward and swung the wood she had with full force at the zombie's head. It made a cracking thud, but the dead man never batted an eye. It leaned forward as Carol tried to get to her feet, moving backward toward the wall behind her.

Betty brought the wood down hard on the back of the zombie's neck. It caught its attention for only a brief second before it once again paid full attention to the warm blooded woman on the ground in front of him. Carol delivered a hard blow to its face with the rear end of the flashlight. Once again it never blinked. Instead, it lifted one of her legs and brought its mouth toward the fleshy part of her calf. Carol kicked out hard and caught the thing under the chin. It flopped backward, but held fast to her leg. Betty once again brought the wood down on its head. This time it had her arm with the other hand. The thing smelled like it had dried piss in its pants for at least a week. The zombie pulled Betty hard, bringing her head up against the seat of the tractor. Her head twisted to one side and she dropped behind the tractor, lying very still.

Carol, by this time, was on one foot and pulling hard with the other. The dead man groaned, opening his mouth to display a disgusting orifice rimed with red and white looking pus that oozed onto its chin. It clamped its teeth down on the side of her foot just as she pulled away.

The blast from Chris' weapon once again sent Carol into another screaming frenzy. A deep red circle formed instantly on the side of the zombie's head, before splattering bone and brain matter over the back of the tractor's seat as the bullet exited.

"Pull your sneaker off! Now!"

Carol obeyed, quickly ripping the sneaker from her foot. Chris grabbed her leg and held it up for inspection. He shook his head with relief. "Thank God, the skin isn't broken."

The cook was now running across the small lawn with a butcher knife. "What the fuck is going on?"

Chris held his weapon up quickly. "Hold it!" He reached into his pocket and pulled out his commission book. "I'm an agent with the Secret Service and this man was dead way before I shot him."

Carol, who was now checking on Betty, looked back at him. "It's all right. He saved our asses."

Chris' cell phone filled the shed with a familiar tune.

It was Marlene Peterson.

CHAPTER 20

Rose aimed the beam of light to the rear. Little beady eyes stared out at them as the rats scurried from one side of the passageway to the other. The rats all seemed to be running from something and kept moving forward. Several of the women had to stifle screams by placing their hands over their mouths. Everyone pushed their bodies against the walls as the rodents ran past without stopping.

Several seconds later, it was obvious what the rats were running from. Water was beginning to cascade down the passageway in a shallow stream. The man with the refurbished pitchfork pushed the business end out in front at the remaining rodents. Kaitlyn grabbed the two kids and kept them moving toward the southern part of the passageway.

"What if there are more rats down here, Aunt Kate?" her nephew asked.

Mikey was the young boy. She knew his eyes must have been as wide as saucers when he spied the rats. "We're okay, buddy. They're just trying to get away from the water. They're not after us."

Courtney was the girl. She kept her hand tightly gripped on her aunt's belt. "I hate those things. They're full of diseases and stuff. I wish we were back home. I wish Daddy would have come to get us. You know what I mean, Aunt Kate, don't you? I don't mean to make you sad or anything. I just miss Daddy a whole lot."

"You didn't hurt me, honey. I knew what you meant. I'm sure he had good intentions of coming over to get you two." She prayed her statement had a bit of truth to it. With Chris, he was sometimes...no, she changed thoughts, he was a lot of the time, no play and all work. "We'll be okay. We'll be outside pretty soon and it'll be just us."

The guide once again took the lead. "There's no more of them following us. I think there was a hole someplace back there where the guys broke the wood up. There're no lights here because, like I've said earlier, it's just not part of the tour."

"I'd like to know just what the hell is going on around here?" one of the men asked.

"I wish I knew." The guide turned to face her followers. "I'm Rose by the way. I've never had any problems of any kind since I've been here. I've been here going on six years now. I can't believe this is happening."

Kaitlyn walked a short ways away from the kids, holding the guide's arm lightly. "Look, I have my brother's kids. He's a Secret Service agent. I don't know much about what he does exactly, but I really need to get in touch with him as soon as I can. I never told him where I was taking the kids. I left him a note thinking that he wasn't going to make it. How much longer before I can get to use my cell phone?"

Rose shook her head. "It's not that far. I really don't know...maybe a bit more than the length of a football field. I can't remember how far they said it was. It doesn't really say on the map I have. They had to make it go all the way out into the lower field. I guess that way no one would be able to see people coming up from the ground. The field is surrounded by dense woods."

"You whispered something bad, didn't you?" Courtney asked.

"No, baby, no. I didn't whisper anything bad. I just wanted to talk to the guard alone for a moment. Please trust me, okay?"

The girl nodded and wiped a tear from her eye.

At another fifty feet there was another small room set into the wall. This one looked as though it had caved in years back. Old boards had rotted where they fell. The smell of rotted wood made it seem as though they were in some sort of ancient mausoleum. The man with the pitchfork poked at something in the mushy earth. It made a clicking sound as the metal tapped the object. When it broke loose, it rolled into the passageway and stared up at them with a deathly smile of old teeth and empty eye sockets.

"Christ all mighty!" The man jumped back and kicked out with his foot. "It's a goddamn human skull!"

The guide grabbed the pitchfork and held the handle against her chest. "I told you not to touch anything down here, right? That could have been holding up something. You want this place to cave in on...." She stopped and looked back. Kaitlyn gave her a look of warning as she moved the two kids farther away. "Just don't touch anything, all right?"

"I was only trying...." the man began.

"Look. If you want to be Mr. Curiosity that's fine with me," the guide said. "But I believe I can speak for everyone when I say that none of us want to be the cat."

CHAPTER 21

Chris drove up a driveway that was more like an airport runway. It led to Marlene Peterson's home. He sat there for a moment looking at a large colonial in a rural section of Huntingtown. There were at least several acres of lawn in the front, and he could only guess how much of the wooded area she owned in the back. Marlene Peterson stepped out on the patio and smiled. It seemed to be a forced smile when he actually took the time to notice and he got out of the car with a bit of uncertainty. What men thought was going to happen on these types of visits usually didn't.

He wasn't one to feel intimidated by money or power, but Marlene Peterson was a woman who called the shots in her life. She was her own boss.

As he was working for the federal government, he was often reminded of that fact. Doctor Marlene Peterson was playing hardball in Camden Yards. He was playing stickball in an alley.

"I hope this isn't a dinner invitation. I stopped at a diner along the way and kind of pigged out on things a cardiologist worth his own weight in gold frowns on," he said.

Marlene smiled. This time it was one with a bit more warmth in it. That smile put his mind at ease for a moment, until she once again became straight-faced.

"We're going to say you're off duty so you can have a drink while we talk. Doctor's orders, and there's no room for negotiations."

Chris nodded and walked up the few steps to the patio. "Let's see if I can come up with your next phrase." He stopped just short of touching her. "You're going to tell me that you're not in the habit of inviting counterfeit patients to your home."

Marlene laughed. "Counterfeit? Okay, so you're a make believe patient. I already have everything set up. Sit down at the table and I'll be back in a moment."

"Marlene?"

She turned in the doorway. "Let's see. You're going to tell me that if it's bad news you won't be staying."

Chris smiled and leaned back. "You're good."

"And when I'm bad, I'm bad." She turned from him and went into the house.

He once again tried his sister's number. There was no answer. Lee Fret would probably be on his way over to the tobacco barns, and here he was hobnobbing with the local physician as the daylight faded.

Marlene came out with a tray that held a small ice container, two glasses, and a bottle of Crown Royal. Chris raised his eyebrows and glanced at her.

"What? We doctors know how to live, too," she said. "A drink once in a while isn't going to pickle anyone's liver. Plus, I want to make sure you're fully relaxed on your few days off."

"How...."

"I called," she said quickly. "Your boss was kind enough to remember me from the news the other night and told me he gave you a few days off. He also mentioned that your sister took the children on a little excursion to a location you weren't made aware of." She held up her hand. "Don't get upset. He mentioned that in passing after I asked where you could be found. He thought you might be looking for them."

Chris shook his head as she fixed the drinks.

"I tried the cell phone and there's no answer," he said. "It's getting dark. I tried her at home and her husband isn't answering."

"It's early, Chris. Maybe they stopped to get something to eat or went to a movie. I think there are a few G rated films down there in Prince Frederick." She sat down and crossed her legs. She was wearing a white, lightweight dress with a see-thru fuchsia scarf. The two ends were draped discretely over her breasts. Marlene Peterson was a beautiful woman, and he realized she simply played her looks down, probably because of her profession.

Chris sipped his drink and continued to look at her. He had the feeling she at first acted as though she wanted to avoid eye contact until she was ready to open up. Finally, she set her drink down on the glass tabletop and looked up.

"I'm going to give up working with both you and Lee," she said. "I think with both of you on this case you can get things done. I'll be there to answer any questions either one of you might have, but it's getting overwhelming. It's beginning to show in my practice and I can't afford to let those people down. They trust my judgment, Chris. I was never actually on the case anyway. I was simply taking care of these people."

He nodded. "That I didn't expect, but I'm glad it's not something horrible. I was thinking maybe it had something to do with my family."

Marlene slowly shook her head. "No. I made my decision when we left the meeting. I can see what all of this is doing to you. Oh, I don't mean to be critical of your business. I just see a lot of myself in your situation. I can get in deep if I let myself. I...." She looked down as Chris leaned closer to her.

"If we're playing our cards here, I'll lay mine on the table first." He lightly pulled her chair over to touch his. She didn't resist when he leaned toward her this time. This time his lips did make contact with hers. He could feel her warm breath on his cheek just like the day on the Yankee Dollar. Her hands stayed down at her sides until he pulled her to him.

"What am I getting myself into?" she asked.

Chris pushed her hair back from her face. "You're not getting yourself into anything you don't want to. If you want me to stop, I know both the letters very well in the word *no*."

This time her arms came up to wrap around his neck. Their lips met once again in a kiss that sent spasms of little electric shocks down his back. His mouth slowly moved to the side of her throat and behind her ear. As she let out a small gasp, they were suddenly rising up from where they sat, standing at the table in a full embrace.

Minutes later in bed, they curled into one another and touched all the secret places that turned pleasure to passion and back again.

It may have been her knowledge of the human body, he didn't know, but her gentle fondling of his genitals made him feel like crying out in ecstasy. He in turn gently parted her vaginal lips and found her little pearl. Her body arched upward as his fingers massaged in circles going one way and then the other. When he entered her, she grasped his buttocks and squeezed hard. Everything in the past suddenly evacuated the inner sanctum of his mind. It was a release and nothing more; he knew that.

Marlene's breath came faster as she clenched him tight, and when he finally let go, it was in perfect time to share her sexual release. They fell away from one another, but he pulled her to his shoulder and kissed her forehead.

"I made you feel guilty," she whispered in his ear.

Chris turned to brace himself on his elbow. "No. No, you didn't make me feel anything but wonderful. I've decided I'm doing the best I can. If that's not good enough for anyone...well, I guess I'll have to take a few steps back."

"So much for our drinks on the patio," she said, laughing softly.

Chris followed suit. "The night's young."

Marlene turned and kissed his broad chest. "Stay. Stay until the night's old and then turns into a new day."

"That sounds like something from an old movie," he grinned.

She smiled back, her eyes partly closed. "And what if it is?"

He stared into her eyes as though it might be the last time he would see her.

"If I'm not really careful...."

She touched her finger to his lips. "Don't. Let's not go there right now. I've decided that I've done the best I can, too. We have a lot to learn about one another. It's only been a short time, but I feel I've known you forever. This was a big step for both of us. Let's go ahead and take our time with the rest."

Later still, they showered together and once again touched one another's bodies in ways that made them both feel as though they were playing finely tuned instruments. Chris dressed in an old robe that Marlene claimed belonged to her father. Who was he to question? He walked out onto the patio in his socks and wrapped in the robe. Finding the drinks a bit watered down, he quickly fixed two more and placed his feet on an empty chair.

"I thought I heard the faint crooning of the Rolling Stones." Marlene came out in her own robe and sat down beside him.

He thought for a moment that it might have been his sister, but decided to ignore the thought of going in and checking. In a while they would be back inside and he could check it then. Together they sat and gazed at the night sky.

The moon was full, and with the light grayish clouds passing slowly over them, it was like watching a horror movie right out of the old Hammer Films.

Though the world was falling apart, tonight everything was just right.

CHAPTER 22

Jennifer leaned back in her chair, totally exasperated. Her ex-husband was one to be a no show fairly often, but he always answered his phone if he possibly could. His dip-shit sister was another tool in the shed altogether.

Picking up the remote for the TV, she switched to another channel and caught another report regarding the problem at the old tobacco barns. What the hell were they talking about when they said 'the walking dead'? Christ all mighty! Was the whole damn world going crazy right before her eyes?

She tried once again to reach her secret agent of an ex-husband, and once again she was handed the booby prize of no answer. The last she heard from Kaitlyn was that Chris hadn't showed up to pick up the kids. That was earlier this afternoon. She rifled through some of the mail on her desk until she came to a white envelope with Chris's name on it. She slid the opener through the top of the flap and pulled out the folded paper.

It said he was going to rent a home with an option to buy down at the point. The beach was there and the kids could enjoy it during the days that he had them.

"Oh! How nice! If only they were with you half the time they were supposed to be." Jennifer looked around the office for a moment. The words just came out of nowhere and she wanted to make sure no one overheard her ranting to herself.

She tried both numbers once again. If she had to listen to the *Rolling Stones' Brown Sugar* one more goddamn time today, she'd throw the friggin' phone across the floor. There was a knock on the door and one of the clerks poked his head in.

"I'm going home, Ms. Kearns. Is there anything you needed before I leave?"

Jennifer put on one of her plastic smiles. "No. I'm fine, Steve. Have a nice weekend."

Realizing it was late; she picked up her bag and coat and left what work remained on her desk for another day.

Jennifer closed everything up and switched off the TV. If she'd have waited a few more seconds, she would have heard the names on the list the front office had at the old tobacco barns.

She'd have known exactly where her children and sister-in-law were.

And she would also have known they were nowhere to be found.

CHAPTER 23

Rose shook her head and patted the man's shoulder. "Look, I'm sorry, okay? I'm the guide and I feel I'm supposed to be the responsible one here. I just don't want to lose anyone in this place. Let's keep moving forward so we can get the hell out of here."

Kaitlyn held Mikey and Courtney's backs against her body. "No one's going to blame you for anything, Rose. We don't even know what the hell is going on. But I do agree that we need to keep moving."

Rose nodded. "We will, but I want to be up front when we do. I noticed that the ground below us is getting a bit soggy. I have a feeling there's going to be a water problem as we move farther toward the other end."

"I paid eighty dollars for these shoes. I'll walk in my stocking feet," one of the women said from behind the line.

Rose turned around. "Look, I don't know what we're up against here. You've seen what we're up against up there." She gestured behind them. "If you cut yourself, there's no immediate medical attention and it could become infected. You can buy another pair of shoes, ma'am. Try that with another foot. All we have are a few little flashlights to see by. It's up to you."

The passageway suddenly shook. It wasn't a violent shaking, but enough to let them know that somewhere something was unstable. Somewhere up ahead the sound of dripping water became louder and louder. A few feet in front of them, the framing along the dirt wall slid down several inches. This caused the shoring that held up the beam going across the dirt ceiling to slide to the side. Two large clumps of dirt fell to the ground with a splattering sound as water began to run down the sides of the vertical beam.

"Move people! Let's get away from this place! Everyone! Move quickly away from the shoring that just caved in. We don't have anything to dig with, so if anyone gets blocked off from the rest of us there'll be hell to pay getting you out." Rose moved backwards as she spoke. The water began to run in the same direction they were traveling. It started as only a fraction of an inch at first, but leveled off to at least four inches.

Up ahead at another twenty feet, two beams had fallen into the passageway. The loose dirt causing the breakage came down beside them about five feet high. The woman with the expensive shoes was now quickly putting them back on. She pushed her way forward until she could see Rose clearly.

"This place is going to cave in on us, isn't it?" the woman asked Rose.

"No," Rose said quickly. "I told you we may be getting into some water problems. The shoring is old, but I think we'll be all right." She surveyed the damage and turned back to her little band of followers. "We're going to have to slide through the opening at the top of this pile. The beams aren't going anywhere because there's no room for them to fall to the side and out of the way."

The water was now getting higher due to the dam created by the cave in. Rose climbed to the top and peered through the opening. It was enough space for someone who was no more than two hundred pounds to get through. If need be, they would have to dig a bit to get the opening to widen even more. "It looks pretty clear on the other side. There's some water, but nothing we can't navigate through." She pointed at Kaitlyn and the kids. "You three go first. What're your names?"

"I'm Kaitlyn. This is Mikey and Courtney."

Rose nodded. "Okay, Kaitlyn. Climb up on the beam just like I did and swing your legs over to the entrance. Slide through belly-side down. I'll hand the kids up to you when you have everything but your head and arms through."

"Did you hear that?" One of the men pointed behind them.

Rose glanced over the group and shook her head. "What did it sound like?"

"It was like a sloshing sound at first and then like a rumbling or something. Maybe someone is coming for us and we can go back the same way we came. What if we get too far ahead and they can't find us?"

"Hello! Hello, is anyone there?" Several of the people began to shout in the opposite direction. There was air being forced into them for some reason. The air smelled twice as strong as what they were currently breathing. It smelled like rotting meat.

Rose shook her head and pointed toward the opening. She remembered the smell of those things...whatever they were.

"Go, get up there fast!" she yelled at Kaitlyn.

As instructed, Kaitlyn twisted her body to one side and pushed her legs through the opening. The dirt and water were cold and smelly, but it was a small price to pay for freedom at this point. On the other side there was a smaller beam that should have been supporting part of the earthen ceiling. Obviously it fell down during the cave in with one end resting on the floor and the other on the opposite wall. Kaitlyn stood in the center and held her hands out through the opening. Rose handed up Mikey first and then Courtney. Kaitlyn pulled them through without any problems and had the kids back away from the pile.

Rose picked who she thought to be the strongest man in the crowd and had him go through next to help the oldest get down on the other side. Trying to make light of the situation, he joked about none of the women wearing skirts or dresses. There were a few smiles and blowing out of the nose laughs, but the somber mood of the situation returned just as quick.

Rose managed to get fourteen of the people through before the surge of filthy water and dead bodies came crashing toward the blockage, with those who were truly dead and those who craved human flesh piling up against the four people remaining. In the darkness, the zombies at the bottom of the pile attacked the living with an insatiable hunger. Those on the other side directed their small lights to the opening, witnessing the horror of flesh and blood mixed with mud and water coming through the hole at the top of the pile.

Several of them threw up what little they had in their stomachs, the vomit splashing down onto the floor to mix with wet earth.

Those who managed to keep their stomachs from turning inside-out herded the remaining people quickly down the passageway.

CHAPTER 24

At the main entrance to the tunnel, the ground gave way under the rush of oncoming water. After so many years, it was little known what was under the earth at the makeshift escape tunnel known as the Underground Railroad. One cave in led to another until the entire area had collapsed into a one hundred yard sinkhole, including burial grounds and what was left of old rotted coffins and pieces of lumber shaped in what resembled storage bins of some kind.

Human bones protruded from the earth in certain areas, and skulls with their empty sockets peeked out from the slippery clay and mud along the sides and at the bottom of the great hole. Police officials who fell in, and were not killed or badly hurt, began to fire their weapons at the grotesque mutations that staggered toward them. Those officials still at the top helped out by firing down into the hole, carefully selecting their shots. Out of twenty-two men to fall into the gigantic pit, only five of them remained alive at the bottom, anxiously waiting for someone to pluck them out.

Toward the southern tip of the cavern, they saw a huge man-made hole in the side of the earth. One of the men flooded the darkness with his flashlight. It was a passageway of some kind, and all five were sure that those zombies who weren't shot in the head had made their escape through the same passageway. News crews were now flying helicopters over the area and sending images over the airwaves to the public. Six different fire departments had now dispatched trucks in case of flash fires, but mainly to help the wounded get back to safety and the dead to where they could be accounted for. The worse was yet to come when the pit started filling with water. When it reached the right height, it began to dissipate from the bottom of the pit into the passageway. The bubbling and churning water made its way into the hole, spitting up chocolate-brown mud like a giant mixing bowl.

The men grabbed onto anything that would keep them from being sucked down into the abyss. The dead were now being pulled down and into the cavern faster than the emergency vehicles could set up any kind of a rescue or retrieval plan. The two hook and ladder vehicles that were included with the others on the scene sent several men down on a winch. They hung the extendable ladders over the giant hole and had the men attach a metal basket to the second one. The men in the water were now holding onto wooden planks made for shoring up dirt ceilings and walls. The men on one detail worked on the other to bring the retrieval basket to one side in order for the trapped men to climb into.

Lee Fret ran to where the front office once stood. Like everything else in the immediate area, it was at the bottom of the humongous pit in shambles. The glass enclosure used for visitors sent large pieces of glass down on several of the men. One man's head was physically split in two, while another bled to death after having his shoulder and arm severed by one of the sharpened panes.

Lee looked frantically around to find someone who might have an idea where the passageway at the bottom of the cavern led to. He looked at the papers given to him some time after he finished his statement with the press. He pressed his finger to three names on the list. Who were these people? For some reason the name sounded familiar. Marlene Peterson advised him right after they heard about the problems here at the barns, that Chris was going to take a break to see his children. For minutes that felt like hours he racked his brain trying to remember the last name. He finally went onto the Internet in his vehicle and looked up constructions companies in the Maryland and Virginia area.

When the name Lambert came up, he scanned through the paperwork. Rather than call the construction company itself, Lee put a call through to the Secret Service's Intelligence Division. He was immediately transferred to the office of the Special Agent in Charge, Aidon Richards. Lee identified himself and asked for the information regarding Kaitlyn and Ernie Lambert and Kaitlyn's relationship to Chris. Aidon confirmed that she was Chris' sister. Lee told Richard's that Chris' children were possibly somewhere under the ground at the site.

It was now time to break the news. It was news that he could have gladly given to someone else, but it was the kind of news that only a friend could deliver.

Whatever it took, Lee Fret would be there for Chris and his family.

He dialed the number for Chris' cell phone.

CHAPTER 25

Ernie Lambert sped up to the police line and jumped out of his company truck. Behind him were Chris and Marlene. Chris immediately displayed his commission book and badge to the officer at the scene, and quickly made eye contact with Ernie Lambert. The officer nodded and allowed the three of them access to the area.

"How long have they been gone?" Chris asked Ernie.

"Since this morning," Ernie said. "Damn it! The whole fucking world is going to Hell in a goddamn hand basket!"

Chris handed him the note. "All I got was this. It was sticking in the door when I got to the house. I left a meeting and went over to get the kids. I wanted...."

"You need time with them, Chris." Ernie shook a finger as he spoke. "This could have been avoided if you'd been there."

Marlene stepped forward. "Mr. Lambert. It would have happened anyway. It would have happened even if Chris did have the children. These...."

"Spare me, Doctor Peterson." Ernie turned to face her. "It might have happened, but my wife wouldn't be in there."

Chris could feel his face burning. "She's also *my* sister, Ernie, and those are *my* kids down there with her. I've never had any qualms with you, Ernie; let's not start now, all right?"

Lee Fret walked up before the heated conversation came to a boil. "Whoa! This is a time to pull together, gentlemen, not slug it out." Chris was still staring a hole through the back of his brother-in-law's eyes. Lee put a hand on both of the men's shoulders. "Let's get over to the side here and try to figure this out, shall we?"

Ernie took a deep breath. "I'm sorry, Chris. But, damn it! You know me and your sister love those kids as much as you do. Hell, I took Mikey on several of the construction sites with me on numerous occasions. He loves it with his sister, but some of those things a father could be doing just as well."

Chris wanted to say a few things to clear matters up, but the lump in his throat at the moment would have made him look foolish. Instead, he turned his head and nodded. He realized no matter how hard you worked, there were times it didn't matter.

Ernie grabbed hold of his arm softly. "Look, I know you're a great dad. I'm not trying to say anything different. I was away from home pretty damn often when I first started this company. There were many a nights that Kaitlyn stayed over her folks' place."

Chris nodded slowly. "There were times I thought you and my sister would be divorced before me and Jennifer." He saw a small smile cross Ernie's lips. "Right now, all I want to know is where the hell my sister and kids are."

Lee pulled out a map of the area. "Okay, now that we have that straightened out. Here's a map of the underground area. The cave is in part of what was commonly known as a holding cell. It was used to keep the slaves from being auctioned off before they could actually get them out of harm's way. That's what they were telling people anyway. However, according to the information I got on the Internet from the National Archives in College Park, those who weren't sold were lined up and killed; execution style."

"You got that information off the Internet?" Marlene asked. She gave Lee a strange look.

"Yes, the National Archives webpage. I made a few calls and got the rest verbally. I have friends in high places," Lee said quickly.

Marlene cocked her head to one side. "No doubt!"

Lee opened the map and laid it out on the hood of his vehicle. The lines drawn in bold were actual tunnels used by the parties who ran the railroad. Thin lines that deviated from the broader passageway markings formed into the actual holding cells. From the design, they resembled horse stalls and were only built on one side. The darker lines ran toward the south and on several occasions smaller lines branched off and formed what looked like rooms of some kind. The lines finally formed into one line and ran southwest until they reached what seemed to be a wide space that didn't look like it was any kind of shelter.

Chris ran his finger over the broad line that started the actual passageway. When he got to the beginning, he once again ran his finger up slowly to where the holding cells first began. The line went through two of them and then branched off into another totally different area. It looked as though the passage it represented went down another level.

Chris tapped his finger on the paper as he spoke. "Ernie, this is another passage. It branches off at least sixty or seventy feet from the main passageway. There's a dip here and then again right over here. You're into construction, so you must be familiar with this type of a layout. Am I right?"

Ernie looked over his shoulder and surveyed a part of the map himself.

Lee answered before Ernie could. "That was the entrance and exit the executioners used after they did their dirty little deed. It comes out into a vacant lot somewhere out back. There used to be an old barn there at one time." Lee shook his head in disgust. "Wine, women and song right before and after their little hit job."

"So what do we do to get into that area?" Chris asked.

"We don't." Lee shook his head. "By now the whole area could be flooded with water. If your family members are down there," Lee gave them both a sympathetic look, "then hopefully they found an area where the water will be held back long enough for them to get all the way through."

Ernie moved a finger along the same lines as Chris. He finally pointed a finger at one particular part. "This here is an escape hatch that's been built about half way to the open field and about fifty...sixty yards off to the west. I'm familiar with this type of layout, even for as old as it is."

Lee checked it out carefully. "I'm not aware of that one. So, what does that mean as far as escape hatches go?"

Ernie shrugged. "Well, if the assholes were found out, they would have a better chance to take the escape hatch and get away nice and quiet like. If I'm not mistaken, this place was shut down not long after it was found to be an underground railroad during the war. This hatch was built...well, more than likely, by the slavers soon after it was taken over. If there's a chance in Hell, we can get to the upper part of the passageway before Kate and the kids."

Chris turned to Lee. "We're going to need support. I'm asking the PD if we can have a few men to go with us when we head down the alternate exit."

Lee brought Marlene, Chris and Ernie over to the cave-in. "That hole you see on the other side is the beginning of the tour. You get underground from the back of the office on a staircase leading down to the passageway. What caved in was the hollowed out portion where the stairs were built. At more than two hundred years old and in today's day and age, I don't understand how the hell this ever passed inspection."

Chris radioed in to the Southern Maryland Dispatcher. It took several minutes before the sheriff was located. When Evans returned his call, he brought the sheriff up to date on the situation at the site. Four more police officers were on their way to the site, as well as two state troopers. It would be around five o'clock in the morning before they could actually get down into the passageway.

Chris slid his phone back in the holder and walked back to the others. Five o'clock was an hour away, but it would seem like a lifetime.

CHAPTER 26

The man Rose had picked to help the others was now leading. The only light they now had was from small keychain lights that only a few people had. Rose's was left behind with the others on the other side of the wall. They moved slowly and were advised to keep to the center of the passageway. Two of the women were crying and holding onto anyone who would stay by their side. They could all still hear the grunts and groans from behind, but were only too glad to keep moving to avoid staying in one place for very long.

Kaitlyn kept the kids close. Every so often they would trip her from getting their legs entangled due to their closeness. It didn't matter; they weren't getting out of her sight for more than an arms length. She was thankful at times for the dim lighting. At least the kids weren't able to see her tears whenever she broke down. She stifled several sobs and told Courtney she was only trying to catch her breath.

The man in front suddenly stopped. "The water's getting kind of deep. I realize it's only up to our shins, but I think it's starting to catch up with us." He directed the light toward Kaitlyn and the two kids. "Sorry, I didn't mean to scare the kids. By the way, my name's Ken Yardley if anyone really cares."

"We're thankful for your help, Ken!" one of the men shouted in the back.

"That's no problem. Glad to help wherever I can. I can't remember what the map looked like as far as the rest of the passageway, but I think we're still a ways away from the open field. The air is getting kind of stale down here, too."

One of the women brushed mud and sweat away from her face. "At least we're still able to breathe. It's not the freshest of air I've ever inhaled, but it'll keep us alive until we can get the hell out of here."

A woman screamed and kicked out violently. Another man with a penlight flashed it down to where her legs were. She screamed again as everyone around her fled to where Ken Yardley was standing. A severed arm did a small water dance by floating several seconds and then sinking out of sight, only to come to the surface once again. Kaitlyn had already turned the kids away just before the woman's legs were illuminated.

"Let's keep moving," Ken said.

The sound of sloshing water grew more intense as they quickly made their way through the passageway in an attempt to keep further ahead of the detached limbs. They traveled like this for almost five minutes. It wasn't until another rumbling up ahead made them stop and listen carefully. Something smacking the water had them straining to see ahead of them regardless of the lack of light. Once again something was falling into the water. This time it was much heavier and sounded as though it might not be more than fifty feet ahead.

"It sounds like mud falling into the goddamned drink," one of the men said.

Yardley looked back and shined the light towards the voice. "We don't know that. It could be a lot of things, but it doesn't have to be mud."

"Ken, shine your light up ahead and to the right." It was Kaitlyn's voice he heard in the darkness.

Ken put the little light where she asked. It wasn't enough to illuminate the entire area, and he moved up a bit. The rest followed behind him, keeping to the center of the passageway and stopping just short of touching him. He once again put the light in that general direction. This time he could see an opening.

The man with the pitchfork moved up to where Ken was standing. "It would be a good idea to keep this handy," he said. "I'm Ralph Lansing." He leaned in and kept his voice down the best he could. *I don't think those things are entirely gone. I have a feeling they're going to get through that opening and damn soon.*"

"Thanks, Ralph." Ken nodded in agreement but kept it to himself. By now he realized the two children Kaitlyn had with her were terrified beyond belief. At the opening to the newfound tunnel, Ken made several passes over the area with the light. It went in about twenty feet and then veered off to the left. Both men walked slowly to the place where the tunnel cut to the left. Directly around the corner was an open room. Ralph moved to the right of Ken and kicked something over. It had a tinny sound when it toppled over.

Ken directed his light to where the sound came from. On its side was a lantern. Ralph picked it up quickly and inspected the frame and glass. "Hot damn! It's all right." He shook it several times. "It has kerosene in it, too."

Ken reached into his pocket and pulled out a lighter while Ralph inspected the wick and what he called the control knob. "Put that light right on top of it," Ralph said.

With enough light to get the thing in working condition they had the wick up to a level that would ignite and stay burning for a while. Ralph let the glass chimney slide down in place and the tunnel was immediately illuminated with a soft yellow glow. Once again, this room was just another type of holding cell. But a tree stump that had been uprooted and sat in the middle of the floor told quite a different story.

The skeletal remains of a human being had been left in a kneeling position, but minus a head. This they found on the other side of the stump. Several calls came out from behind them as to where they were and if they were all right.

Ralph quickly went back and told the rest to stay behind for now, explaining that it was just an old room. On a makeshift shelf in the back of the room was another lantern. This, too, was in working order. There was no exit door to the room from either side, and both men agreed that there was no sense in hanging around. In this room, the water had no place to go and would be a bit higher.

"Bastards," Ken said.

"Fucking bastards is more like it," Ralph said, holding the lantern up for one last look.

Kaitlyn hugged Courtney and Mikey to her side. "Look, guys. We have a lot of light now. See, things are beginning to look up."

The statement was no longer valid as the first zombie came up the passageway. The rest of the party ran up toward the room. Ken Yardley, now holding the pitchfork, lifted it up over his right shoulder, left hand in front of the right. His first thrust sent the metal tines through the dead man's chest with little effort. He pushed hard to back it up and pulled the pitchfork out for another shot at it. By this time two more had showed up and were hungrily making their way past their battling comrade. Ken once again sent the tines into the zombie's chest and again received the same results; the thing refused to die.

Kaitlyn moved to the back of the room and huddled in the corner with Courtney and Mikey. They were now both crying for their mother and father. The feeling of guilt that she hadn't left a better message for her brother left her crying along with them. The rest of the people moved back against the wall opposite where she and the kids were. The men took up pieces of wood heavy enough to use as weapons, while the women tried their best to comfort the young boy and girl, while at the same time maintain their own sanity.

Ralph kicked over several pieces of furniture that had been broken over the years. In the corner and covered with an old confederate flag that was now well worn and tattered, was an old sword. The zombie closest to Ralph reached out for him and he swung the old sword in a sweeping motion, then down over the thing's neck. The head lolled to one side for a brief moment before plopping into the water below.

Ken had now found a solid mark by sending the pitchfork into the face of the man he'd already stabbed several times. This time the tines found their way through both eye sockets and into the brain. The zombie dropped to the floor like a sack of potatoes and stayed put.

Another man, who was closer to the entrance, hit another one on the side of the head with a piece of hardwood. The blow was so strong it actually caved in its skull. This too proved to be effective. The thing staggered for a moment and then fell silent into the filthy water.

"Kill the brain!" the man yelled. He looked at Ken Yardley in the yellow glow of the light. "It's the brain that has to be destroyed! I don't get what's happening here, but I know that it works. Who the hell ever thought that all those zombie movies would actually have a bit of truth attached to them?"

It wasn't a real question and, if it was, it was treated as hypothetical; no one answered.

With the last zombie put down, they all breathed a sigh of relief. For a few seconds no one spoke; then a question was raised.

"Does anyone have the time?" The man with the hardwood board asked as he leaned against the dirt wall and looked up the passageway.

"What difference does it make?" a woman asked. "We're not going anyplace in a hell of a hurry."

The man nodded. "Yeah, I know. I just would like to know what time it is, that's all."

Ralph glanced at his watch. "It's four-fifty. That's in the morning, by the way."

CHAPTER 27

The repeated burglar alarms going off in the shops in California, Maryland had the PD headquarters people jumping through their asses. The large, plate-glass windows in every store front were smashed in and littered with the undead. It could have been out of memory that they came to the stores, but their lust for human flesh overrode anything else their feeble minds could remember. Anyone working in backrooms or storage areas who couldn't get out in time were food for the insatiable appetites of the living corpses.

The well lit establishments were hit first. The police found the body of the dry-cleaning owner in a pile of blood and torn flesh between the cleaning and the sewing repairs. Rubbing salt into the wound meant shooting these unlucky people in the head. It was either that or end up having them getting up again and running with the pack.

In the back alleys of the eateries, old discarded and maggot ridden foodstuff found its way into the stomachs of those zombies who ventured into the old dumpsters. Officers from several different stations formed a barrier of squad cars, pulling their vehicles into the alleys and loading docks, making well aimed head shots to keep the dead from moving off in other directions.

Another block down, they could hear the sound of more gunshots. All night liquor stores and gas stations were not left unmolested. Young men and women behind the thick security glass of the filling stations stared in horror at what stood staring back at them. Supervisors were woken up in the wee hours of the morning with threats of employees quitting their jobs on the spot. By now, Maryland, parts of Delaware, Pennsylvania, DC and Virginia were under a state of emergency.

Just over the state line in Delaware, Green's Funeral Home had prepared an unembalmed body for a morning viewing the night before. In the cooler, the body laid dormant for practically eight hours. Josh Green was up at five o'clock sharp to get the body dressed and ready for the last visitors he would never be aware of.

Green was a master at his trade and had the body ready in forty minutes for an eight o'clock viewing. By five-fifty, he was in the back of the building washing the hearse.

Green's wife came over and listened to her husband as he came up the stairs. She was always asked to give her opinion on the final look of the deceased. It wasn't something she was very fond of, but she knew it meant a lot to her husband, as it did those who survived the deceased. After marrying Josh, death had become a big part of her life. This morning it would be an even bigger part.

She got up and glanced out the window to check on what kind of morning it was. She intended on calling to her husband as he made his way to their bedroom, putting on her best smile and mentioning how it was going to be a beautiful morning and God given day for the deceased's sendoff. The funny thing about it was, Josh was washing the hearse and not in the house.

Ida Green had never seen the deceased, living or dead, but as the dead man walked through the doorway and made his way toward her, she could tell that something wasn't quite right about this man.

She screamed as the stranger with his skin as pale as pure driven snow continued to slowly advance on her. The man's eyes were rimmed in red and sunken in. Even though a bit of makeup adorned the lower part of his eyes, they still looked lifeless, discolored and dead.

She screamed again as he forced his mouth open, tearing the staples through his lips and growling at her through cigarette-stained teeth. Ida Green stumbled over the hassock she so often sat on while putting on her shoes as the man's dead weight fell on her before she could regain her footing and stand up. Her blood was warm and fresh as it left her body in pulsating spurts and slid down his throat.

Josh Green had worked with the dead for many years so he ignored the news flashes that were popping up at every commercial break.

The dead were just that; dead.

Zombies were in the minds of those who made millions of dollars for telling stories in books and films. But Josh Green would have memories of this horror for the rest of his life.

Hearing his wife's second scream at the last minute, he made his way into the house in record time. Passing through the blue room, he found an empty casket that had tumbled from its bronze-colored bier and now rested sideways on the floor.

Upstairs, he found the cause of the screams, and a corpse who had soiled his brand new suit with the blood of his loving spouse.

CHAPTER 28

It was well after five in the morning when they formed a line at the entrance of the escape hatch. Two more unmarked cars pulled up near the entrance. Several seconds later, four men emerged from the vehicles. They made their way toward the others and flashed their credentials. Two were Secret Service and two were FBI. Five minutes after they arrived, another two cars pulled up with two locals and two state troopers.

Chris nodded to his comrades, suddenly recognizing who they were and what division they were from. Everyone introduced themselves and offered the same explanation. They were sent to lend a hand when the crew went underground to find the lost tourists. Jackson and Bateman, the two Secret Service agents were sent from Investigations. The two FBI men, Bordon and Lederman were sent from forensics. The two deputies passed on their apologies to Chris from the Sheriff's office for the lack of the other two men.

Lee moved back to where Marlene was standing. "I'll stay here with Doctor Peterson in case anyone else shows up."

It was Chris who opened the old wooden door. It was wrapped in old band iron and held together with old rusted bolts. The smell of stale air and the putrid stench of hundred year old body odor had him quickly back up for fresh air. Bateman offered a light that sent a beam down into the hole bright enough to see that the ladder was old and rusted. Several of the metal rungs were split in two as well as several more missing completely. Water was flowing past the last few rungs, but it was hard to tell from up top how deep it actually was.

Bordon flipped on his own light and stepped up to the entrance. "I've been in this situation before. Tell you what. I'll go down first and the rest of you will know exactly how deep and what we have for a floor. It's kind of hollow sounding down there in case anyone hasn't noticed. It sounds like it opens up a bit wider as it heads south."

Lederman clipped the end of a rope to Bordon's belt just before he descended. The metal ladder wobbled in all directions with the man's weight. The hookup at the top was still fairly solid, so there wasn't too great of a chance for it to break loose anytime soon. Bordon stepped down to the last rung before dipping his other foot into the water. The bottom of his leg disappeared to the top of his knee.

"It's pretty solid under the water." Bordon unhooked the rope from his belt as he looked up at the faces peering down at him. He let the beam of light open up the passageway in front of him. Once again he looked up at the rest of the crew.

"It's exactly as I thought. It looks like some of the shoring, top and bottom, has caved in. One of the side walls is gone completely and there's an open area about the size of a garage. Then it looks like it goes off to the left and down some."

Chris was already half way down. The rest took their time until everyone had safely made their way into the shaft. They waded through water that at times smelled like it had passed over dead animals that had been baking in the sun for days. The opening described by Bordon was a cave-in that dropped off to the left. Water cascaded down the passageway like a small waterfall, but was still passable. Chris tied another piece of rope off at one of the fallen beams and went down along with Bordon. The rest followed, using the rope as a makeshift banister.

At the bottom, they continued straight ahead for almost a hundred feet until the passage wound its way to the right. Chris pulled the map out of its dry container and carefully opened it under the light that Ernie held up. "It looks like it goes on for about another hundred feet or so. It appears to go off to the left again and then heads upward. That must be where the exit is," Chris announced.

Ernie put a finger somewhere in the middle of the line. "Anywhere from where we are to this point could be where the others are. We don't know that, but if they're down here, it's slow going for them because of the water. Our only hope at this point is that there are no blockages anywhere," once again he pointed out sections, "from this point to here. If there's no place for the water to go," he shrugged, "they could all drown."

Before they could move again there were other sloshing footsteps coming from somewhere else. Chris held up his hand for silence. Each man took slow easy breaths, listening quietly with their mouths slightly open. There was definitely movement from someplace behind them. The splashing of water suddenly ended up getting mixed with voices that were unrecognizable. As the noise of the water being disturbed got louder, it became apparent that the voices were merely grunts and groans.

"Shit, we left the door open and the wrong dogs came home!" one of the troopers shouted.

CHAPTER 29

Ken and Ralph positioned themselves one in front and one in back. They would move at a slow pace and then stop for several minutes to listen. The water was now knee high, but seemed to be moving a bit slower. Kaitlyn stayed in the middle, keeping the two kids close to her side. It made her sick to her stomach knowing they would probably have nightmares for the rest of their lives. She should have taken them for ice cream at the mall. There were other people at the mall. What could happen? There was safety in numbers. What the hell was happening above ground? All these thoughts went through her mind in a rapid succession.

One of the women patted her shoulder and tried to smile. "We're going to get to the end of this place. You'll see. This is just a temporary setback for us. The children will have a lot of stories to tell their children when the time comes."

"Who would believe this?" Kaitlyn said. She tried to keep from being choked up, but the current situation made her words come out as sobs. "These are my brother's kids. He's a Secret Service agent and I know he'll be looking for us. My husband owns a construction company. Lambert Construction."

The woman's eyes brightened. "Oh?" Her mouth suddenly dropped open. "Oh, my dear God, what a coincidence! My son works for him. He's been there for about six months now. He says the work is hard at times, but he does like it. It's been God sent as far as I'm concerned. He stays out of trouble and he's able to keep up his child support. Your husband's Ernie, right?" She held out her hand. "I'm Beverly Carlisle."

The world suddenly opened up with the conversation. Kaitlyn took the woman's arm and held her close. "Hi, Beverly, I'm Kaitlyn. And yes, he started it in a garage with one van and five helpers." She laughed and it suddenly felt good. The kids looked up and listened to the conversation, too. Other people began to loosen up and strike up their own chats. "It's amazing what you can do when you put your mind to it."

Beverly nodded. "Your husband set up some classes for him. I know my son didn't want to go, but he realized that someone was actually trying to help. I'm going to sit down and write a letter to your husband. Edward, my son, he doesn't have to know anything about it. I'd just like to thank him for taking the time to care."

"Are you afraid?" Mikey asked Beverly.

Beverly smiled down at him. "Well, I was a bit afraid a little while ago, but now that I've met your aunt...no, not any more. You're not afraid, are you, dear?"

"If my dad was here, he could shoot them. He would shoot those things for trying to kill us. He protects the President sometimes."

"Sometimes I think he believes that's more important," Courtney said.

Beverly shot Kaitlyn a concerned look but said nothing. Kaitlyn hugged her niece a bit closer. "Courtney, that's not true at all. The President is an important person, but so are you and Mikey. Your father loves both of you very much. He has a very important job, but he would never choose his job over you and Mikey. Never!"

"Did you hear that?" Ken Yardley turned to the rest of the group. "Everyone be quiet and listen. I thought I heard something like an explosion." Several more muffled pops went off. "There they go again."

Ralph Lansing nodded. "I heard it that time. It sounds just like gun shots."

One of the other men in the group walked to where they were standing. "Yeah, it is gun shots."

Kaitlyn held the kids closer to her. "That means someone else is down here. If they have guns then it means that there's a good chance it's the police."

"It seems that those *things*...whatever they are, are mindless corpses. I don't know if they have the intelligence to run the other way. But if they do, they could just as well be heading this way." Ralph pointed down the passageway. "I say we keep moving just the way we've been moving. The water's getting deeper now. That hole we came through could have opened even more."

Ken signaled to move forward with a wave of his hand. "I agree. If I remember right, the passageway goes upward. If that's the case, then we might be in a lot deeper water when we get to that point."

One of the beams across the ceiling began to rumble in the middle of the group. Water dripped down from it like a large open faucet. Six of them got through before the waterlogged plank gave way. It slid sideways and into the wall on the other side. There was a scream from behind them. Rose was caught directly in front of the heavy piece of wood. It dragged her to the other side with it, smashing her solidly in the chest.

Another plank slid into the water from the opposite side. Beverly Carlisle moved toward the woman, but was taken by the arm. Ralph Lansing pulled her back to the other side of the group. "No. She's gone. Those planks are heavy by themselves, never mind that they're now soaked with water, too."

"But we can't just leave her here."

Ken shook his head. "Mrs. Carlisle, we can't drag her with us either. I don't like doing this any more than you do, but it's something that has to be done for the rest of us to survive."

With one last glance behind her at the fallen woman, Beverly had to agree he was right, and she moved forward with the rest of the group.

With one of their number lost, they once again moved down the passage.

Kaitlyn turned back one last time, a twinge of guilt and pity for Rose filling her to the point she had to turn away.

The muddy water had now risen to the tour guide's eyes, since she had fallen over in a slumped fashion.

Several seconds later, only the beam was left to hide the horror beneath it.

CHAPTER 30

The undead staggered and stomped through the water with only one purpose on their clouded minds; get to where the smell of the living originated. Where they came from was a question none of the rescuers could answer. There were no others around before Chris and the crew entered the shaft. Chris and the four other agents knelt down in a single file and picked their shots. The deputies and troopers took their places behind the agents in a standing position. Flesh and bone sprayed into the water as each bullet found its mark and collided with their heads.

After three or four minutes of shooting and reloading, it appeared that at least twenty or thirty of the bodies were piled up on top of one another with others still coming. Chris had the officers back up twenty or so feet, and once again they took another stance. The zombies were now climbing over their own to get to the warm flesh and blood in their path.

Ernie Lambert kept a light frozen to the area from behind. It gave the agents and officers a chance to get a good bead on the advancing zombies. He also kept an eye out for danger behind them. If the zombies came from both sides, the crew would have one hell of a time shifting back and forth, especially with just head shots.

The smell of gunpowder mixed with dead flesh filled the passageway. After another four or five minute volley they stopped coming. They could hear grunts and groans from around the corner, but the rest of the undead would not come forward.

"Let's keep moving back!" Chris shouted.

All of them agreed and kept moving in the opposite direction. One or two of the undead would show up from around the corner, only to be picked off by the agents. The passage now wound its way to the left again and finally came to a solid dirt wall with broken timber for its shoring. The passage here was much larger and the water remained the same depth. Ernie and Bordon sent a beam of light down in the opposite direction. It was empty, but there was something in the quietness of the moment that seemed to hang in limbo. Something or someone was moving in the other direction; coming toward them.

"What if it's them?" Ernie asked.

Chris turned to the rest of them. "We're going to have to go back the way we came. That means if it's the tourists, they're going to have to pass the bodies we just left behind." Chris suddenly raised his hand and shook his head. "Let me put it this way. No one can stay behind. If those things come out, and they will, we're going to be shooting one another in a damned crossfire."

Jackson and Bateman moved up to the front with the two FBI agents following. "We were sent here to help you find your family." Bateman looked over at Ernie as he reached into a pocket on the side of his thigh. "I don't know how legal this is, but ask me if I actually give a fuck at this point. Shit, everyone else down here has one." He handed Ernie a gun and a second clip. In ten seconds or less he showed Ernie the basics. "Ernie, you keep an eye out from behind us just in case. The rest of us can do exactly what we did during the last volley with those things. We'll get down in the front while you guys fire over our heads. If it's the tour group we can only hope that they'll hear the shots and, hopefully if they already have, they'll stay back."

The four agents led the way back to the outlet where the bodies lay. The stench was almost overpowering; the water clinging to their pants legs left a residue to dead blood that reeked of decomposition. Climbing over the bodies was a whole new thing. Each man tried not to touch the corpses they stepped over, which proved to be damn near impossible. The passage they came out of was now clear. The undead had gone in another direction, and Chris had a feeling it was the same way they were headed.

CHAPTER 31

Jennifer Kearns, upon stepping out of her car, was immediately approached by police officers monitoring the police line. The whole area had now been corded off with yellow tape. Her complaints about her children being underground fell on deaf ears. "I just heard the names of the missing. My son and my daughter are down there with my sister-in-law!" she screamed.

One of the officers took her back to her vehicle. Others who had arrived because of hearing the names of their family members came to the same ending. They were not allowed anywhere beyond the police line.

Jennifer held the officer's arms with tears streaming down her face. "Please. Please tell me what's going on. All I want to know is if my children are still alive. Is that too much to ask? They're just babies and probably scared out of their minds. I can't just stand here and do nothing."

The officer nodded in sympathy. "Ma'am, there's nothing you or any of us can do until we hear from the search party that went down after them. Just as soon as *we* know something you'll be the first to know. There's a vehicle over there with some hot coffee and cocoa. Why don't you go over there and get some? I know it's not what you want to hear, but that's the way it is for all of us at this point. Please, let us do our job, okay?"

Several shots were fired from the other side of her vehicle and the officer quickly turned to see what the commotion was. When he drew his weapon, there were at least twenty zombies approaching from behind, all of them moving toward the other family members. Jennifer could only stare off into space. The radio broadcast announcing the horror of dead cannibals walking around had finally crept into her line of sight; in the sour taste of reality.

One of the undead bit down hard on the space between the neck and shoulder of one of the women. The blood spurted out uncontrollably until she fell quietly to the ground. An officer close by sent a bullet from a.357 magnum through its forehead. Another put a bullet into the woman's brain before her dead body could become a gang member to the legion of the undead.

Jennifer screamed again as Lee and Marlene ran up to her.

"We heard you. You're Jennifer Kearns? Chris Kearns' ex-wife?" Marlene asked.

Nodding her head violently, Jennifer held onto both their arms. "Please. My children are down there. I just...."

"Jennifer, Chris is down there, too," Marlene said. "There are a number of agents, troopers and deputies with him. They'll find the tourists. They'll find your children and get them out of there before anything can happen."

Around them more shots rang out. Four more cruisers pulled up with more deputies and state troopers. They took a stance behind their vehicles and picked off the zombies before they could actually breach the police line. The ground in front of them was now littered with dead bodies. Two deputies pulled the slain woman to the side and placed her in a body bag behind the lines. The undead now came from the wooded areas, backyards, and even behind store locations. In the distance, sirens blared as the emergency vehicles raced to several different fires throughout the area.

Jennifer sat with Marlene and Lee at one of the police-line stations. Lee brought her a cup of coffee and sat down at one corner of the table beside her.

"You said you heard what's happening on the radio?" Lee asked.

Jennifer nodded. "I was just getting ready to turn off the radio when the announcer said something about a critical announcement and to stay tuned for more information. I thought it might be something about the war in Iraq. I have a friend with a son over there. I always try to listen just in case. They said they were setting up emergency shelters for people who were homeless or whose homes were susceptible to being broken into. They mentioned something about a mysterious parasite making people go crazy.

Then they mentioned the cave-in here and gave a list of missing persons. My sister-in-law and my kids...."

Lee passed her several napkins and held her hand. "Chris will find them. We've been working on this case for quite some time."

"What the hell is happening? What the hell are those...*things*?"

Lee and Marlene looked at one another for an answer. Marlene took a deep breath and answered first. "To be honest, they're zombies. I know it sounds crazy. I'm a doctor by the way, so you can imagine how I felt when I first came in contact with this...whatever it is."

Lee let go of Jennifer's hand and offered a further explanation. "It's a parasite that attacks the human brain. You can't catch it like a cold, but you can ingest it as far as we know, and you can be bitten by one of them. That's why they had to shoot the woman. It appears that it's now out of control. I guess your sister-in-law took the kids on the tour and unfortunately there was the cave-in. The only way out is to follow the route to the other side of those woods. They found an extra entrance or exit, whatever you want to call it, and figured they could head them off before they actually got to the other side."

Jennifer's eyes went wide with fright. "And if those things are down there? They don't have any weapons. How the hell can they defend themselves from people who are already dead?"

Marlene was just coming back with refills. "They can't. But hopefully they've been able to stay out of harm's way. Hopefully there aren't any of those things down there. You have to be optimistic, Jennifer."

"What about the water?" Jennifer asked. "I saw water down in that huge hole. What if they became trapped and drowned?"

Lee nodded. "I understand, but the water isn't rising in the crater. That means it's moving along at a certain depth, which is probably knee deep; max. As long as the crater doesn't fill with water they should be all right." Marlene gave Lee a quick glance. It wasn't exactly the truth, but it was something to keep the woman from going over the edge.

Lee's cell phone rang and he quickly flipped it open. "What's that?" He listened into his phone for a few minutes. Marlene never took her eyes off of him. "So, you're telling me we had it all wrong?

Well, in a way that's good news, but it doesn't shed any light on how Dale Brant got sick. If we..." Lee suddenly leaned back and exhaled hard.

"What?" Marlene asked.

Lee gave Marlene a look and shook his head as he spoke into the phone. "I guess he thought his life was worth fifty thousand dollars. Now, neither one of them are around to collect it. They're both dead. We were wrong about the daylight as well. The damn things are running all around this place."

Marlene and Jennifer watched as Lee ended the call.

"What were we wrong about?" Marlene asked.

Lee gave her a half-ass smile. "The parasites are harmless in sea water when altered the way they were. There's no immediate danger of ingesting anything from the Chesapcake Bay, for example. Brant was told he'd be paid fifty thousand dollars if he'd use himself as a human guinea pig. Oberbraun gave him a line of bull about how if he got sick he would be given the antitoxin and be paid another fifty thousand."

Marlene shook her head. "So, Oberbraun lied to him. That was just another nail in his coffin, and another reason why he killed himself. The charges against him were just stacking up on a regular basis."

Lee ran his hands through his hair. "The Pentagon didn't know about this part of the scheme. According to what they found in Brant's home, it was a private deal between Oberbraun and Brant. The CDC is going on live all through the rest of the day and into tomorrow about the food sources. Meanwhile, those who are already infected with the strain are simply making others just like them. It appears they don't have that much of a fear of sunlight either," he motioned toward the commotion, "as you can see."

Marlene sipped her coffee with a look that had 'dumbfounded' all over it.

Lee shook his head. "Don't let it get to you, Doc. If a week ago, someone told me I'd be sitting around someplace in Maryland while zombies were literally being shot all around me, I'd tell them they needed to fit me for a straight jacket and rubber walls."

CHAPTER 32

With the lanterns throwing light from behind, Ralph Lansing swung his sword continuously back and forth, dropping advancing zombies in their path. The heads of the oncoming dead cannibals often tumbled into the murky water, followed by its body falling in the opposite direction. Ken Yardley busied himself by repeatedly ramming the pitchfork into their undead faces, aiming the tines for their eyes and into their brains. When one of them went down, several more took their place.

Two of the women in the group fell, tripping up several others who were desperately trying to back up. Ken tried to help them to their feet, but it was fruitless. The lanterns cast eerie shadows of the zombies in front of him, making the passage appear to have more of the things than there really were. It also made it difficult to actually know who was who. It took constant jabbing with both hands to guide the pitchfork to its deadly destination. He also had to keep a continuous lookout on the malevolent sword Ralph was swinging in order to keep out of the way.

The undead fell on the living who went down and couldn't regain footing. Beverly Carlisle and Kaitlyn kept to the rear, keeping the kids behind them and free of any chance they might be trampled by the rest of the group. When Ralph fell, it seemed like that particular moment in time stood still for Ken. Two of the zombies had him by the legs while one of them ground its teeth into his calf, even though the sword had taken off one of its ears and made a gaping slash wound through part of its shoulder.

There were now nine of them left. One of the other men had taken up the sword after Ken was able to snatch it from Ralph's death grip. Watching Ralph Lansing being eaten alive was something he could have easily done without. One of the lanterns was now gone, but the light from the other was still enough to keep the undead from mingling with the living.

Kaitlyn turned Mikey and Courtney toward the wall when Beverly Carlisle suddenly yelled up to Ken that something was in their path. The light opened up the shadows behind them and three dead bodies lay face down in the water. A short distance away there was another pile of bodies lying in various positions. A hand reached up from the filth and grabbed Courtney by the ankle with an iron grip. The head of the undead woman surfaced; the hair hanging down over the face in matted clumps. Kaitlyn repeatedly stomped down hard on the dead woman's face. Beverly now had Courtney's foot, pulling it toward her and making sure it got nowhere near the thing's mouth.

Beverly was finally able to pick up Courtney while Kaitlyn held Mikey. Both of the kids were now screaming out of control. Ken rammed the pitchfork down hard on the woman's head, ending her thrashing and growling beneath the weight of both Kaitlyn and Beverly.

"I'm not climbing over those bodies!" someone yelled from behind.

Ken looked around frantically for a target and then kicked out hard with the bottom of his foot, sending one of the zombies crashing into the others. Ramming the tines into the face of another sent it quietly into the water below.

They were now at least twenty feet from the escape passageway leading to the outside. Beverly Carlisle lost her footing and fell with Courtney. Both their bodies rested on a dead zombie before Beverly was able to push herself to a sitting position.

One of them had Ken by the shirt with its mouth inches away from his face. Grasping the pitchfork's handle at both ends, he came up hard from underneath the thing's jaw, sending its bottom teeth into the top. Coming up from the bottom once again, the tines found their way through its throat and out the back of its head.

Kaitlyn now had Beverly by the back of her shoulders, pulling up hard to get both her and Courtney to their feet. An older man who had been holding back to stay out of the way of the younger ones in the group came forward. A woman in the group followed him, and both led Beverly and Kaitlyn six or seven more feet toward the escape route.

The exhausted Ken Yardley fell to his knees. Less than six feet away, the zombies swarmed in for the kill. It was like battling with a set of barbells. Ken's arms could no longer lift the pitchfork. He fell backward just as the passageway was flooded with an intense light.

"Get down!"

Kaitlyn and Beverly turned to see only the silhouettes of the people behind them. In the illuminated passageway, the zombies were lit up to show the actual horror of their being. In every case, their eyes were rimmed in red and yellow-green teeth were enhanced only by their pyrea infected gums.

"Get down! Everyone get the hell down!"

It wasn't an order any of them cared to follow, but the outline of their rescuers guns behind the intense beams of light gave a whole new meaning to getting out of deaths frightful grip. Kaitlyn and Beverly dropped with the two kids first, followed by the rest of the group, leaving the zombies directly over them. The sound of exploding weapons was ear piercing. The weight and the smell of decomposing dead bodies falling directly on top of them became totally gut wrenching.

A disfigured, dead face landed in front of Courtney. She screamed before Beverly could get her twisted around and away from the hideous spectacle. Trying to keep her own face out of the water, Beverly pushed the zombie's head to one side to prop herself up on an elbow. It was then that the thing bit down hard between her thumb and index finger. The zombie stood up once again, bringing Beverly up with him. His grip on her chest was like that of a madman who had finally found his way free.

Kaitlyn screamed for her to get back down, but the dead man moved forward toward the shooters. Gunshots rang out again; several bullets ripping through the zombie's head. Beverly held her thumb tightly over the wound and staggered towards Kaitlyn. Her intension was to reach down for Courtney and pull her to one side and out from under a body. From a distance and to the shooters, it was a blind threat. The bullet that hit her in the back of the head came out her forehead in a gaping hole mixed with bone and brain matter.

The silence was almost as deafening when the gunshots ceased. The seconds ticked off like hours as the rest of the group lay in the filth, all in fear of getting to their feet.

"We made it! We're alive!" Kaitlyn finally yelled.

"Get up! All of you, up!" a voice commanded.

Slowly, each person rose to their feet.

Chris could see Kaitlyn, Courtney and Mikey standing off to one side and his heart felt like it was being torn from his chest. Ernie moved a few feet forward and called out to Kaitlyn. They turned down the intensity of the lights and brought their own images into full view.

"Daddy?" Courtney said.

Chris nodded and quickly moved toward the group, followed by Ernie and the rest of the team. The frail arms around his neck brought the lump in his throat to the surface. Soon they were all in a group hug before turning toward the escape route.

Kaitlyn had Ernie by the arm before they could get too far into the passage. "We can't leave one of the women here with them. Beverly Carlisle. Do you know her?"

Ernie looked back at the dead bodies. "Carlisle," he said aloud. "I had an Edward Carlisle on the payroll."

Kaitlyn nodded. "She's his mother. She was a lifesaver, Ernie. What do they call it in time of war when someone is killed by accident?" she asked, pausing for a moment. "Friendly fire?"

Chris looked at Ernie and then back at the rest of the group. Taking off his jacket, he pulled Beverly to the entrance of the escape route and covered her head and shoulders.

"We'll send someone back down to get her body," Ernie said. "After that, we're going to blow this damn place shut."

"What about the rest of the dead in the group?" Kaitlyn asked.

Chris shook his head. "They all just became part of it, Kaitlyn. There's nothing anyone can do at this point. This could very well be their grave. We know that none of them asked for this, but things have gotten a lot worse topside since you've been down here."

CHAPTER 33

When the escape hatch was finally flipped open a huge passenger bus was positioned near the exit. Smoke was billowing up from various locations with the sound of shots and explosions ringing throughout the area.

Police officers had positioned themselves at both ends of the bus while the others were boarding it, and police cruisers and other vehicles that were left unguarded were now surrounded by the undead. Inside the bus, radio news flashes were bombarding the airwaves with supposed safe houses and the news that the National Guard had been called in to secure certain areas was the talk of the hour.

Outside, a crowd of dead cannibals had gathered, all of them making an attempt to get as close to the bus as possible. Officers on both sides maintained a vigil of constant firepower with others taking their place as they reloaded. The zombies took no time in pushing and rocking the bus when the shooting stopped, and the officers and special agents finally got inside, the driver closing the door with relief.

An Army helicopter flew overhead as the bus made its exit, and when it was a safe distance away, the chopper locked in the target and fired directly into the pit. The explosion sent debris into the air in the shape of a huge black cloud of wood, bone, and the flesh and blood of those it silently harbored.

From the air, the crew of the aircraft could see the passageways crumbling and caving in until the entire area looked like an unrecognizable maze.

The next set of missiles carried firebombs that exploded in a mass of mushroomed shaped blazes. When the smoke and flames cleared, charred and maimed bodies twitched and rolled for several minutes until their brains were truly fried.

Heading down the small county roads to safety, those inside the bus watched in horror as homeowners defending their property from the undead fired weapons from rooftops and second and third floor windows. Vehicles had been flipped, some of them burning. There were no other cars on the road with the exception of the occasional emergency vehicles and police cruisers. It was sometimes only the sound of them coming and going in some cases, but there was no sight of the vehicles themselves.

Chris called headquarters in an attempt to get the SAIC of Intelligence. The agents who answered were there only to take emergency calls regarding protectees. The buildings that housed law enforcement and other federal locations were locked down in a need to know or enter basis. Washington, DC had been shut down. The J. Edgar Hoover building proved to be no different. The two FBI agents both made calls that ended with the same results.

More news flashes came over the radio regarding the hundreds of people in both Iran and Iraq rejoicing in the streets over the situation the war-mongering Americans faced. An Iraqi spokesperson was heard saying that the Americans have sowed the seed of death for many years, and now the dead have been reaped upon them. Several TV stations were still broadcasting throughout the state, but they were only broadcasting news of impending horrors that still awaited Maryland and its contiguous states.

Kaitlyn leaned against Ernie while hugging Courtney close to her chest. Chris had Mikey on his lap, still shivering from the horrors that would now plague both he and his sister's dreams for a long time to come.

Jennifer was leaning back in the seat next to them, exchanging teary-eyed glances at her ex-husband. "I was wrong in saying the things I did. When careers come in the way of children, there's something terribly wrong with that marriage. I should have seen that coming a long time ago. For what it's worth, you saved their lives."

Courtney climbed into her mother's lap and nuzzled her face into her aunt's neck. That was when more tears began to flow.

Jennifer turned away for a second to catch her breath and wait for an answer. Marlene listened silently and then turned away, embarrassed that she felt she had attempted to share the moment.

Crossing her forearms over her medical bag, she stared out the window at a world gone mad.

"We can beat ourselves up, Jennifer, but it won't do any good," Chris finally said. He repositioned Mikey and looked out his window, catching Marlene's reflection on the other side of the bus. "There was a time I thought that I'd never be a husband, let alone a father of two kids. These are things we should have worked out before hand, Jen. Like I said, there's no need to beat ourselves up. What's done is done. All we can do is make what we now have a whole lot better." He motioned to Courtney and Mikey. "For them."

As the bus made another turn onto Solomon's Island Road, the National Guard stepped out onto the roadway and had them pull over. On the side of the road, in one of the several huge parking lots, was another vehicle with hot and cold food and drinks. The driver pulled the bus close enough to smell the fresh-brewed coffee and pastries.

A guardsman stepped up to the open door and nodded to Chris. "You made it. I was confident you'd be okay, but I was concerned none the less."

Chris recognized one of his colleagues from headquarters who was what they called a 'weekend warrior' in the National Guard. "It was close. They didn't waste any time leveling that place, did they?"

The guardsman shook his head. "No. As soon as we heard you were all clear of the area we radioed in. There was nothing that could be done down there. In some areas it's swarming with those things. Are you still with the CDC on a temp?" he asked.

"Yeah, but I think that tour of duty is just about a closed case." Chris nodded and clapped him on the shoulder as he walked away.

Once again they sat at a table and shared drinks and eats. Courtney and Mikey sat with their mother, quietly sipping hot cocoa. Chris sat with Marlene and Lee, discussing what the new plans were going to be, if any. Ernie and Kaitlyn went off by themselves to another table. Ken Yardley sat with the remainder of the tour group, while the rest of the agents mingled with the National Guard.

The parking lots along the shopping centers were littered with cars; some parked in strange positions that no one could figure out. Store front windows were broken into, and in a way that might have suggested human bodies simply crashed through them. Glass was scattered both inside and out on several locations. Periodically, shots were heard from inside the stores. After a half hour or so, National Guardsmen came out through the storefronts and signaled that everything was secure.

Chris tried to reach Aidon Richards on his cell phone and was still left with a ringing tone and no answer. Lee and Marlene did the same with their own staff. No one was answering their phones.

"This can't be happening. The whole world just can't come to an end this way with no one answering their damn phones," Marlene said.

Chris started to say something, but his own phone began to chime. One of the agents from Intelligence Division received a message from the SAIC. Chris listened as he was told that Richards and a number of agents were on assignment to get the President over to Camp David. The rest of the workforce had gone home, leaving those still on duty taking on other assignments with protectees under the Dignitary Protective Division. Anyone who was not on duty or on any other particular assignment was on twenty-four hour call.

"It's like the whole place is deserted," Lee said.

Marlene sipped her coffee and gave Chris a concerned look. "Anything good?"

Chris relayed the information he'd just received. "Why is this happening? How can so many people become infected in so short a time? The whole country is on red alert."

Lee nodded. "What better time to strike than at an open wound?"

Bordon from the FBI walked up behind Chris. "We just got word that a train coming from Stadium Armory became disabled. There was a power outage somewhere along the line. The train was stopped dead at Eastern Market. Chris, someone got their wires crossed and...lack of communications I guess, there was a collision. Your father was on the train that collided with the disabled one. He's unconscious."

Chris jumped up immediately. "Is there some way I can get into DC?" Chris looked over at the driver of the bus who was busy with several other people.

Bordon shook his head. "That's not all. The authorities said that the tunnels are crawling with those...*things*, whatever they are. The last message they received was that many of those things in the tunnel are looking pretty strange. The messages were broken up, but the dispatcher caught something that sounded like hairy animals. Different than what we have here."

"What the hell does that mean?" Chris asked.

"Their features," Borden said. "They were described as looking like some kind of an animal; facial hair and elongated teeth and facial structure. Almost like...muzzles is what they said."

Lee Fret quickly walked over to the two men. "Anything else?" he asked.

Bordon shrugged. "That's about it. They just said that the things in the tunnel are animal-like." Bordon looked at Lee. "Wait! There was something else. Those things in the tunnel are a lot more agile than those who look more human. They can move pretty damn quick."

"They're changing," Lee said. "Something is happened to them genetically. The parasite must have something to do with it. It's...it's morphing the body into whatever the host eats; other than human."

"Rats," Marlene said.

Chris shook his head in disbelief. "Christ, you don't know that, Lee. Right now that's...well, an intelligent guess, but a guess none the less. My father could be dying."

"I understand, Chris, but you have to understand that there's a lot we haven't found out about this parasite. We haven't had a chance to really study exactly what it is and what it does to the human body. Yeah, we know about the brain thing, but this might be something totally different."

Bordon jumped in again. "There's radio communications between the Metro Transit Police and other personnel, and there's a metro worker with a walkie-talkie on the second train. As far as any of the passengers are concerned, they can't get to them. The last report said your father isn't bleeding."

"As far as they can see," Marlene said. "Look, I don't want to be the medical pessimist here, but that's not saying he isn't bleeding internally."

Bordon nodded. "That's true. So, why don't we talk to the National Guard and see if they can get a chopper to land here. If those things get into those trains...."

"I'm coming along," Marlene said. "There's no answer at the office and I'm not getting anything from the hospital either. If there's anything that can be done with your father, Chris, I want to be there to handle it. I have a second medical bag in the bus. All we have to do is get to the train site without anything going terribly wrong."

Lee stared down at his car keys in his right hand and then tossed them to Chris.

"I'd be glad to do the honors, Marlene," Lee said with a smile, "but I'm afraid my vehicle has...ah, gone missing."

Marlene smiled back, as did Chris.

Jackson, Bateman and Lederman were now mingled in with the group.

"I'm heading over to the roadblock. I'll see if I can get one of those guys to hook up with a chopper that did the job at the site," Jackson said.

Bateman smacked him on the shoulder. "Good. I'll tag along."

CHAPTER 34

The passengers huddled together in the derailed train that had collided with the disabled one. Each tried to imagine a huge rescue team coming in a short amount of time. They were in the second car, the one behind the lead. They watched in horror as those who never made it to the other cars in the first train were met with creatures that poorly resembled anything human.

For now, the mutated creatures were content with their human meals; the first being the train operator whose body was halfway through the glass. The rear of the first car was completely demolished, as was the lead car on the second train. Some of the things were pressing their paw-like hands on the windows. They would bang and paw at the glass in an attempt to get through to the next car. It appeared that the only saving grace of those trapped within the trains was that the things couldn't figure out how to operate the metal handles on the doors.

Joseph Kearns lay on his back, his chest slowly rising and falling in shallow breaths, his head resting on a folded suit jacket. Someone else had taken off their jacket and laid it across his chest. A large bump on his forehead was turning a purplish color and the skin under his right eye and down to his chin was swollen. A small blotch of dried blood was in his right ear.

A woman knelt down next to him and continually monitored his condition.

"He has a concussion. They say you're not supposed to sleep after you've banged your head, but I don't know what this means. I mean, being knocked out cold. There's no alternative for this poor man."

"Does anyone know him?" one of the men asked. He looked around the car. Those that responded simply shook their heads.

A Metro employee who was constantly on the radio nodded. "I was talking with him before the crash. He was telling me about his son, Chris. He's the father of a Secret Service agent." He pointed down at the prone, unconscious man. "His name's Joseph Kearns. I dropped the name when I called for help. So hopefully that means we should have a rescue team being formed as we speak. All I can do is relay information for now. They wanted to know if anyone else was hurt. I told them no, outside of a few bumps and scrapes. Was I right?"

A young woman involuntarily changed the subject as she ran to the back of the car and threw up. She pulled a handkerchief from her purse and wiped her mouth. Looking back up toward the front of the car, her face was as white as snow. "I can't stand all that blood in the other car. I have to move to the next. I can't stand watching those...*things*. What are they and where did they come from?"

"They're wearing clothes," another man said. "They must have been human at one time. I've never seen anything like this in my life. I do remember the news saying something about how dead bodies were walking around, but they never mentioned anything like this. What happened to those who were supposed to be monitoring these trains?"

"Some of the stations have been closed down because of all the attacks," the Metro employee said. "DC is closed down all the way to Roslyn. They're trying to figure out how to get a team through the tunnels. One idea is to bring a train in from Addison Road."

"But won't they still have to get out of the train in order to get to us," a woman said.

The Metro employee shook his head. "I don't know, ma'am. I'm just relaying information the way they deliver it to me."

An older fellow in one of the side seats pointed to him. "Why do you have that earphone in? I think everyone would like to know what's going on."

"Look, I'm just trying to keep the noise level down in here, okay?" He listened for a moment and continued. "The rest of you can hear what's going on around the car without the squelching of the radio. I think that makes pretty damn good sense."

The rest of them either nodded or spoke out in agreement. There were noises under the train and, in some cases on the sides, but there was little room between the side of the train and the tunnel wall for any of the attackers to actually get up to the windows.

One man pulled out a pack of cigarettes and began to light one. The older fellow quickly pointed to the sign on the overhead. "There's no smoking, eating or drinking. Can't you read?"

"Christ all mighty!" the man snapped. "Here we are in a goddamned disabled train with who the hell knows what those things are outside, and you're worrying about the fucking rules!"

The Metro employee pointed to the back of the train. "Go back there if you have to smoke; just don't make a habit of it by chain smoking. I don't want to breathe that shit anymore than the rest, but I agree with you."

One of the older women pointed to the rules on the overhead. "I guess you could call it ironic if we all died of starvation or dehydration."

"Roger that." The employee let go of the radio's call button. "There're soldiers outside and waiting on a team coming from Southern Maryland. Maybe we...."

A loud noise from outside hushed his final words. Between the cars, a face appeared in the front window. The thin hairy fingers of the creature grasped at various places to hold on to while it moved from side to side. Two of the women screamed, while the young woman in the back went through to the next car. She ran down the isle until she was in the center of the car and sat with her legs bunched up.

In the back of the car, a window was broken, which was the reason no one was in that particular car. Several of the passengers were running to the back, waving their hands and screaming to get her attention. One of the rat-like creatures came through in one bounding leap. She ran, but it was far too late. She was less than half way to the door when it pounced on her, biting her squarely in the back of the neck and shoulders.

She screamed and looked up into the eyes of those who could only stand there and watch her die.

CHAPTER 35

The military chopper landed amidst a squall of gunfire. The team kept low as they exited and made their way toward the train station. Soldiers fired continuously until they were finally behind the lines. The undead had taken over a good part of the area and were still making a strong fight of it in periodic attacks every fifteen or twenty minutes. Addison Road Station was void of any employees who didn't carry a gun or didn't need to be there. The parking area and road itself was littered with dead bodies; some of them with head wounds made by the soldiers after the victims were bitten by a zombie.

A soldier turned to the team. He spoke to Chris since he was the closest to him. "I'm Colonel Hapshire. The men you see here will be assigned to your team. I'll command the soldiers and you can figure out who's in charge of your group. Who is Agent Kearns?"

"That's me," Chris replied and the two men shook hands. Chris quickly pointed out his team. "We have two FBI agents, three Secret Service agents, including myself, a medical doctor, a doctor from the Center for Disease Control, two state troopers, and three county officers."

"They won't be armed?" Hapshire asked, pointing to Marlene and Lee.

"No, Doctor Peterson is here to help my father. I've been assigned to the CDC and have been working with Doctor Fret since the start of this disaster. I want him with us so he can let his superiors know what's going on. He'll also be a big help to Doctor Peterson."

Hapshire nodded. "So, your father is a passenger on the train?"

"Yes, his name is Joseph Kearns."

Once again Hapshire nodded. "Okay. We'll follow your lead. I suppose you all have a plan of action to get to the tunnel at Eastern Market?"

Chris nodded. "We decided that it would be best if we can take a train and back it down all the way to the last car of the first train we come to. Hopefully it's not derailed. We can have a few of the Metro people come with us and ready a hook up or whatever has to be done to get the unhurt passengers and any wounded onto our train."

"Sounds like a plan. Have you notified Metro?" Hapshire asked.

"Yes, Metro seems to think it would be better and safer that way, and I agree. We're going to have a lot of panicky people coming through those doors. Sort of like being in the water after a shipwreck and waiting your turn to be airlifted before the sharks arrive."

Hapshire pointed to his men. "We can get the soldiers into the car on the disabled train and have them assigned to keep some kind of order. That would be best to keep anyone from getting trampled just in case there *is* a rush."

Chris nodded. "Excellent. All we have to do now is...."

Gunfire cut short his last words and Chris turned to face the road with the rest of the group. The zombies once again started across the road and toward the train station. Some made it as close as twenty feet to the soldiers before they were cut down from a shot to the head. The parking lot was still void of any walking dead, but soldiers formed a firing line around the iron gates in case the undead began moving in this direction. The attack lasted no more than five minutes before all the zombies making the rush were laying still on the pavement.

"They've been doing this every fifteen or twenty minutes. It's strange. It's almost as though they have some sort of battle plan. The gates to the station are closed and locked just in case there were any of them in the tunnel, and the battalion is lined up in front of the station and along the parking parameter," Hapshire pointed in each direction. "The rest will stay here until we get the train back and rescue everyone who needs it. I'll also put some men down on the loading platform for when we return. And with the mercy of God by our side we *will* return."

All of the team acknowledged their understanding.

"Do we still have communications with that Metro employee on the train we plan to back into?" Chris asked.

"I'll have my radioman call in and give him the plan," Hapshire replied.

Chris looked at the rest of his team. "Okay then, we all know what we need to do. I don't think we need anyone shouting orders here. It's simple. We back the train down and hook it up to the last car of the first train we come to. Any questions?"

No one did, everyone was ready to do what had to be done.

Hapshire signaled to his men and yelled to all who were heading out. "Let's lock and load, people!"

CHAPTER 36

Inside the crashed train, the Metro employee nodded and smiled. "Hey, we have good news! They're on their way. The bad news is my battery in this thing is going fast."

The rat creature that had just killed the young woman was now beating and scratching at the glass in the next car back. Finally realizing it wasn't going to get at the humans this way, it then moved to the door itself.

They could hear the thuds of its paw-like hands banging on the metal sides and the glass. It ran its hands down the length of the door and suddenly stared down at the metal handle. It was sure the strange looking thing moved in some way but the thought quickly went through its dull mind and once again it resumed its pounding.

"It's gonna get in here! You know that don't you?" the old man said and then pointed to the back of the car. "What happened to that young lady is going to be all our fates. The only lucky one in this car is that man." He pointed down to the unconscious form of Joseph Kearns. "At least he won't know the horror of our demise."

The woman kneeling down next to Joseph looked up at him. "Why don't you just hush up, all right? My goodness! It's bad enough we're in this situation without having to listen to some pessimistic old coot sending invitations to the angel of death. Now, what we should do, at least the rest of you, is to get close to those doors. If one of those things figures out how to open one of the doors, that doesn't mean the rest are going to. Once you pass through them they close up again."

The man with the radio nodded. "She's right. Our bodies pressing against the door will keep at least two of them from getting in here, maybe three. Christ, the worst thing about dying is the sitting around and waiting for it to happen. Okay, so let's split up. Each of you takes one end of the car. Ma'am, you had a good idea there."

The woman smiled. "I'm not going to leave Mr. Kearns unless you need an extra body in an emergency. I wish we had some ice. This lump looks awfully discolored. I hope the rescue party gets here soon."

The old man gave off a laugh that ended in a toothless smile. "Now who's the damn pessimist?"

"Shut up and go over there by the door," she replied." They probably won't want you anyway, you're too damned ornery."

CHAPTER 37

At the train yard, Metro police officers and DC police surrounded one of the cars that would be taken to Eastern Market. The undead made their way across the roads, stumbled across tracks, and pushed on fences only to be shot down for their trouble. The continuation of the covering fire let the others get close enough to board the lead car once the operator had everything in order.

FBI agents Bordon and Lederman stood inside the open doors and fired whenever the zombies came in range. Secret Service agents Jackson and Bateman took the rear car and placed themselves in the same position until Chris and the soldiers were all on board. When the doors finally closed, the operator advised the team they wouldn't have to back down; he would be heading up to the other end to make the first car the lead. From there they would still be able to hook up with the rear of the disabled train.

The undead refused to move from the tracks. Banging and pulling at whatever they could on the metal cars, they fell underneath the shiny-steel wheels with the sickening sounds of crunching bone and flesh.

When the train was ready, they closed all doors and spread personnel throughout the cars. The lights moving into the tunnel sent eerie shadows over the walls and tracks. It was strange how all of a sudden the beady eyes of the creatures appeared out of nowhere. In the suffuse light, they glowed just as any animal out on a darkened country road. The train passing through the tunnel left them little room to move out of the way. In the time it took them to pass Potomac Avenue, there was blood mingled in with pieces of clothing and flesh smeared across the elongated windows of the cars.

The operator slowed the train down to almost crawling speed as they entered the next tunnel heading for Eastern Market. One of the creatures was hanging on the back of the car and pulling against the door. When it opened, Chris fired a shot through its forehead and sent a spew of bloody-brain matter and bone shards onto the tracks.

Moments later, the lights from the rear car showed the bleak details of the crash. The second train had slammed into the first to become twisted in a zigzag pattern even with the little space it had between the walls and cars. The good news was that the last car wasn't derailed.

The undead were now a mixture of various forms. They crowded in the area and made attempts to pull the car apart with their bare hands and claws. They bit and screamed with rage when none of the metal or glass would give up the treasure it held inside. Hapshire moved some of his men into the lead car and positioned them off to the sides. When the door came open, it was obvious there was going to be a battle to keep the strange looking beings out.

"I have the train positioned so that it will latch when I push into it," the operator said. He stood in the center of the car and spoke to Hapshire. "The only problem is that the train we're going to be pulling out of there is derailed. We can't really tell what cars if any are on the tracks, but there's a good chance that some of them are."

Chris stepped beside Hapshire. "But we can still pull it, right? We have to get these people out of here and my father to the hospital. Base says the guy in there with the radio is no longer answering. I have no idea what condition my father's in at this moment, but I think it's better if we plan for the worse to be on the safe side."

The operator nodded quickly. "Yeah, we can still pull it. But if it's derailed anyplace it's going to be one hell of a bumpy trip, though. I can't really make any promises. I've never had to do this before. You guys will have to make sure I can go on back and make the rear car the lead car again."

"What if we can get everyone over to this particular car?" Chris asked. "No one really knows how many people are injured in the car in front of the disabled one."

Hapshire placed his hand on Chris's shoulder. "I think for the sake of life threatening injuries and everyone concerned, it would be a good idea to see how many people we can actually get into these cars. If we have to cram them in like sardines, then so be it. Shit, I've ridden on these things like that just heading downtown."

Chris turned to Marlene. "Do you agree?"

"Of course, this is really out of my field of experience so I have to say I defer to you gentlemen." She looked at Hapshire as she said this.

"Good. Then that's the plan," Chris said. "We get the people in those two trains into this one and get the hell out of here." He pointed to the last car on the disabled train. "Those things are going to be piling in here as soon as we open a door. The whole ass end of that train is busted in." Chris looked to Hapshire. "How do you want to work this with your men? I think it would be best to move the train forward a bit and then shoot our way back again. We need to get rid of as many of those bastards as possible."

Hapshire exhaled hard. "Yeah. We make sure the rear car is clear so the operator can make it the lead again. We move forward and blast our way back up. We get into the first train and move through, clearing those creatures out as best we can. We get the people from that train onto here, and then we do the same with the train in front. I don't see any other way to go about it. We don't have enough space down here to do it any other way."

The other four agents nodded in agreement. Hapshire sent two soldiers to pass the word and waited until he could actually see them passing from car to car. When they were positioned in the last car, he gave them the plan and once again gave them the order to lock and load.

It was amazing how agile the rat creatures were, while the regular zombies were so lethargic they could barely climb onto the hookup. The first round of shots was strictly aimed at the rat creatures that appeared to have defied all laws of genetics. They looked like the animals they had somehow caught and devoured. Several of them managed to get inside the car before succumbing to a bullet or two in the head. Most of the creatures and, some of the regular zombies, managed to get under the cars. They clawed or crawled their way along the bottom until they reached a place which they felt was reason enough for them to be there.

The dead were thrown out onto the tracks or into the operator booth of the damaged last car on the second train. Soldiers went through first, followed by Chris and the four agents, then Marlene. She was last so there would be no chance of her being attacked.

The rest of the officers stayed behind to make sure none of the creatures got behind them. That would mean shooting in a cross-fire and the possibility of injuring or killing personnel with friendly fire.

Going from car to car, they managed to get through to the one car that held the dead young woman. Blood was splattered over the windows and seats. The rat creature feeding on the female corpse was more than willing to take any bullets the men had to offer. Chris was the first to send a .357 through the back of its skull, the insides of its deformed head landing in a frothy mess on the car's flooring.

When they reached the car holding the passengers, Chris knelt down next to his father and touched his cheek.

"Dad, can you hear me?"

"He should be fine if we can get him to a medical facility," the woman said. "I've been monitoring him closely."

Chris looked at the woman and smiled. "I appreciate everything you did or tried to do. It'll be a few minutes before we can check out the next set of cars on the other trains. Did he blink or anything?"

The woman shook her head. "No, but the bump on his head is getting awfully discolored. I don't think there's anymore bleeding in the brain because the blood is still dry in his ear." She pointed it out and shook her head again. "I'm not a nurse. I just...."

"You did a great job just being here," Marlene said, now standing behind Chris. "He more than likely fractured the front of his skull. Probably a small fracture, but one that will require more than a few days in a hospital. He's been lying here way too long, Chris. We need to get this show on the road and get out of here."

In the other car, several of the rat creatures pawed at the glass. They could detect the smell of any spilled blood that was present and it made the situation even worse. Marlene took Joseph Kearns' vital signs and gave him a shot. Taking another jacket from the floor, she braced it under his shoulders to level out the areas between his head, neck and shoulders.

Chris and the rest of the crew were already following the soldiers through the next car and into the first train to become disabled. This one had more damage than the one before it since it had more broken windows. The undead couldn't get through them only because there wasn't enough room on the sides. The third car in had two dead bodies that appeared to be untouched.

The fourth told a very different story.

CHAPTER 38

A police escort brought Ernie, Jennifer, Kaitlyn and the kid's to the Lambert home, where it was a battle to just get out of the car, let alone into the house. Ernie had taken the time a few years back to put framework around the windows to support metal bars. They would be safe here for only a short while, or until they eventually had to come out to get supplies. It wasn't going to work all that well and they knew it. The entire area was now crawling with the undead. Some never bothered to come near the residence, while others were shot trying to get to anything that was living.

In the back lot were two full size campers. Both were built for full size occupancy, but one required the need to be towed. The other was built in the same fashion as a bus. It was a bit rough on gas, but it was far better than moving back into a house that eventually would become not only their prison, but their tomb as well.

Jennifer stayed with the kids in the vehicle while Kaitlyn and Ernie finally got everything they would need from the house. The first thing Ernie went for was the guns and ammo he had. They then packed away food, extra clothes, and various bathroom and kitchen utensils. All forms of currency was removed and placed in secure compartments throughout the RV. Ernie suddenly thought how this could quite possibly turn out to be their life for a long time to come.

It wasn't what his life was supposed to be. After four or five years of just getting by, he finally made something of himself, but it was over in the blink of an eye and seemingly all too fast.

Kaitlyn sat at the corner table, looking out the window. Tears streamed down her cheeks as Mikey and Courtney did their best to comfort her. Jennifer sat on the other side. It only took a few minutes for her to feel the hurt that was so deeply buried in her soul. It wasn't only for Kaitlyn that she cried, but anything that had happened involving this horrible nightmare. It was for what she once had in life that seemed so brief. She covered her mouth as she inhaled a loud sob. What was it that life wanted? What was it that God wanted?

Courtney immediately ran to her seat and hugged her mother. The faint smell of perfume and shampoo drifted up her nostrils as she nestled into her mother's neck. All four of them were crying now. In the front seat, Ernie buried his face in his hands and upped the count to five. It was Mikey this time who went up to the front of the bus and hugged his uncle. Before the escort made ready to depart, one of the officers carefully made his way to the driver's side of the vehicle and waited patiently for Ernie to open the window.

"Are you all ready, Mr. Lambert?"

Slightly embarrassed, Ernie brushed tears away and nodded. "Listen, thanks for all your help. I think we can get out of here."

The officer nodded and tried to smile. "It'll eventually get better. I don't see how any of this can get any worse."

Ernie nodded. "I once worked out of my garage with a few guys. We used to do roofing jobs and sidewalks. I eventually built up a small empire." He waved his arms so that they spread outward and around him. "It's like they say, isn't it? Empires do crumble."

Ernie watched the cruisers leave his driveway. The undead were now coming out of the wooded area and heading for the house. He couldn't help but think of the zombie movie he saw in black and white at the drive-in with his first girlfriend. The only differences were, this one was in living color, and this one was for real.

As he pulled the RV out onto the street, the odd thing about some of the zombies was that they seemed to have changed. Some now had the features of a cat or dog. It wasn't a drastic metamorphosis, but subtle changes that hinted at what they were. Perhaps it had something to do with a new species of man.

Ernie slowed down as they ran into the path of the RV. This he allowed to go on for only a few minutes. Clamping his jaw tightly, his eyes squinted as he gave it the gas, cursing the day the son's of bitches who started this shit were ever born.

Looking into the rear-view mirror, a possessed smile crossed his lips as he felt their bodies thumping under the wheels of the huge vehicle. Around them, the other homes were left with front doors wide open. A few cars were still in their driveways, but every home outside the immediate area looked abandoned.

Feeling little Mikey on his arm brought him back to a more sane personality. The boy had his face buried into his uncle's bicep. Ernie quickly shook his head several times. "It's either them or us, buddy. We've lost enough for one day, right?"

Mikey looked up and through the vehicle's large windshield that tilted inward. "I just want things to go back the way they were, Uncle Ernie. I don't like it like this. Those things can get you and eat you. Why are they like that?"

Ernie shook his head. "I don't know, Mikey. Some people thought they...." He looked down at his nephew. "It's just something that happened, buddy. But you know what?"

"What?"

"We live in the bestest country in the whole world. It's more gooder than any other place on Earth. We'll get out of this mess and we'll be all right. You'll see."

The boy smiled for the first time in a long time. "There's no words like *bestest* and *more gooder*, Uncle Ernie."

CHAPTER 39

The soldiers started firing first. There were broken windows on the front and rear of the train that the undead managed to get through. Small children as well as adults were either shot as zombies, or shot as they lay dead from the original assault; not yet revived as the living dead. In other cars it remained the same. It appeared that the passengers attempted to escape by going from one car to another. The undead followed close behind and managed to get through the doors as well. At the end of the train there was no other place to go but back the other way.

They were about to turn back when Chris heard a noise in the small operating room of the first car. Behind him and to the left was a light orange seat. To the right, the door had been closed, dividing the small space between the control room and the seat. With the windows of the control room designed to be darkened, he couldn't see in. Chris pounded on the door and announced himself with the rest of the squad standing behind him. The door opened slowly, and staring into the barrel of his .357 was the large brown eyes of a small girl; the train operator was directly behind her.

"We heard the shots but we were afraid to come out. I thought you might shoot us, thinking we were one of those things," the operator said, holding onto the tiny waist of the child.

The girl looked to be six or seven and had obviously been crying. The tears left a trail of clean skin down her small, dirty face. "They got my mommy," she said.

Chris knelt down and brushed the hair away from her face. "It'll be all right. You're safe now and we'll make sure you get someplace where you stay safe. What's your name?"

In an almost inaudible voice she said, "Amanda."

Chris smiled. "Okay, Amanda. We have all these soldiers here and some agents from the FBI and Secret Service. I think you're gonna be well protected." He looked at the train operator. "And you?"

"Carlton Abel," he said, looking out the door and at the entourage Chris had brought. "I didn't have time to do anything. When the second train plowed into us, I went out to see if there were any major injuries or worse. People were on the floor and leaning over the backs of the seats, and then all of a sudden those things; Lord God all mighty, those things."

Chris tapped the man on the shoulder. "You did the best you could. It's just as bad above ground. We brought a train in from Addison Road. We can get everyone in the second train onto the first. Everyone on this...." Chris looked down at Amanda. Several more shots were fired and Chris turned to survey the situation. He turned back to Carlton Abel. "We have to get moving pretty quick. Those things are going to be getting in here through the windows that are broken." Chris cupped the girls chin in his hand. "This child has seen enough horror, and I have two of my own."

The operator picked the girl up and was positioned in front of Chris and the rest of the agents on the way back, which was just as bad as the first time. In the other cars, the creatures once again started eating the dead. Once again the soldiers shot and killed any of them that didn't make it back out. The train operator kept the girl's face buried into the fleshy part of his shoulder.

When they arrived back to the next train, Chris' father had already been moved into the working train. He was placed on a wheeled stretcher that was lowered close to the floor. The only complaint from Marlene was that she didn't have an IV to keep his strength up. Joseph Kearns blinked his eyes a few times and Chris knelt down beside him.

"Take his hand," Marlene said.

Chris took his father's hand in his. "Hey, Dad."

His father squeezed his hand slightly and smiled. Marlene nodded. "That's a good sign."

With a jolt, the train once again started toward Addison Road. In the other trains, the dead would be devoured, but they wouldn't add to the multitude of undead the county already had to deal with.

CHAPTER 40

When the train pulled back into Addison Road, the state police already had a helicopter ready to transport Chris' father to the Breezy Point Medical Center. Chris flew with his father and waited until they had him checked in and under Marlene's care. It was time to find out exactly what the story was on going back to work, as Washington, DC was still closed down on all points of the compass.

Chris immediately contacted his sister while he waited outside the medical center. When she answered, the conversation started out with more tears and apologies. Chris had all he could do to swallow the lump he had in his throat. When she was able to get control of her emotions, she advised him that they were now entering parts of Delaware and passing rural areas with little or no one else in sight.

"So where exactly are you headed?" Chris asked. There was a silence he didn't particularly care for.

"Ernie has family in PA.," she finally said.

"And what about Jennifer?"

Once again there came a pause until his ex-wife got on the line. "We're not doing anything behind your back, Chris. We just want to get away from the area. Maybe farther north this isn't happening. Although, we've passed a bunch of rural areas and there's not a single person either driving or walking. The only place we found any other cars was on the major highways, like the Beltway and 95."

Chris waited for a moment. "And the kids? You'll tell me where they are so I can come and visit, right?"

"When we get to where we're going, yes. Ernie seems to think New York State might be a bit safer. The radio stations are all talk shows up this way."

"What about your job? Has anyone contacted you? DC is closed down tighter than a drum. Everybody who is somebody or even thinks they're somebody is out of town. As of right now I don't even know where my next paycheck is coming from," he said.

"There's no one there. The whole area is on red alert. How's dad?"

Chris was taken aback for a moment. She hadn't called him that for a while. It was always, 'How's *your* dad? How's *your* father doing?'

He thought about how their divorce first took place. According to statistics, in first place for divorce was a money problem. Second was abuse, and running a close third was infidelity. In what place was not being there?

"Chris?"

"Yeah. He's...he's doing fine. He's in the medical center. It's probably the only place where it's safe right now as far as Southern Maryland goes. They're working on putting bars on the glass doors and metal roll-up doors on all vehicle entrances."

"I forgive you, Chris."

"Forgive me for what?"

"For all the things you think were your fault. And I'm sorry for all the things that were mine." With the last part of the sentence she trailed off in tears.

"It just happened, Jen. It happens to the best of marriages when...I don't know, when certain things get in the way; like careers for instance. Mine took me away and kept me away."

She sniffled. "I thought that by keeping the kids closer to me they would have a full time parent. I know you were away on assignments a lot, so I thought it would be better if you could pick your own time to see them. I was...."

"That doesn't matter now, Jen. What matters is that these kids get a safe place to rest their heads at night. We could go over what was wrong and what was right forever and never come up with a foolproof solution. Nobody can, Jen. Nobody!"

"Hey?"

It was his sister's voice again. "Hey, yourself."

"Look. We're going to stay at Ernie's brother's place. He has a farm with a pretty big house and a foreman's quarters down the road. That's where we'll be staying for a while. I don't know how long, but I'll give you the number when we get there. Okay?"

Chris nodded as if she could see him. "Yeah, that's fine. Can I talk to the kids before you hang up?"

"Of course, just hold on a minute."

It was Courtney who got on first. "Hi, Daddy."

"Hey, baby. Are you doing all right?"

"Yeah, we're okay. Are you all right? Please be careful, Daddy. We haven't seen anyone walking up here or anything. I think everyone is afraid to go outside. All the schools we passed only have a few cars in the parking lots, and all the lights are out."

"Well, they're probably taking precautions, honey. You just make sure you don't go anywhere by yourself, okay? Stay close to the adults. Tell Mikey the same."

"I will. Here he comes now."

"Hi, Daddy."

"Hey, big guy. You make sure you take care of the ladies, ya hear?"

The boy gave off a boyish giggle. "I will. Are you gonna come up here when you can get off from work?"

"I'm gonna try, buddy. I have some things I need to take care of up here. And then I'll make a beeline up there lickedy split."

"Bye, Daddy."

Chris waited for a moment before he could answer. Special Agents of the United States Secret Service were human, after all. "Just so-long, buddy, not goodbye."

PART TWO: AFTERMATH

CHAPTER 41

There were very few things left the same throughout the country. The government ran as best it could under the circumstances, but it was chaos and greed that kept it from ever coming back to its rightful place in society. Chris drove down major highways as though they were simply country roads out in the wilderness. Many major highway repairs were halted in their tracks due to lack of funds and manpower.

Ships coming into the United States were stopped well short of their destination to check for the cannibalistic creatures who were now the new minority. The US Customs seemed to be the only agency doing a job that had never changed. Those who refused to be boarded and searched were sunk after several warnings. These were usually the drug lords and other bottom-of-the-barrel lowlifes who learned quickly that there would be zero tolerance for failure to obey a lawful order. The influx of immigrants all but ceased. No one wanted into America. All the news that was to be aired during the day was about the deaths of citizens at the hands of creatures who were half animal and half human. It was like listening to the coverage of the old Vietnam War of the sixties when it was at its peak.

Radio stations that still bothered to play music were frequently interrupted by news flashes of possible attacks by the new breed of terrorists. A government council was formed similar to what was put together after the JFK Assassination. Fingers were pointing in all directions to cover up those who were actually guilty. A general and a scientist were far from the only culprits responsible for turning America into a war torn apocalyptic country.

The FBI and Secret Service were now no more than paid assassins. New offices within each agency were formed with a new precedence set for both. All agencies now came under the Department of Homeland Security. The newest office was designated as TLC (The Lazarus Culture). Those who could still find something to laugh about did just that. It was laughable. The new breed of man had finally arrived. The funny part was that technology was soon lost.

All that had taken place over hundreds of years would be reverted back to the savagery and ignorance of witch hunters and dunking stools.

The price of gas no longer mattered. Driving to and from anyplace was now a privilege for law enforcement personnel, the military, and the rich and famous. The military had somehow kept up its strength over the past months from the time when the outbreak first began. In that time there were no longer any foreign wars to fight. The United States was now at war with itself. It was a time for foreign nations holding grudges with the Americans to sit back and watch it begin to crumble. The Cold War was back, and more vigorous than ever.

Chris caught sight of the huge barn in the center of a fairly large field. On the side was painted a rather awesome American flag. This was where he would make a left turn. He was all but ten minutes away from putting his arms around Courtney and Mikey. They must have grown like weeds over the past seven months, he thought. He immediately thought of his father who had died of complications due to his head wound; an aneurism that somehow avoided being detected at the medical center. Marlene was beside herself when she had to deliver the news to him. It was something that happens and he was told that from the start. He immediately started missing Marlene.

It was just over a hill that the creatures came out from the thickly wooded area. Chris gripped the handle of the specially designed Uzi located between the windshield wipers. The Washington Navy Yard still held the finest designers for weapons and communications owned by the Secret Service.

The creatures that had mutated into animalistic beings were no longer put down with just head shots.

They could now be killed by a bullet penetrating any vital part of their bodies. He squeezed the plunger with a steady pull of his index finger and rotated the weapon so that it swept to the right. The first to be hit was a pig-like being complete with tusks. It was strange how some of them still wore old ragged clothes that were now weather beaten and dry rotted rags. The horror was just looking into the eyes of once human beings that now took on the similarity of a grotesquely formed pig or cat.

They weren't exact features, but facsimiles of something that gave a hint of where they had received their animal traits. Creatures that resembled dog and cat faces peered into the vehicle from a distance. They were smart enough not to come into full sight, in fear of the awesome weapon that left their cohorts bloodied and lying still on the ground; knowing it would ravage them as well. They crept back into the foliage in low murmuring grunts and growls.

With a click of a button, Chris switched to the second Uzi located just above the right passenger side mirror. A snake-faced creature balled its fist and made ready to slam it into the front door window. Dark red blood squirted from the side of its throat as the 9x19mm shot ripped its head all but off.

There was a sound as he drove away. A sound that made his skin feel as though tiny spiders danced across the hairs on his arms. He was sure it was a voice. Maybe it was the way one or two of them screamed with rage, but he could have sworn the voice was yelling a single word.

"Death."

CHAPTER 42

Ernie and Kaitlyn watched the vehicle as it came down the road, the dry ground leaving a trail of dust behind it. The road leading to the house was a quarter mile long and had never been paved. Phil Lambert's private property turned out to be a lot bigger than Ernie first thought it to be. His brother had made big plans to build a farm and deal with the locals in produce and various kinds of meats, but the only meat ever to get delivered was human. Phil gnawed on his wife's dead flesh until there was only skin and bone. Ernie Lambert shot his brother in his brother's favorite room; the den.

They were on the porch when Chris stepped out of the vehicle. "I heard some excitement down the road. Everything all right?" Ernie asked.

Chris checked his firearm and smacked the clip back into place. "Just a few of the locals who looked a lot like something out of The Island of Doctor Moreau, but no big deal."

Ernie pointed to the house. "I put bars on every window. I also set up some small charges out in the fields. It keeps the animal looking ones at bay. The regular zombies don't give a shit if their balls get blown off."

Kaitlyn smiled at her brother. "See, even the females of the zombie clan are a lot smarter than you guys. How's the good doctor?"

Chris shrugged. "She's fine. She's back at the medical center, or what's left of it. They get what they can from Uncle Sam and a hope and a prayer gives them the rest. The latter isn't working too well, however." He shook his head at Ernie. "I'm sorry about your family."

Ernie looked toward what used to be the foreman's residence. "The foreman got sick first. Phil went to check on him one morning when he didn't show up for...well, there's really no sense in telling you the rest."

Giving her brother a hug, Kaitlyn held his arm as they went into the house. "It's cold out there. I've made some coffee and I'm fixing some pancakes and eggs."

Chris watched her walk away with tears in her eyes. "Where are Jennifer and the kids?"

Ernie cleared his throat. "Chris, we had a bad scene here when we first arrived. The whole place...."

"Ernie, where are my kids?"

Ernie raised his hand to the house. "They're upstairs getting cleaned up, Chris. The kids are fine, but Jennifer was pulled through one of the downstairs windows trying to lock it. We didn't know how smart these new fuckers were then. We found out they can surprise you. Some of them can form words and small sentences. This is only the animal looking ones, of course. The others are still mindless corpses. There are a surprisingly small number of them around. It's like they morphed into the friggin' critters they're eating. If you think you had nightmares when this shit first started then you've got another thing coming."

"So, my children's mother is more than likely dead?" Chris asked.

Kaitlyn turned and wiped tears from her eyes. "We don't know if...well, in the shape the country's in right now, if that's the politically correct term, Chris. They dragged her off into the woods out back. Those animal things are powerful. Ernie tried to get a few of them with the rifle. He got a couple of them, but the ones dragging Jennifer, they went behind one of the small sheds and were hidden from view until they finally made it to the woods. It was just too dangerous to go after them."

She brought her brother a cup of coffee just as Mikey and Courtney came bounding down the stairs and heading in a beeline to their father. "Daddy! Daddy! You finally got here safe and sound!" Courtney got to him first. "I love you, Daddy," Mikey added.

"I love you guys, too. Man, you guys have grown over the past months. Pretty soon I won't be able to bounce you on my lap anymore. You'll break my kneecaps."

Courtney giggled and held on tightly. Mikey laid his head on his father's shoulder and drew a breath. "Mommy is gone, Dad."

Chris kissed the back of his head. "I know, son. We'll make out all right. There are a lot of people working around the clock trying to get things right again. It'll take a while, but you'll see that things will go back the way they were. We'll live as a family again and no one, or no *things*, will ever threaten your lives ever again."

"Okay, everything's ready. Let's get to some serious eating here," Kaitlyn announced.

They ate for a while in silence. It took a little time for Chris to realize just what he'd lost over the last few months. They talked about neighbors and helping hands around and outside the farm. Ernie mentioned that there were several homes in the area that could be taken seriously as fortresses of some kind. Everyone who had any sense was busy building up their homes for any sort of attack.

"So, what does it look like as far as new members of the dead race?" Chris asked.

Ernie chewed a piece of sausage and swallowed. "It looks like no one else has been affected or infected as far as this area goes. I tend to think that most of the people know what to expect, and know enough to not go anywhere alone or unarmed. The things come out mainly at night. The zombies are few and far between anymore. I tend to think they've more than likely begun to rot into the ground. Those animal looking things seem to be in fairly good shape. I know they're part of this thing because some of them are still wearing clothes."

Chris nodded. "I saw that when I first arrived. The whole process of changing into another form of life is too hard to believe, but I've seen it with my own eyes."

"The kids go out on the back porch during the day. They go out into the yard only when Ernie is out there with a gun," Kaitlyn said.

"I miss the hell out of my business, Chris." Ernie said as he finished the last of his coffee and then poured another cup. "I need to get back to what I was. I want to eventually get this place sold and see if I can work things out back in Maryland. This place is too wooded and we can't keep the kids cooped up like this. It's only a matter of time until they start coming out in broad daylight. Can you pull some strings in Washington, Chris?"

Chris leaned back in his chair. "I don't see why not. I can tell you that things in Maryland are getting better. Those things are running out of ground, Ernie. I feel like a deserter leaving the area. My whole life is in Maryland, and so are my kid's lives. I could get you a great deal in Washington and Baltimore if you're willing. It's up to you, but I have to give it to you straight."

Kaitlyn bit her lip as she waited for the next comment. Ernie crossed his arms over one another on the table. "I'm all ears."

"I'd want my children close to where I am." Chris looked his sister in the eye. "Look, I know you've been great with them, but I can't live from day to day and not know that they're all right. I need them in my life more than ever. I'm sure you can understand that, Katie."

Kaitlyn's eyes filled with tears. "Of course I can, Chris. They're your kids." She looked out to the front porch and took a deep breath.

Ernie took her hand and looked over at Chris. "I used to think that you and Jennifer were in a tug of war with both your careers. I used to believe that perhaps Mikey and Courtney were just two little people who tripped both of you up. I know better now."

Chris twirled the cup around in the saucer. "I used to think that I'd lose any rights I had to those two kids. I would lie in bed at night and try to tell myself that I was doing everything the right way." He shook his head. "Sometimes you have to take a step back and look at the big picture."

"Yeah, well, we're on your side, fella." Ernie tapped Kaitlyn's hand softly. "So, what are your plans for work? Are you still with the service?"

Chris nodded. "More or less. They're rebuilding everything to fit around this entire problem. As a matter of fact, I meant to tell you earlier that two other agents are coming up this way to do a little job. Farther north of here there's a huge estate they believe has been overrun by those creatures; some kind of clan, if you want to call it that. They've been attacking the locals in the two towns surrounding the farm. We used to have a Resident Agency set up in the area, but it's been closed down for some time now."

"If I can do anything to help, all you have to do is ask," Ernie said.

"Thanks, brother-in-law. But, I'd rather you be here with my sister and my kids. I wouldn't be worth a damn if I knew they were here alone."

Kaitlyn played with her husband's fingers. "And you wouldn't either. You'd be thinking about us the whole time you were supposed to be shooting the bad guys."

They finished eating and then went inside the house to relax and catch up some more. Courtney and Mickey hung on their father like leaves on a branch, happy to have him in their lives again.

That evening, Chris turned in early and listened to the light rain hitting the roof of the back porch. When he finally drifted off, it wasn't a peaceful sleep. Something moved in the room that his mind was now occupying. His eyes slid back and forth under the lids until the shadow passed directly over his face. Jennifer's pointed teeth bore down on his throat and broke off his wind. When he was finally able to inhale, he sat up with a loud gasp.

Mikey jumped back, pulling his nightshirt around his throat.

"Are you okay? You were making noises in your sleep, Daddy."

CHAPTER 43

The animal things feasted on the dead flesh of a small deer. They were like a pride of lions when they hunted in packs. The woods were overgrown with all types of vegetation, making it a perfect and natural hiding place for the new breed of carnivores. They very seldom fought with one another. Instead, they would hunt down whatever crossed their paths and lay bare the spoils of nature to all those who chose to dine with them.

The zombies kept to themselves. They were simply walking dead with no will or mind of their own. Until they were introduced to the blood and tissue of some poor critter in the wild, they would continue to deteriorate in body until they finally collapsed in a pile of putrid skin and bone. This residue of a once human being was one meal the pack would not devour, despite how intense the hunger had become.

Off in several directions, there were males who chose to sow their newfound oats. They would gladly hump any female in any state of mind or body in an attempt to relieve the pressure on their swollen testicles. In them, the parasite was no longer present. They were a host to nothing that could be categorized as a foreign body. Already, just in this area alone, they had impregnated in droves the younger females of their species.

More and more deer and other wildlife were seen in open spaces due to the multitude of creatures that migrated from other parts of the county. Trucking companies that were still in operation would log in many road kills along their primary routes. These creatures were a new breed of animal, and just as dangerous as any grizzly bear or cougar. Once bitten, the victim would gradually feel the change taking place by the intense pains of bulging bones and sinews. It was believed that the ones who had eaten the flesh of a coyote were the most feared. They were werewolf-looking creatures with a voracious appetite.

The being that was once Jennifer Kearns stared out of the forest and onto the house where her children were peacefully sleeping. Her body ached from the strange substances that were introduced into her bloodstream. Already, her teeth were beginning to show the first signs of growing canine fangs. Her eyes had become oval shaped after the first few days. Jennifer slowly ran her thin, elongated tongue over them in slow, suggestive movements.

She woke from her stupor, feeling the closeness of the beast standing behind her, grunting as he pushed his thick manhood between the cheeks of her ample ass. He was the reason for her change in body and mind. On the first day of her captivity, he claimed her as his own, stripping her naked in the midst of the meadow that was embedded deep into the wooded landscape. She screamed and dug her fingers into the cold ground, grasping handfuls of foliage that simply tore out of the soil. When he entered her, she howled in instant pain from the mere thickness of his huge member. Her screams and pleadings drove him on even harder and faster in his sexual attack. Soon, she felt the warm liquid of his ejaculation deep inside her. It was his very seed that brought about the change.

She gave in to his cravings. Leaning forward she once again allowed him to enter her, this time from behind. She held tightly to a small birch while he lifted her ass to his swollen member. Her body thrashed back and forth in a rhythm attuned to his violent thrusting. Her nails dug into the soft bark of the tree as he let out a wild gurgling sound from the very bowels of his throat. When he let out his final roar, she once again felt the flushing of his testicles into her waiting human commode.

Tears slid down her cheeks as she kept her eyes riveted to the place that held the two most precious things in her life. Two precious beings she would more than likely never get to hold again.

CHAPTER 44

Jim Jackson and Pete Bateman arrived early the next morning in time to have breakfast with the rest of the family. Small talk went around the table like a business meeting at a general assembly. Jackson carried a letter from Marlene Peterson to give to Chris. She was looking into moving to another part of the county and wondering if there was any chance of them coming back to Maryland any time soon. The rest was personal and for his eyes only.

On the way to the estate in question, Chris wrote down his thoughts about what he would write back to Marlene. He missed her far more than he actually thought. Jennifer's death hadn't sunk in all the way either, but he knew there was no reconciliation there anyway; it was over and he just wanted to move on just as she had.

They turned onto an old dirt road with woods and swampland on either side. After crossing over a small bridge, they took a sharp turn to the right and into an open area that looked as though it had been a cornfield at one time. Just above the field loomed the fortress-looking Abernathy Mansion. For a few years it was patrolled by the local sheriff's office and county police department. When it appeared no one had an interest to getting into the monstrous building, with the exception of a few crack heads and drunks, they finally kept their patrols to three or four times a month. A few arrests were made for trespassing, but over the years those soon died down as well as the patrols.

Around the mansion were pine trees that stood tall and full. Between them were clumps of wild bushes of various types, with the earthen floor littered with long dried out needles. To the left was an oval shaped pond the size of two footballs fields. Below the pond were several living quarters that were probably built for the servants. According to the public records, Abernathy was built in the early eighteen hundreds. It was first built as a hotel with more than sixty rooms and three stories high. Chris shook his head with uncertainty as he followed the other two agents' car around back. It was then that a smile crossed his lips.

Lee Fret opened the door to his hummer and stood on the side step. He looked carefully around before letting his eyes rest on Chris' vehicle behind the two agents. A few seconds later, Trace Bordon and Tom Lederman popped out from the front and back seats with grins similar to cats successfully eliminating the ever tweeting canary.

Jackson looked back at Chris. "Hail, hail, the gang's all here."

Lee walked forward and took Chris' hand in both of his. "We miss you back in the real world my friend. Marlene sends her best."

Bordon and Lederman made their rounds of greetings as well before piling into the modified hummer that Lee was all too hyped up to show off. "Okay, we got the Uzi mounts front and back with one on each side. The rocket launcher is under the seat there," he pointed to the back of the vehicle, "and it's always ready to go. Well, it's not loaded, but it's all set up to be."

Chris folded his arms. "Uncle Sam is still spending money I see."

Lederman sat down on the passenger side's swivel seat. "What Uncle Sam wants, Uncle Sam gets, Chris. You should know that. And what he wants is to rid the fucking country of the walking dead...in any state of mind or body."

"How do we work this out?" Chris asked. He opened up the layout of the structure from inside and out and placed it on a small table inside the vehicle. "This place has a shitload of rooms. It started out as a hotel and then was given a facelift by the Abernathy family quite some time ago. These damn creatures could be anywhere in there. It also has a basement that was used for storage. The Abernathy family kept a lot of the hotel's larger equipment and stored it down in the basement. We have...what, six people here to go through this whole place? As for you, Lee, not that I'm not glad to see you, but you're not even in law enforcement."

Lee nodded. "That doesn't mean I'm not a good shot."

Chris laughed. "True."

Once the basement door was unlocked from the outside, they went in and unlocked any other doors that were included in the area. Anyone who got into trouble in any one area could hopefully escape through the closest unlocked door. Chris and Jackson went off in one direction, while the others went into another room. Most of the furniture and anything else that was included in the hotel scheme of things was covered with white sheets. It reminded Chris of a movie he couldn't remember that starred Sharon Stone.

"Do we look under the sheets, too?" Jackson asked.

Chris stood silent for a moment. It was a logical question and one that deserved a logical answer. "I don't think they would hide under a bunch of sheets, but it kind of makes me wonder what the hell is under most of them."

Jackson lifted up a sheet that was draped over something long and narrow at the top, and had sort of a seat at the bottom. When he had it half uncovered, it turned out to be an old piano. Another was a large credenza with the doors placed on the top instead of the side. He lifted one end slowly and then the next one over. There were two more on the other side of an ornate piece of wood of the same polished material acting as a divider.

Slowly lifting the one next to the divider, Jackson got it half way open when the piglet looking thing barely missed biting his arm. It made a jump for him just as Chris sent a slug through its chest. It only took a moment to realize it was a midget at one time.

The three others came rushing into the room with guns ready. "What the hell?"

Jackson nodded. "Damn near got my arm. Hell? Yeah, that's about as good an analysis of where this thing originally came from as I can get."

Chris lowered his weapon. "We have our work cut out for us, gentlemen."

Bordon moved toward several cabinet spaces on the other side of the room. Behind him, Lederman moved off to the right so he would be at an angle as the thin wooden doors were pulled open. The door beside it appeared to have flung open by itself. A kick from another of the animal creatures, this one looking a lot like a raccoon, grasped Bordon by the wrist of the hand that held his weapon. The other went to his throat and squeezed hard enough to block the airflow to his lungs.

"Keep his head away from you, Trace!" Lederman yelled.

They rolled several times in one direction and then the other. Trace Bordon kept the butt of his hand pressed hard into the thing's chin. From another room, six more of the creatures entered the room and circled around the covered furniture and out of sight. One of them leaped for Bateman and caught a .357 under the chin, taking the back of its head completely away from the rest of the skull. Lee Fret put three slugs into one of the wolf-looking ones and two more into something that looked like the face of an over-sized owl.

"Hold it still, Trace." Lederman leaned against the far wall and cupped his hand under the butt of his weapon. The thing turned his way in time to catch a bullet in its screaming mouth. The floor, cabinet doors, and white sheets around the area were now less than artistically speckled in red.

The others ran for another room and never came back. It took more than forty-five minutes to remove sheets from covered items and double check rooms. It was now time to shut down the elevators that ran from the basement to what was once the lobby. All but one of the other elevators had been closed down long ago and the doors walled over.

Bordon wiped blood from his arms and wherever else it splattered to make sure none of it was his own. The sink at the other end of the room gave proof that he wasn't cut or bitten anywhere. It didn't take long for them to find and eliminate the rest of the beasts.

"Where the hell's the National Guard when you need them?" Lederman quipped.

Chris laughed as he turned the key inside the ground floor elevator and rendered it inoperable. "They're busy doing other things and baring the brunt of our own situation. I would have loved to have ten or twelve of them here. Let's relock the doors down here before we move on."

On the next level, the lobby was now a huge foyer. Plants long dead bent awkwardly in all directions. Once again they split up into two groups and surveyed the remaining rooms. The kitchen was amazingly untouched. A counter in the center of the room had a sink and various contraptions that were used for prepping meals. Above the countertop were hooks and runners with stainless steel cookware hanging in perfect unison.

At the side of the counter a wooden board was attached supporting slits and various sized holes for holding kitchen utensils. Several of the slots were empty. It was obvious by the thin slits that they were the holders of sharp knives.

Bateman pointed to the board. "You thinking what I'm thinking?"

"Yeah, exactly," Chris said. "Some of these bastards are packing. We lucked out in the basement. Every door in every room has to be carefully opened with extreme caution. These fuckers aren't as dumb as their zombie predecessors."

Jackson opened several closet doors, revealing different types of equipment, most of which was for cleaning floors. Another was a huge walk-in closet for storing linens for tabletops. It was obvious that the Abernathy's took advantage of the paraphernalia left behind when it was a hotel, deciding it was good enough for home use.

Once everything was secure, they went up to the next level. A winding staircase took them to a long hallway at the very top. The Abernathy's had blocked off more than half the rooms on each level by removing the doors and framing, and then continuing with a wall where the doors had once been. This was accomplished by alternating every other room to be blocked off on both sides. Each floor now had twelve rooms on each side of the corridor, with a total of twenty-four on each side of the level; all of them were locked.

A well placed foot just above each of the doorknobs took the place of any well-meaning skeleton key. Three men took a side and began the kicking process. In one of them, Tom Lederman opened fire on four of the creatures kicking one of the walls in to get to the other side. Chris and Pete Bateman narrowly escaped being jumped by three of them who were actually waiting for the door to be kicked in.

On several occasions, the creatures had constructed a hole inside the closet walls to gain access to the rooms that were sealed on the outside. This was one of the biggest problems in cleaning out the room. The crude entranceway had to be checked out carefully before one of the men was able to crawl through. Any slip-ups and they would end up joining the ranks of the creatures and end up being shot by friendly fire to avoid such a fate.

In an hour and a half, they finished the second floor and dragged the dead out into the corridor to be taken to the first level when the job was completed. The smell of the things was horrendous. A few of them had ticks that were engorged with blood, and several of them actually had fleas that would every so often bounce around on their dead faces.

It was now late afternoon and they took a break in one of the larger bedrooms. Some of the wooden furniture left over from better days was used to build a warming fire in the fireplace. It was one of the perks in renting one of the larger rooms when the place was a hotel. Lee and Chris came back with coffee and sandwiches. They took turns being lookout at the door while everyone had their fill and warmed up.

Chris poured more coffee into the cups of Trace and Tom. "You guys are on your own at this point?" he asked.

Tom Lederman nodded. "Trace and I were assigned to the terrorist section two months after nine-eleven. When this happened we were moved out into the field to work with investigators at the Pentagon. When DC was more than three quarters closed down, everything was changed around. Most of us went off in different directions with various assignments. The pay is a little slow in coming, too. What about you guys?"

Chris laughed. "With Congress closed down for now, the Capital Police are now assigned with the protection of them and their residences. The Secret Service took agents from the field offices and put them on various assignments in regards to this shit. Jim and I are no more than paid assassins, as are a lot of the other agents from the big field offices. It's now been learned that the west coast and mid-west states are now coming up with either these God forsaken things or the undead. If it wasn't for our nuclear power we probably wouldn't be the United States anymore."

CHAPTER 45

While Kaitlyn put a Scooby Doo movie in for the kids, Ernie went out to get more wood for the living room fireplace. The house was heated with electric, but the fireplace was something that couldn't be ignored. Both he and Kaitlyn found it soothing in the middle of the night when they couldn't sleep. The day was quiet so far. Kaitlyn looked out into the woods and wondered how long the creatures would torture Jennifer before they actually got around to killing her.

She watched Ernie pile wood into the wheelbarrow and kept her eyes peeled for any of the things coming out into the open. They never did anything like that during the day, but there was no doubt that the creatures were getting braver and a bit smarter. As far as the zombies, they would stagger about at any time. They were now few and far between, but there were still some of them left.

The Butler place was just a few miles from where they were, and the locals mentioned that the other day they killed three of them in the lower pasture. She wondered how long it was going to take for the country to clean up after the idiots who were responsible for this catastrophe.

Her eyes caught something out of her peripheral vision and she turned her attention back to her husband. Ernie was swinging a piece of wood at the head of one of the biggest creatures she ever saw. There were now three of them coming out of the small shed.

Why hadn't they checked the shed?

She screamed, bringing Mikey and Courtney to the kitchen window. As they reached the window and saw what was happening, they started to cry.

The rifle Ernie brought out with him was leaning up against a small tree just out of reach. Kaitlyn ran for the front door and around the house. The three creatures were now no more than twenty feet from where Ernie was violently holding his own against another who had attacked from the tree line at the same time. The thing that took the blows her husband had to offer wasn't affected by them. The wood might as well have been a plastic baseball bat.

"Aunt Kate!" Courtney ran to the door and locked it. She then ran back to the window in time to see her uncle fall to the ground. The thing had a muzzle in front of its face that resembled the likeness of a pony. The wide nostrils flared as it bent forward and hoisted Ernie up from the ground and into the air.

A shot rang out, and then another. The beast threw Ernie Lambert more than twenty feet, slamming his shoulder hard into one of the trees. It turned to Kaitlyn who had already cocked the lever once again and fired into the creature's throat. It grasped at the front of its neck and spun violently around. Spurts of arterial blood sprayed the dried leaves and over the wood that had been collected in the wheelbarrow. It fell face down and didn't move again. The others were already leaping into the wooded area directly behind the shed.

Kaitlyn ran to her husband's side. He was unconscious and breathing in short raspy breaths. Each exhalation brought a frothy glob of blood from between his lips. Kaitlyn knew from taking first aid classes that it meant he had some kind of a lung problem; more than likely he had broken ribs with one puncturing one of his lungs.

"Aunt Kate, what's wrong with Uncle Ernie? Is he going to be okay?" Courtney's small voice was wavering with sobs.

"I need you to get inside, honey." Kaitlyn said, dumping the contents of the wheelbarrow onto the ground. "Get the cell phone and call your daddy. Tell him we need him here as soon as possible. Go quickly."

She watched her niece run for the house and brought the wheelbarrow over to where Ernie was laying. It then occurred to her that trying to get him into the contraption could make matters worse if he indeed had a lung puncture. Mikey was standing by one of the bedroom windows when she looked up. She made a motion with her hands that suggested the opening of the window. Mikey slid it open.

"Mikey, throw one of the heavy blankets through the bars, honey. Please do it quickly for me, okay?"

Mikey pushed the blanket through the bars and watched his aunt open it up and then fold it in half. Kaitlyn brought it over to her husband and laid it down at his side. Her idea was to get him on the blanket and move him as close to the front of the house as possible. His eyes suddenly fluttered for a few seconds.

"Aunt Kate?"

"Just a minute, Mikey. I need to see if I can...."

"Behind you, Aunt Kate! Behind you!"

Kaitlyn spun around and immediately went for the gun. She leveled it and stood completely still. She wanted to cry, but the anger simply had her grinding her teeth as she stared into the eyes of what used to be Jennifer. "We saved your life. We saved the life of your children as well. Look what they've done!"

The Jennifer thing stared back at her. Her teeth had now become more animal-like and coarse hair began to sprout from the sides of her shoulders. Her eyes slowly went down to the monstrous being lying on the ground. No more would this particular thing penetrate her in unwanted and violent sex. Her eyes stayed there momentarily before looking at the limp body of her sister-in-law's husband. She let her eyes roam over the weapon and then up into Kaitlyn's eyes.

"Go back into the woods, Jennifer. Leave us alone or so help me God I'll shoot you fucking dead."

"Kateeee...lassst...lasssst tiimme talk." Jennifer shook her head. "I...I heeelp get innnnsiiide, Errrrnnneeee."

Kaitlyn stood silent as Jennifer walked slowly to Ernie. She touched the blanket and looked back over her shoulder. Kaitlyn followed her every move with the gun, but made her way over to the other side of the blanket. Both of them were able to scoop him up slowly and lie him down on his back atop the blanket. Each taking a corner, they slowly pulled his body around to the front of the house.

Mikey was at the top of the stairs at first, and then behind him came Courtney. The girl began to cry softly. "Mommy?" Courtney's small voice ached with the pain of losing her mother. "Mommy, don't hurt us, please."

Jennifer turned her head away from her daughter's pleas and tears. She slowly shook her head as her own tears slid down her cheeks. In another few seconds she was making her way back around the house. She stooped low as she passed the body of the creature that once tried to claim her as his own. She quickly touched her clawed hand to the ground to pick something up.

A siren was blaring in the distance and it was getting closer. Jennifer knew for a fact that her ex-husband would shoot her dead. At the edge of the woods, she once again looked back at the house. It was over; there was no turning back the clock. The world as she knew it had been changed and locked itself in this situation for all time. It was only a matter of time before they were all hunted down.

Jennifer Kearns held the object she had scooped up from next to the dead body of her tormentor.

Kaitlyn saw something gleaming in Jennifer's claw.

Jennifer lifted the knife and gave her best smile before once again disappearing between the trees.

CHAPTER 46

Chris and Jackson made their way toward the house. As soon as they spied Ernie lying on the folded blanket next to the steps, they knew it wasn't good. He was pale and making low gurgling sounds.

"What the hell happened?" Chris asked.

In her excitement, Kaitlyn ignored his question. "Chris, I saw Jennifer. She helped me pull Ernie from the back of the house to here. She knew exactly who I was. She recognized everyone and she spoke. It was...broken up, but she told me she would help bring him around to the front of the house. He would have been inside, but I think the sound of the siren scared her off. We have to get him to a hospital, Chris. I think he has a punctured lung."

Jackson grabbed a makeshift table made of plywood that was off to the side and broke off the top. He brought it over next to Ernie. "We turn the blanket up on one side and slide this flat board under his back. We don't want to pick him up so that his back is arched. If there is a rib puncturing his lung that might make it worse."

Kaitlyn held him to one side while both men slid the board under him. "What do we do about getting him to a hospital?" she asked.

Chris looked around. "We don't have much of a choice. We can try to call someone from the hospital five miles from here, but considering the way things are that's probably a totally ludicrous idea. We'd be better off taking him there. That, I think, would be the better deal." He looked back at his sister. "You never answered my question, sis. What the hell happened here?"

Kaitlyn shook her head. "He was outside getting some firewood. Everything was fine, then all of a sudden he was attacked by a bunch of them. One was huge, the biggest bastard I've seen yet. They attacked and Ernie was using a piece of wood to fend the big one off. He picked Ernie up like a sack of potatoes and threw him against a tree."

"And, Jennifer? Where did she go?"

Kaitlyn pointed toward the other side of the house. "Back into the woods. She picked something up on the way. I saw something gleaming in her hand. I think it was some kind of a weapon. Maybe a knife, I don't really know."

After getting the keys from Kaitlyn, they lifted Ernie and took him to the camper. In a few minutes they were turning around and heading down the road. Jackson followed in the car and stopped off at the old Abernathy Estate. Lee talked Chris into putting Ernie into the Hummer and Tom Lederman headed back to Ernie's place to stay with Kaitlyn and the two kids. He immediately looked out the back window, checking the area for any more of the creatures; such as the grotesque body that lay on the ground, taken down by Kaitlyn.

He went back into the next room and smiled at Mikey and Courtney. Looking at Kaitlyn's face gave him a good idea of her mental state. "You know...you could have gone along with your brother," Tom said.

"I know I should have gone with them, but I didn't want to leave the kids with you, Tom. No offense, I don't mean that...."

"None taken, Kaitlyn. You don't have to apologize. Actually, I think the kids would be better off if you were here. Ernie's in good hands. I have an idea though. If I can get through, we might be able to get Doctor Peterson up here. I think the National Guard would fly her up in no time. There's really not much she can do in Maryland right now. They've got an all out war going on. The good thing is that the mutants aren't capable of shooting back at anyone. It's like going after cavemen. There are very little injuries or deaths reported in that regard so far. If she's willing to make the trip, we'd be in good hands. We'd be a true group of professionals." Lederman dialed Pete Bateman's cell phone number.

Bateman answered the phone just as several more shots were fired from directly behind him. "*Yeah, but you'll have to hold on a moment, I...yeah, here it is.*" Pete read off the number quickly before turning around and taking one of his own shots. "*What the hell are you going to call Peterson for?*"

"We need her here. Chris needs her here, too. This isn't going to last forever. How's it going over there? You guys sound like you're in one hell of a battle."

"*I was able to get several state troopers over to the mansion during the time Chris was gone. The third floor proved to be an all out war. They're everywhere, Tom. It's like they thought we would have known they'd stay at the bottom floors. And there's some of them that show a great deal of intelligence. What's going on over there?*"

"One of the bastards got Ernie Lambert. It looks like he might have a collapsed and punctured lung. Chris is on the way to the hospital. What about Trace?"

"*He's fine. I have to go. I'll get back to you as soon as these bastards have all bought it, or at least a good part of the farm.*"

Kaitlyn held the two kids to her side. "I took you away from your duties."

Tom smiled. "Yeah, well, I'll forgive you if you make a fresh pot of coffee."

CHAPTER 47

Chris drove past a playground littered with dead bodies. Several of them recognizable as zombies were feeding on the flesh of dead creatures.

Jackson warned Chris that he would hear a few shots as he opened a gun portal at the back of the Hummer; then he fired off several rounds.

One at a time the zombies dropped like sacks of flour.

"There's no use in letting them morph into more of those disgusting freaks of nature," Jackson said.

To the right was an abandoned school. Almost every window was broken or missing. Again, the parking lot and campus were littered with rotting corpses. The zombies there no longer feasted on the dead flesh. It was cold, and all they wanted was the taste of warm blood.

Jackson once again sent a bullet through each of their heads.

They had another twelve miles to go. Somehow the calculations given to him were off by at least six or seven miles.

Chris looked back at Jackson. "Why the hell are those things out during the day? Did they get all this shit wrong? First it was 'don't eat the fish,' now it's this daylight shit. Kaitlyn told me the damn things were wandering around during any time of the day. It wasn't like this in the beginning."

Jackson fired another few shots at several more creatures. "I think they were, more or less, grabbing at straws. This whole mess is fucked up, Chris. We were never told they were going to morph into these animal things either."

The hospital at Cotterville was closed. Chris cursed and glanced back at Ernie. Jackson pulled the blanket down a bit and looked at Ernie's complexion.

"He doesn't look any better. And he's got kind of a blue complexion now." Jackson felt for a pulse. "He's still alive, though."

The only other hospital was now over seventy miles to the north. Chris used the phone in the Hummer to call his sister. Everything was fine so far, she told him, and the kids were now convinced their uncle would be all right. Chris told her about the hospital at Cotterville being closed and that they were now headed for the one just outside of Altoona.

He checked the map and turned onto another major highway. It was strange to see cars overturned on the side of the road and bodies strewn about like road kill. The stench was enough to gag a maggot. There were vehicles at a dead stop in the center of the highway, while others appeared to have been parked to the side, intentionally abandoned for one reason or another. Both Jackson and Chris took it that the vehicles ran out of gas and the drivers took their chances on foot.

Both men thought it was strange.

"Why the hell are they still there? Why didn't they come back as zombies or the other creatures?" Chris asked.

"Maybe the parasite doesn't exist anymore," Jackson said.

Chris nodded. "That could be true, but there are also those animal looking things lying around, too. They were probably killed by the police or military. But the bodies of men and women still looking human didn't make much sense. If we weren't involved in an emergency here, I'd pull over and take a look at those things."

"What the hell do we have here?" Jackson asked, pointing straight ahead.

On the side of the road, there were bodies stacked up as though they were deliberately placed that way. Chris swerved to the right and steered around several of those that were lying away from the others. A steady stream of dark smoke billowed up from someplace over the rise in the road and the stench of burning meat almost made them vomit. When the Hummer crested it, Chris could see that the locals had a bonfire going in a parking lot next to a small marina. To the right of the marina was a narrow bridge. Men were carrying bodies to the fire and tossing them into it as fast as they could carry them.

"Let's just keep going," Jackson said.

Chris slowed down as he approached the sickening smell of burning flesh. Those who were working at burning the bodies looked curiously at the Hummer. One of them held up his hand in a manner that requested Chris to stay where he was.

"If you're headed down the road...well, you're in for a surprise." the man said, stopping just short of the open window.

"What's the surprise?" Chris asked.

The man pointed down the road. "The damned things came out of a barn. The rest of these folks thought they were regular people at first, but I knew different. I know just about everyone in the area and I knew there wasn't anyone on that farm. They sold it several years ago." He then pointed off into a dried up cornfield on the right. "These damned things came out of the field. By the time we got them under control, the rest of them came across the bridge. We didn't get the rest of the bodies down that way. The surprise is a bunch of these God-for-bidding things still roaming around, and a bunch still lying all over the road."

Chris thanked the man for the update and continued on. He had Jackson check on Ernie once again and was told Ernie had taken to blinking continuously. A quarter of a mile past the bridge, he found what the man was talking about. Bodies were strewn all across the road. A good part of them were the animal creatures, with six or seven zombies. The smell was enough to seep into the closed windows of the Hummer.

Making his way around the corpses, Chris got no more than sixty or seventy yards before several people stepped out onto the road in front of him.

One of the men held a rifle up to his shoulder, pointing it at the windshield. The other two slowly and cautiously made their way down the sides of the vehicle. Jackson quickly ducked out of sight, thankful that he'd closed the weaponry lids on the roof. Chris stopped, not wanting to run the men down, and knowing that it was probably something he was going to regret before the day was out.

"Get the hell out of the vehicle! It's ours now!"

One of the men on the driver's side held a pistol to the window and at Chris' head.

Chris immediately thought of Ernie in the back. He also thought about making a break for it. The man in front might get one shot off, but the others would no doubt be shooting for the tires.

Chris tried not to move his lips as he slowly lowered the window and spoke to Jackson. "Are you seeing this?" he asked.

Jackson was moving up toward the rear Uzi and positioning the target. "I see the sons of bitches. Give me about thirty seconds."

"I ain't gonna ask you again, mister," the man said.

Chris pointed down the road. "I have a very sick man in here. He needs to get to a hospital. I'll give you three a ride wherever you want, as long as it's heading in this direction."

"No, that ain't gonna do it. We'll take the fuckin' rig and go where the fuck we wanna go. Now get the hell out of there or this gun is gonna make one hell of a nasty mess out of your head."

Chris quickly thought about buying time. Just enough for Jackson to get into place for whatever he had in mind. "This isn't going to help whatever has your shorts in a twist, pal," Chris said as he flashed the man his best smile.

The man nodded with a shit-eating grin. "Yeah, well, that's what you say, asshole. Now, open the other fuckin' door and let my friend in. You make one wrong move and you're gonna get a few ounces of hot lead in the brainpan."

Chris was screwed and he knew it. There was a strange noise in the back and he thought he heard Jackson making his way under the back seat. There was enough room for a person and some more weapons. If there was going to be a shoot out, it was going to be at close range, Clint Eastwood style.

Chris unlocked the passenger door and waited for the other man to step in.

"Holy shit! This thing is a rollin' arsenal," the second man gasped.

"Anybody else in there?" the man at the driver's side window asked.

"No. Not that I can see," his buddy replied. "There's a guy layin' here lookin' kind of like he's on his last legs, though." The carjacker put the gun next to Chris' head. "What's wrong with him, mister? He got some kind of shit that we can all catch?"

Chris thought for a moment. This could be a way out, but it could cost Ernie his life if they moved him.

"Yeah, in a way he does," Chris replied. "He was in a fight with one of those things. We think he has a punctured lung. That's why we're trying to get him to the hospital. He's my brother-in-law. They have some kind of a shot now. It may keep him from turning into one of them," Chris lied.

"Yeah? That ain't gonna happen," the man at the driver's side window said. He slowly opened the driver's door as the man with the rifle climbed into the Hummer from the passenger side. He aimed the rifle at Chris' chest.

"Now, get the hell out of here and you might live to see another day. Your brother-in-law, however, now that's a different story. His ass is comin' out of there, too. You're gonna carry him. I ain't catchin' no fuckin' diseases from his sick ass."

Jackson kept his body rigid under the seat. He would have to come up from behind the seat to get off a shot. If one of them came back behind the seat, he'd have to take him out no matter what. Jackson hoped like hell that Chris still had his weapon.

It was like a curse just thinking of it, as if the carjacker had read his mind.

"First of all," the man with rifle said to Chris, "get down on the ground so I can check you for any other weapons."

CHAPTER 48

The creatures were coming toward the house in full force. Tom Lederman checked all the doors and had the kids go up to the small gable at the right side of the house. It had a hidden staircase that went down to the ground floor in case they needed it, but inside, the gable was only accessible from the attic. Zombies simply grabbed at the bars, but the animal creatures were more aggressive. Even the wrought-iron bars in the front and back of the house were not left out when it came to abuse.

Kaitlyn fired several shots from one of the bedrooms while Lederman fired from the living room. The noises from the pounding, grunts and groans of the creatures were enough to drive both of them crazy. In the front, a huge pig-like creature pulled the iron door away from the latch. It swung open, leaving the heavy wooden door now exposed. This was no more of a problem for the beast than the hollowed out type of door normally used for most home closets. When it crashed in, Lederman shot the thing through the head. Behind it, the others quickly navigated their way through the kitchen. Kaitlyn screamed as she fired repeatedly until the gun refused to fire again.

Lederman tossed Kaitlyn his empty rifle and pulled his service piece, letting loose with a volley that dropped seven or eight of the beasts in a matter of seconds. He slammed another clip up into the handle while Kaitlyn fumbled with loading bullets. Some of the bullets dropped on the floor and she simply screamed in frustration at them for not cooperating.

When a gun finished, she tossed it back to the agent who was now working his way over dead bodies and toward the front door. He finally got it closed and turned the deadbolt. There was another noise from someplace outside. Then it registered. The kids were screaming.

It was Kaitlyn who went up to the attic and into the gable. One of the things had climbed up the side of the house by using the windows. It looked similar to a rat, or perhaps a squirrel.

"Get the fuck away from my kids!" Kaitlyn screamed. The shot that rang out from the rifle took the top of its head clean off, but it held onto the frame for a moment before dropping down to the ground.

Once again there a was commotion downstairs. This time Kaitlyn took the kids into the attic and told them to run into the gable only if necessary. If the things came up into the attic, she told them, it was time to get out of the house and run to the north. She pointed out the direction and hugged them to her. They were hers just as much as they were her brother's. In the back of her mind, she had a bad feeling about Ernie. It was only bits and pieces that she remembered from the fight, but she could have sworn she saw blood on her husband's arm.

Coming down off the ladder and into the bedroom, Kaitlyn could hear more gunfire from outside. As she came through the doorway and into the living room, Trace Bordon was coming through the front door, followed by Peter Bateman and Lee Fret. Tom Lederman was on his back, not moving.

When the pantry door swung violently open, it was Bordon who shot the thing through the chest. Another beast came down the staircase from the second floor and met the same fate. To the right, a window had been smashed in and the bars broken off at the bottom and pushed inward. Kaitlyn realized since the thing coming from the pantry was huge; it must have grabbed Tom as he passed by on his way to help her.

Bordon knelt at his partner's side for a long moment while the rest of the crew came into the kitchen.

Lee Fret came quickly to her side. "Are you all right?"

Kaitlyn nodded. "Yeah, I'm fine. Oh, God! I'm so sorry, Agent Bordon. If it wasn't for Tom and the rest of you guys, the kids and I would be dead right now."

Bordon shook his head. "It must have grabbed Tom when he went to unlock the deadbolt. It's not your fault, Mrs. Lambert. The important thing is that you and your children are safe."

"I have to get the kids." Kaitlyn was in tears as she turned and went back up into the attic to retrieve her niece and nephew.

Her life was like a nightmare that would never end.

When her cell phone rang on the way back down, she could hear her brother trying to catch his breath as he talked.

She collapsed against the wall with Mikey and Courtney hugging her as she slowly slid down to the floor.

CHAPTER 49

Chris slowly took his place on the ground next to the Hummer. The man climbed into the driver's seat and held the gun so that it pointed at Chris' head.

Jackson held his breath for a moment before slowly and quietly turning as far onto his left side as possible. A box of Uzi ammo was the only thing keeping his face from showing. He kept his knees bent so that only half his legs were visible, but not in plain view.

The man with the rifle held up Chris' commission book.

"Well, lookie here! We got ourselves a real live secret agent man. Now, I tell ya, this poses a real threat. Any old dude ridin' along in a Hummer is one thing, but a secret agent man is totally another. We'd be in real trouble if you was to ID us, asshole. I guess you're just gonna hafta end up as another freak on the side of the road."

The man in the passenger's seat backhanded his friend on the shoulder. "Never mind that shit. Is he packin' any heat?"

The man shook his head. "Nah. But I find it real strange that he ain't. What's a secret agent man without a gun? That's like a fish without any gills."

The other man climbed over the seat and looked down at Chris'. "Where you keepin' the gun? Come on! I know you got a gun somewhere, G-Man."

Chris turned his head to look up at the man in front of him. "I don't have a fucking job anymore. Have you looked around you lately? The whole damn world is coming to an end."

The man nodded. "Yeah, I been lookin'. I say we get Mr. G-Man off to the side of the road before anyone else shows up."

Chris saw something move in his peripheral vision inside the Hummer. The blanket lifted up slightly and then back down again. In front of him, he could see Jackson's weapon peek out from under the seat. It was going to be a close one.

"Let's get goin'," the man in the driver's seat said. He leaned out of the Hummer and grabbed Chris by the back of the neck and pulled him to a kneeling position. "Come on, G-man! Get movin'!"

When Ernie sat up and twisted toward them, he wasn't the same. To the men in the Hummer, it was something out of their worst nightmares.

Ernie immediately grabbed the man in front of Chris, sinking his fingernails into the man's arm. It was then that Jackson's gun went off. The man in the passenger seat grunted and flipped out backward and onto the road. Chris jumped up, got the man in the driver's seat by the wrist, and hit him solidly on the left side of his jaw. His back went over the steering wheel just as Chris slammed another right hand into his ribcage.

The man Ernie grabbed first had just finished screaming in agony. Ernie raised his head and howled as though he was suddenly the head of a pack of wolves.

The man in the driver's seat was still fighting and he pushed his thumbs into Chris' eyes as the rifle got between the two men. The pressure on Chris' eyes was something that lasted for only a few painful seconds. The barrel of the rifle pushed the man's chin upward and out toward the open door, and when Chris managed to get his finger around the trigger and squeeze it, the rifle went off. And so did the top of the man's head.

"Chris, watch out!" Jackson was now halfway out from under the seat. Chris turned just as his friend dropped down flat in the back of the Hummer.

Chris's eyes met Ernie's for a few seconds.

"Do it!" Ernie croaked.

It was merely a whisper, but Chris heard Ernie's plea as plain as day. Through the grotesque features and raspy breathing, there was still part of his brother-in-law in there.

"I'm sorry," Chris said, pulling the trigger on the rifle and sending the bullet through Ernie's forehead.

"Holy shit!" Jackson screamed, coming up to the front.

That was when Jackson saw Ernie's arm and the elongated wound on it. It was festering and discolored beyond recognition. The creature that had attacked him must have scratched him sometime during the scuffle, and sometime during the attempted carjacking, Ernie had temporarily died.

When they finally cleaned up the mess, both Jackson and Chris sat solemnly on the side of the road. The men who were burning the bodies on the other side of the bridge made their way toward them, the gunshots attracting them to the Hummer.

While Jackson filled in the other men on what happened, Chris pulled out his cell phone and made the call to his sister he was dreading.

CHAPTER 50

Lee Fret knelt down next to Kaitlyn. "What's wrong, honey?"

Mikey started crying along with Courtney. "Aunt Kate, is my Daddy all right?"

Kaitlyn's heart was breaking as she hugged both their heads against her. "Daddy is all right but Uncle Ernie became very sick." She looked up at Lee. "What am I going to do here, Lee? Ernie was everything to me, and now I have nothing."

Lee shook his head. "You have a business back home. You have a damn good brother who can find someone trustworthy to start it back up again. Everyone who knows what's going on in the country knows how to take care of the situation. The military is rebuilding as we speak. It's going to be like another war for a while, but the good thing is that our military will be the only ones shooting guns."

Courtney buried her face into her aunt's bosom. "Uncle Ernie's gone, Aunt Kate. I thought he was going to be all right. You said so."

Lee stood up and looked down at them. "I'll be right here in the other room. Talk to them, Kaitlyn. They'll come around in a few days. There'll always be someone here for you no matter what."

Kaitlyn sniffed several times as she nodded. "I know, Lee. You've all been here for us, every one of you." She kissed her niece's head gently. "I know, Courtney. I know I said he would be all right, but he was a lot sicker than I thought. The main thing is that your daddy is all right and you'll be seeing him very soon. We're going to try to go home soon. You can live with me for as long as you want. As long as I have you two, I have my sanity. Everything's going to go back to normal. Not today or tomorrow, but soon enough. I'll see that you have a family to come home to when you get out of school each day."

Kaitlyn called out to Lee, who came into the room immediately. "Lee, agent Lederman called Doctor Peterson. I think the idea was that she was going to meet them at the hospital; the one Chris said was closed down. Someone has to contact her."

Bateman nodded as he stood in the doorway. "Yeah, he called me and filled me in. I already called Chris and told him. He should have attempted to contact her by now. Hopefully, he got through to her."

CHAPTER 51

Colonel Hapshire fired several blasts from his automatic rifle. The zombies were now walking in direct sunlight. Soldiers surrounded one of the developments and moved in slowly to close in the circle. Front lawns and backyards were the battlegrounds that would suffice for the cemetery plots of the dead. Creatures of various sizes and shapes came out of several of the homes. Once again, this meant entering some of the houses to disinfect them of whatever the dead occupants would become.

Hapshire moved to the center of the road and backed up to a stalled vehicle. "Hapshire here." He held the cell phone to his ear while plugging the other with his finger. "A flight to where? You've gotta be kidding, Doctor Peterson. I'm in an all out war here. The whole state of Maryland is in Armageddon. You understand that don't you, Doctor? This is the battle of good and evil the bible talks about in Revelations."

Marlene Peterson took a deep breath and continued to close up the torn arm of a man who had run through barbed wire.

"They're in Pennsylvania, Colonel. How long would it take to get a helicopter to their location and then back here?"

Hapshire shook his head. "That's only a...what, six hour drive, Doctor?" He quickly turned and fired several more shots, exploding the heads of zombies trying to sneak up on him. "Yeah, I know you were asked to be flown there, but that was iffy as well. You can understand that, can't you? I have a whole regiment here to take care of. As a physician who works in a hospital setting, you should know what that's like."

Marlene wrapped the man's arm. "Keep it clean and change the bandage every day. I'd like you to use a cleaning agent on it as well. Peroxide would do." She walked to the other side of the room and sat behind one of the desks.

"Yes, Colonel Hapshire, I can. The thing that bothers me is, well, they lost two of their people. They have two children as well. The fear is that the dead will occupy the highways en masse. It's happening all over the country as we speak. Four hours, perhaps a bit more, Colonel Hapshire. That's not too much to ask, is it? I can make it up to you and the military in general at one time or another."

Hapshire gave off a deep sigh. "Let me get back to you, Doctor Peterson. I can't make any promises here, but I'll see what I can do. Right now I have to look to my men. You have to understand, Doctor, I can't bring the wounded to you, and you know that. Anyone wounded by those things is as good as dead. I don't take kindly to killing my own kind. I'll get back to you."

The sounds of gunshots from automatic rifles filled the air once again. Soldiers came from homes and yards as though they were weaving some kind of tangled web throughout the area. It was getting worse now. Pulling the cell phone from the casing, he dialed the number for security and thought about the old saying of getting worse before better. It was then that he saw the reflection of a mutated zombie in the windshield of a stranded vehicle.

It came down from one of the bigger trees on the side of the road. Without thinking about where it would land, it tumbled backwards and rolled to one side. The animal-like creature gave off several loud squeals as Hapshire's bullets ripped through its hirsute body.

Hapshire once again picked up the phone and redialed.

If he had to, he knew he could do it.

He could blow his own head off rather than become one of the damned.

CHAPTER 52

Chris stared at his sister's face for as long as it took to register the feeling in his tired brain. The rest of the group left the room and waited for them to get out any emotions they had. Kaitlyn sank into his arms and let him hold her weight for a few minutes. It was as though her knees refused to bear the brunt of her upper body.

"I'm so sorry, sis. I had no idea he was infected by that thing. It was only a matter of time before he turned. In the last few moments of his life," Chris held her face in his hands, "if it's any consolation at all, he saved our lives. Through him we now know there's still a spark of intelligence and good in some of them. I guess that would be one of the sad parts of becoming one of them."

Mikey and Courtney held onto their aunt's waist. Chris knelt down and pulled his two children into his arms. His eyes roamed over their faces equally as he spoke. "I know what it's like to lose your most loved family members. First it was your grandfather, and then your mother and uncle. I can't bring any of them back, and I can't tell you that the hurt will go away any time soon, but I can give you every ounce of love I have left in me. We're going home. I'm not going to run anymore. Pennsylvania can take care of itself. We're going back to Maryland and reclaim what's ours."

Kaitlyn shook her head and gave a mock laugh. "Wait until this shit is all over and they have to sort out who owes whom what. Mortgages, rentals, auto loans, private loans, hell, it'll take them a few years to figure it all out. I don't even know if I have a home to go back to at this point. Even if I do, the memories are just going to add on to the hurt. What if everything Ernie worked for was all pillaged because of this frigging war?"

"I can't answer that, Kate." Chris turned away and gazed out the window. "We all have to hope for the best. This is like waking up in the middle of the night and realizing that everything we went through was for real and not a nightmare."

Bateman walked up and handed Chris his cell phone. "Chris, it's Colonel Hapshire." "Kearns here." Chris continued to stand and stare out the window. At the edge of the woods, he thought he saw something moving along the edge.

"Your Doctor Peterson is a fast talker, Kearns." Hapshire's voice came through as though he were standing in the next room. Chris smiled slightly. *"I think she believes the army is running an air taxi service. So, what's it like up there? I understand you lost a few people."*

"My brother-in-law and one of the FBI agents. It's not a lot of fun having to shoot family and friends, but when these bastards kill or injure you, there's nothing else you can do."

Hapshire waited a moment before answering. *"I tried to tell your doctor friend that same thing just a little while ago. I'm just about finished with this particular area. We're moving on to the south in a bit. Saint Mary's County is as bad as any of them. I'll tell you what I can do, Kearns. I can send a chopper up that way for your sister and the kids. One of you can come with them. I'll send a few of my men over to the old homestead; your brother-in-law's place. I think that area's pretty well taken care of. Let's say, half an hour immediately after you tell me where they need to land."*

Chris gave him the directions that one driving a car would follow. The landmarks from the air were easy enough for Hapshire to follow, since he also had relatives up that way. As soon as the conversation regarding the directions was over, Hapshire assured him the helicopter would be in the air and on its way in half an hour.

Chris moved away from the window and up to his sister. The rest of the group was standing in the doorway. "They're sending a chopper from Maryland to pick up my sister and the kids. I'll be going with them. They can only take the three of us. The rest of you will have to take to the highways. I'd put the cars between the camper and the Hummer. This way you'd have a fighting chance in case the roads are blocked for any reason."

Kaitlyn touched his arm. "Chris, where the hell are we going to stay?"

Raising his hand, he kept her from getting any more emotional. "The colonel is sending some of his men over to check out your place. He thinks the area is pretty well clear. Most of the residents in that area have moved back in. Kaitlyn, it's going to be slow going, but we can't just keep moving away from our problems. We can't let them take over. In a year, maybe a little more, things will be a lot better. Everyone is going to have to rebuild, from the government on up." Chris handed the cell phone back to Bateman.

Trace Bordon moved into the room and slid his cell phone back in the holder after using it.

"I just got word," Bordon said. "Parts of California are burning out of control. Firefighters are not only fighting the blazes, but the mutants as well." Bordon nodded to Chris. "It won't be long before your agency gets in contact with you. Congress is back in session and the President is on his way back to the White House. We have funding and we're back on the payroll. Right now, though, as far as anyone can understand, we're all still pretty much a mercenary group."

Chris nodded. "Well, there you have it. It's time to get our asses in gear and finish this mess once and for all. When we're assigned duties again, we'll have to leave all this macho soldier bullshit to the army. Until then, I'm going to take back as much shit as I've lost. I have my kids," he winked at Mikey and Courtney, "and that's a damn good start."

CHAPTER 53

It took less time than they thought to pack things up and head out. Tom Lederman's body was placed in a body bag and loaded into one of the trunks. Chris watched the small caravan pull out and head up the road. He turned his head toward the woods and had the sudden feeling that his weren't the only eyes watching their every move. Somewhere in the distance there were gunshots. The hunting parties he'd run into earlier were moving even closer to the residence. Any of the remaining creatures in the surrounding areas would be coming out of the woods in hordes.

It was now over forty minutes after the initial phone conversation with Hapshire. Chris made his way to the small buildings on the back lot and checked each one. Kaitlyn told him earlier that Ernie's brother kept tools and garden equipment in them. He kept the Uzi ready to fire in case his exit was blocked by either the undead or the animal creatures.

The first one was mostly bags of grass seed and various types of soil for planting. Along the walls were different kinds of pots and other containers. It was secure; virtually no place for anything but a small animal to hide. Satisfied, Chris made his way to the second one.

This one was a lot bigger. The padlock was open and turned so that the hole in the top was facing away from the hooked shackle.

"Chris, no one's been in there for quite some time," Kaitlyn said.

Chris raised his hand and nodded. "I'll be all right, Kate. I just want to see if there's anything we've missed during that time."

Kaitlyn and the kids watched closely as he made his way into the shed. In his job, it didn't matter that he would throw his body in front of someone he was protecting, but now it was the thought of being attacked and wounded by one of those things that was stuck in the front of his mind.

Chris switched on the light for good measure. A lime green John Deere tractor sat in the middle of the floor. On both sides of the shed there were various gas and electric powered tools hung on the walls. Being an agent, the first thing he noticed as he slowly moved around the area, was that the back door was unlocked from the inside. He carefully pulled it open and found the hasp has been pulled from the wood. There were no gouges around the outside of the hasp, as though a crowbar had been used on it with care.

A thought went through his mind. Two inch self-countersinking wood screws didn't get ripped out by a human hand. He pulled the door closed and latched it from the inside. He realized whoever or whatever broke the outside lock would have no trouble ripping the door of its hinges, but he locked it anyway.

"I caa...can't doooo it."

Chris whirled around and leveled the Uzi. Jennifer stood next to a large cabinet that held various hand held garden tools. Her face was covered with thick hair, making her look like she was made up for a horror movie. She was Lon Chaney, The Wolfman, in full makeup. In her clawed hand she held a heavy looking Bowie knife.

"Christ! Jennifer?" It was the only thing he could get out at first sight of her.

"Chrrriiisst, nothiiiing tooo doooo wiiith meeeee."

Chris shook his head. He could hear the gunshots coming from the woods even though he was inside the shed. "They'll be here. I can't...."

"Kiiilll meeeee, Chriiiisssss."

The lump in his throat was hard going down. The shots grew louder and soon there were strange voices, inhuman voices, out-side. Chris backed away from his ex-wife, looking over his shoulder as he neared the door. She followed his every move; her eyes carefully studying him. It was as though everything went into slow motion when Jennifer took one powerful leap over the tractor. There was rage in her growl, but in her eyes was the soft glow of pity and pleading. Chris gave a short burst from the Uzi that sent blood splattering over the smooth finish of the tractor.

As her limp body landed on the shed's floor, her sobs of both pain and thankfulness melted a heart that had grown cold over the years. He was lost in thought until a shot rang out from outside. He once again whirled, ready to face the situation.

A zombie stood and stared at him for a few seconds but then a dumbfounded look came over its face as a small gray hole appeared in its oversized forehead. At the same time, the back of its skull exploded outwards.

Kaitlyn lowered the weapon and looked into his eyes. "I've lost enough. I'm not going to lose any more."

Chris quickly took out his handkerchief and waved it over his head. The hunters acknowledged his signal and continued to shoot the remaining creatures and zombies that were now scattered about the field. Several of the hunters looked up toward the sky. The sound of rotor blades floated down from somewhere above a low overcast made up of thick white clouds. Seconds later, the helicopter finally swooped down below the blanket of white and slowly settled down between the two sheds.

Chris remembered one of the hunters from the human funeral pyre. The man stood no more than ten feet away from him. "Those men you killed were friends of mine."

Chris nodded. "Those men tried to take what belonged to me. You need to pick your friends with a bit more acuity. If you're thinking about using that rifle on me, you'd better think twice. Those are military men in that helicopter and they mean business. When that chopper leaves here, you'll be laying here amongst the dead." He leveled the Uzi, grasping the clip firmly with the other hand.

By now, a small group had gathered around the two men. Chris reached into his pocket, retrieved his commission book and let if flop open. With his badge now on display, several of the group took a few steps backwards.

"Is there a problem here?" Two of the men from the chopper in military dress approached the group with hands on their side arms.

Chris eyed his accuser and gave a sly smile. "Well, is there?"

The man shook his head. "No, there's no problem. We were just checking out the place when this fellow came out of the shed. We didn't know what we were up against." As he turned away, his expression was an arrogant *this isn't over*. But it was.

"What was that all about?" one of the soldier's asked.

Chris shrugged. "It seems I blew away a few of his undesirable friends. It was something that happened while I was trying to get my brother-in-law to a hospital."

"Chris Kearns?"

Chris nodded and put out his hand. "Yeah. That's my sister there, and the two kids are mine. We'll be ready to go in no time. Can you give us ten minutes?"

The two men nodded in unison. Before Chris could get himself turned around completely, he caught sight of a smiling face walking towards them.

"I talked them into taking me along. You know, just in case." Chris smiled and nodded at Marlene Peterson. She was a welcome sight.

In the house, they kept things on a business type deal, but Chris wanted to take Marlene in his arms once again. The world as it was right now didn't matter. There had to be some kind of meaningful relationship along the road to recovery. For him, Marlene was it. Even Kaitlyn looked at them with smiling eyes, though the pain it sent through her heart when she saw the looks they gave one another made her want to collapse where she stood.

It took exactly eighteen minutes for them to head on out to the chopper. The house was once again closed up tighter than a drum. That was, with the exception of a few broken windows and some of the bars that had been torn out.

Chris closed his cell phone and slid it back into the holder. A vehicle would be waiting for him at the base.

Five minutes later they were lifting off the ground and heading for Andrews Air Force Base in Maryland.

CHAPTER 54

In the District of Columbia, gunshots rang out every few minutes. Zombies and mutants were now taking to hiding in the basements of any building that were closed down, but still accessible from other unknown and unguarded entrances.

On some blocks the streets were lined with dead bodies ready to be picked up by flatbed trailers. The stench of decomposition was overbearing. Most of the zombies were well on their way to being fully decomposed even before they were shot. Some were actually crawling their way around thanks to festering limbs and brittle or broken bones.

The White House and the Old and New Executive Office Buildings had twenty-four hour security set up inside and out, as well as the block surrounding them. The Secret Service's Uniformed Division swept the designated areas, while agents and uniformed division personnel changed places frequently around the White House grounds.

The rural areas of Maryland and Virginia were still heavy with mutants. Rockville Park was a war zone with the Army working a V shape through the wooded areas. Many of the mutants were making their way to Maryland by way of Great Falls from the Potomac River, which many didn't realize was actually in Maryland. The state boundary followed the shoreline on the Virginia side of the river and the National Park. The Park Service maintained the area for viewers of the Great Falls cataract. Though visible from the Maryland side of the river, access was from the Virginia side.

The crossing of state lines involved a bit of thinking, showing authorities that they weren't always dealing with ignorant animals. The mutants were quick to find a hiding place where no human would want to put their body. They would leap from rocks and trees where cover was plentiful. In a few cases, zombies were found dead for unknown reasons. It was now believed that the parasite couldn't stand an overabundance of direct sunlight and would eventually die, leaving the host with no further direction or guidance.

Several hours after receiving the phone call from the rest of the team, Chris, Marlene and Kaitlyn met at the waterfront in DC. Several of the restaurants were now open again, all of them hiring security personnel to secure the outside areas and make the diners feel safe.

When they were finally able to get a table, they all sat in the back and had a quiet, early dinner. Tom Lederman's body was cremated and the remains sent to his family. No one talked about the time spent in PA. It was over and done, and nothing could change the outcome. Dead was dead.

Chris reached under the table and took Marlene's hand. It wasn't a secret gesture, just one that he wanted to keep soft and caring. When she turned her head to look into his eyes, he once again knew love. But the thoughts of killing his mutant wife were still in the back of his mind. The image of Ernie rising up in the form of a mutated human being would haunt his dreams well into the morning hours of sleepless nights.

Kaitlyn smiled and carried on as though nothing had happened, but her facial expressions gave away the facade of happiness that no longer lingered there.

*　　*　　*

Chris started to say something to keep her smiling, but he stopped before the words could escape his lips. Aidon Richards came through the doorway leading into the dining area; he was shadowed by two other agents. Slowly scanning the room, he finally located the group. A small smile spread across his lips without losing his somber facial expression. The two other agents accompanied him as he made his way over to the table.

"Don't get up; I think I know everyone here." Richards nodded at Kaitlyn. "I'm sorry for your loss, Mrs. Lambert."

"Thank you, Mr. Richards."

"Aidon. Aidon is fine." He stuck his hand out toward the two agents. "These two characters, Powell and Honeycutt, as well as you and Jackson, are going to be reassigned to TLC. The good news is that we're back in business. The bad news...well, we're still a long way from eliminating the threat. If we can keep this...disease, or whatever it is at bay, we'll have a good chance at getting both feet in the door to recovery."

Lee Fret nodded. "I'm told that the parasite is slowly dying off. The overexposure in the direct sunlight...." He shrugged. "For one reason or another, it's killing them off. It seems the brain has a certain awakening of its own. It doesn't know any better. Evidently the parasite doesn't correct that problem."

Richards cocked his head to one side. "More good news. Thank you, Doctor Fret."

Chris pulled three chairs over while the waiter brought another round of iced tea.

"Is there a way we can get Doctor Peterson a position on a temporary basis? She knows quite a bit about what's going on," Chris suggested.

Richards nodded. "I agree. Perhaps it can be on a consulting basis. Would that be to your liking, Doctor Peterson?"

Marlene leaned back in her chair, her mouth still agape and searching for words. "Well, I really never considered it. I have a practice to think about. I don't know if I can truly and diligently give a fair amount of time."

"I spoke out of turn," Chris said. He gave her a small smile. "I was just thinking about what kind of practice you had left."

Richards sipped his tea. "I think everyone involved would understand if you declined the invitation, Doctor Peterson. Just like they would understand the time, or lack of, that you were able to put in. The offer stands if you're interested."

"Thank you, Mr. Richards." Marlene looked at Chris. "Okay, let me see what I have back at the office. Maybe I can do some morning hours for a while and then switch to afternoon appointments. I can't promise anything, but I'll do my best."

Richards folded his hands on top of the table. "That's all anyone could ask for Doctor Peterson. Now, there's bad news and then there's worse than bad news. The bad news is we don't have enough military power to take away from working in the field. The worse than bad news is," he took a deep breath, "the mutants have taken hostages in an old abandoned military building." He nodded toward Chris. "It's a similar situation to what you got your sister and children out of, Chris. The difference is that it's more of a huge basement area. It's massive and, from the looks of our maps, it's got a bunch of different rooms. They're taking both male and female hostages, but we have a sneaky suspicion they're using the males for food and the females for breeding. They're also targeting children because they're easier to capture and manipulate. This is probably our biggest and most dangerous assignment to date."

Chris shook his head. "Why the hell are we learning about this now?"

Richards leaned back in his chair. "No one knew about it until now. The Department of Homeland Security's TLC agents followed some of the mutants who had captives. They didn't take them then and there because they figured they'd lead them to where they were keeping the hostages. They disappeared underground. We checked the area by air using spy equipment and found the tunnels. At one time the county used the tunnels for something I'm not quite sure of. Personally, I don't think I want to know. What's even worse than worse is that we don't know much about what kind of space is provided."

"Count me in," Lee said.

Richards smiled. "Consider yourself counted."

Marlene took a deep breath and nodded. "I'll be there in case of any injuries. But nothing can be done with bites. Anyone bitten will have to be quarantined until we can figure out...."

"There is no figuring out, Marlene," Lee said. "You know that. At the risk of sounding disingenuous toward the cause, anyone infected will have to be put down." He sipped his drink and shrugged.

"They're not really animals, Doctor Fret." Marlene said with a touch of annoyance in her voice.

Lee shook his head and once again shrugged. "They're not really humans either, Doctor Peterson."

"So, when do we get started?" Chris asked, quickly breaking up the minor quarrel.

Richards tapped his knuckles on the tabletop. "As soon you've all been given time to rest up and get your heads together."

Lee Fret raised his glass. "I propose a toast to working together once again."

They clinked glasses atop the center of the table and drank.

In the quiet of the moment following the toast, the echo of gunshots drifted in from somewhere in the city.

CHAPTER 55

The following Friday, a military helicopter was used to get the team to the drop zone to once again do battle. Just as the spy equipment had projected on the screen, the area had several places where tunnels were used to enter the old building from thirty or forty feet away. Two of them were closed off and one was similar to a trap door type entrance. The hole had an old steel ladder that went down at least ten feet. The walls were made of rock, similar to an old well.

Chris was the first to load up and descend.

The entrance was similar to a parking garage with a vast open space that was reinforced with wide pillars of cement and steel to support the ceiling. Various pieces of clothing were scattered about the cement floor. The string lights were covered with a wire cage around each of the bulbs and gave off an eerie spectrum of darkness and light when they blended in with the shadows of the team. At the far right end was an old mattress that was ripped and bulging with the cotton padding within. Chris picked up a torn blouse with the muzzle of his Uzi and held it up to eye level. It was splattered with a dried reddish-brown blood.

In the distance there was a dripping sound similar to a leaky faucet. The flooring was dry with the exception of a few wet spots where the cement had taken on water and left odd shaped blotches of dampness rather than tiny puddles. The team separated and moved slowly and cautiously along the pillars. Once the room was completely secured, they made their way around the corner into the next. A ramp was to the right that brought them one more level below.

Jackson, Fret, and Bordon went up one level and took a quick look around. It was the last level going up and took only a few minutes to make sure it was secure. Chris, Bateman, Marlene, and two army privates stayed behind at the ramp going down. When they were all together again, they began to move slowly down the ramp. Looking over the railing, Chris found an old battery and a few bald tires. Off to the side, was a car with broken windows and flattened tires.

Somewhere in the distance was a sound that resembled a crowd of people whose voices were muffled by some kind of barrier. It was faint, but it was audible enough to catch at the right time if one stood quietly with their mouth slightly open. An escalator type ladder with wooden slats stood motionless in front of them. There was another level below them, but it wasn't accessible from the way they just came. Going down the ladder was definitely out of the question.

"There's another level below us. That's where the sounds we keep hearing are coming from," Chris said.

"There must be a door or some kind of entrance besides that ladder contraption," Lee said, pointing in the general direction with his weapon.

Bateman looked off to the left and pointed. "There's an elevator behind that little housing. If there's an elevator then there's got to be another door. It's a fire hazard type deal. This place may be made out of cement and steel, but there's gasoline in the cars parked here that can easily catch fire. Noxious fumes and all that shit. I'll lay you ten to one there's another small housing similar to that one somewhere on this level."

The two soldiers came back and made their report. "What we're looking for is right around the corner and towards the middle of the parking area. He's right, there's a small housing with double doors made of metal. It can't be seen from where we came in because it's hidden by the escalated wall. The housing is actually built out of the ramp itself."

Chris nodded. "Evidently they don't know we're here yet. If they did, they'd be on us like fucking white on rice. That's our point of entry. All we need...."

"Excuse me, sir." The other soldier shook his head. "It's locked."

"Damn it!" Chris swung at the air. "That's exactly what we need. We're lucky we got this far. We can't be banging around trying to open it. If they didn't know we were here, they will by the time we get it unlocked."

Bateman reached into his pocket. "Wait a second! Check this shit out." He brought out what looked like a small jackknife and opened it to reveal a set of lock pick tools. Chris and Jackson gave him a strange look.

"What? Look, I carry a badge. We can't always break into a place and make a big racket, right? Sometimes we need stealth."

In a few seconds he had the door swinging open, squeaking slightly as the entrance became totally accessible. A set of cement stairs with metal edges went down and curved to the right. Chris and Pete entered first, followed by the rest. Marlene was busy taking mental notes from one of the soldiers on how to load, fire, and hold the gun she carried as they descended into the dim light.

Around the corner, a small child sat and listened. It was a girl; a child of about seven or eight years of age. Below her on the next step was a puddle where she had apparently peed herself. She stared at a closed door that immediately registered in Chris's mind as being locked from the other side. Pete Bateman squatted down several steps from the girl. She seemed to be barely breathing.

"Hey, there, honey. Are you all right? What's on the other...."

When she turned his way, her eyes were milky white. She began to cry and move her tiny body toward the wall next to her. "Are you the bad people? Are you going to kill me like they did my daddy?"

Marlene made her way down past the two men. "No, darling. No one is going to hurt you today or any other day. Why are you here? Why are you sitting here all alone?" The smell of urine assailed her nose as she leaned forward.

"I get in the way," the girl said. "I can't see like the others. I can only see colors and shadows in front of me. I was in a room with big lights when they found me. Even with my eyes closed so tight, the lights hurt them so bad. They took my friend, Bobby. He was just like me."

Bateman reached for the door handle. It turned downward more than halfway, but he went no further with it. "It doesn't seem to be locked. Why couldn't they just put her someplace inside out of the way? Why here?"

The sound of footsteps ended the conversation for a moment. "They had her in a hospital on an operating table," a deep voice said and a moment later Colonel Hapshire rounded the corner and stood with a group of men behind him. "She was probably one of the first of those they tried to use a reverse procedure on. The little boy she was talking about is in the same shape. The military interrupted them and they left the kids there in the room. They had those lights shining in their eyes for quite some time."

"What procedure? And what happened to your all out war up there?" Chris asked, pointing upward. Marlene looked his way as if he took the words right out of her mouth.

"They were trying to work out a reversal for the new breed. The zombies they couldn't do anything about, but the animal-like creatures they felt could be reversed with time. The only catch was that it would take a small bit of bone marrow from a child. It didn't have to be a match like for other diseases. It just had to be implanted within a very short time." The colonel shrugged. "As far as my all out war, I have that covered."

Marlene turned to address the colonel. "So, you're saying they planned on using children to...what? To put...." She shook her head. "Those sons of bitches. If it was going to be successful, they were going to use it on those they *wanted* to be cured."

Hapshire nodded. "That was the plan. Any high ranking official that got caught up in this bullshit would be on the list for reversal. We also found out there are a lot more of these underground cellar locations throughout the country. They have a leader of some kind. They just can't do it on their own."

Chris knocked on the closed door. "We have other fish to fry. We'll worry about that when the time comes. Right now, we need to clear this one out."

Hapshire turned to the soldiers behind him. "We're going in."

Marlene took the girl and wrapped her eyes with a scarf. "I'm taking her out of here. I'll be up here and out in the open. If there's anyone injured you know where I am."

Bateman turned the handle once again, but this time pushed it down to the max. The door flung inward with no one on the other side to greet them.

The smell of death and bodily functions was enough to gag them. Hapshire's men fanned out from right to left as Chris brought his team down the center of the huge room.

At the far wall were double doors and, beyond them, the sounds of both human and humanoid voices.

Colonel Hapshire's men took to both sides of the entrance. When it was flung open, all hell broke loose.

CHAPTER 56

The stench of decomposed flesh assailed their nostrils, making them want to vomit. In the immediate area, zombies turned on the intruders immediately. With the double doors, the team was allowed to move quickly into the area and spread out. They couldn't see beyond the dead things that were attempting to surround them, but they could hear in the background the voices of those who were taken prisoner. Some of them were wailing as though they were being cut open without the aid of anesthesia.

Zombies hit the floor one after the other. The main problem was the hundreds of animal-like creatures that began to drag their captives to another part of the room. Soldiers made their way to the center of the room and fired when they felt the captives were out of harm's way. Without warning some of the creatures dropped from the ceiling and landed on unsuspecting soldiers. They tore out gouges of flesh from either throats or shoulders.

Chris was up against the side wall firing at a group of creatures who were making their way toward another door marked with a busted red and white exit sign. Some of them were fast. They made their way toward the soldiers with leaps and bounds that completely stunned the men.

Chris pointed to one of the soldiers. "That door they're trying to get into! If it opens, throw a grenade through it. We'll take our chances that the building won't collapse on this side. I don't want any of them leaving this room!"

The soldier glanced at Hapshire who nodded in approval. "You heard the man!"

The soldier shouted back his acknowledgment amongst the gunfire. Chris and Bateman moved closer to the end of the wall. Making their way to the other side, they stopped dead center of the room and blasted ten or twelve of the creatures who dropped down from the ceiling. Bateman noticed the pipes overhead were large and low enough to allow a creature to wedge itself between the ceiling and the pipe.

Chris turned in time to see several of the creatures coming up from a staircase they hadn't noticed. It was a circular hole in the floor off in the corner. Bateman spun to meet their advance, but one of them had already grabbed his leg. The teeth bit deep into his calf and tore flesh and cloth off in one quick tear. Bateman let out a shriek of pain as blood began to fill his boot.

Chris sent a half dozen Uzi rounds through the thing's face. "Get upstairs to the doctor! You can't...."

But Bateman had already decided his fate. By his own hand, the bullet ripped through the underside of his jaw and out the back of his head. He knew there was no way out. Once bitten, that was the name of the game.

Jackson was busy firing at the same exit door the soldier was directed to blast. When they finally got the door open, the GI threw the grenade with a hook shot. It bounced once inside and then through the open door. The blast sent the wall crashing down, but only part of the ceiling inside the main room. When the smoke and dust cleared, the dead had been thrown in various places leaving them in positions that assured the team that no one was getting back up.

Colonel Hapshire had at least twenty men firing across the room and into a corner. A group of creatures were attempting to get out through one of the vents built into the wall at least twelve inches from the ceiling. In the next room, Hapshire found most of the civilians the creatures had captured. Most of the kids were naked, and several of the women were given a soldier's shirt to cover their naked breasts.

Outside, the flight of the half-human creatures met with another platoon of soldiers who fired repeatedly until all of them were lying dead. Marlene had left word with one of the sergeants to inform the Secret Service agent named Chris Kearns that she had flown the little girl to the shock trauma center in Breezy Point.

Back under the huge dwelling, the rest of the team cleaned up anything left that had to do with hostages.

Reports soon came in from over the rest of the country that similar teams such as Hapshire's had mirrored his attack and cleaned out nests holding more than three or four hundred of the creatures. There were lives lost, but in every war fought, it was one of the best used sayings.

"It's the sacrifice a soldier faces in the time of war."

CHAPTER 57

Marlene walked out into the hallway and headed for the elevators. Chris was already waiting for her and she gave him a short smile. After numerous tests, it was found that the captives were not infected in any way. However, the test results of the bone marrow research proved to be a false hope. They waited in silence as the elevator door closed.

Marlene scanned the lighted numbers above the closed doors as they flashed on and off. Her face told a story, but Chris couldn't begin to read it clearly. Chris Attempted to speak to her several times before finally breaking the silence.

"There's something you're not telling me, isn't there?" he asked.

Marlene nodded. "I wanted to make sure all the tests were in and all of them were in our favor. I've had enough of these crazy research programs wasting money and everyone's valuable time." Her face grew serious. "It's one of the women."

Chris nodded. "Don't stop there."

Marlene turned and looked into his eyes. "She's pregnant, and the tests are showing an abnormal reading. It's different this time. I mean, someone high up in the chain of command called a few minutes ago and asked that the child be delivered regardless. They want to see exactly what we have here. I wanted...."

"Yeah, of course they do. It's someone else wanting to do more damn experiments to fuck up the rest of the normal world. They want to see what the kid's gonna look like. Maybe he can dig holes in the ground faster than any human. He might be able to leap tall buildings...." Chris shook his head, slightly embarrassed. "I'm sorry, Marlene. It seems like this shit never ends. No one ever gets the point; the moral of the story. I can't make that call and neither can you. None of use can make that call except the mother."

Marlene shrugged as the doors opened. They stepped out into the lobby and made their way to the cafeteria.

"The Center for Disease Control wants it aborted," she said. "They're now saying that this isn't the only case. Hundreds of women are turning up pregnant all over the country. Several have turned up in the United Kingdom and Germany. If the military thinks they have this under control, they have another thing coming. This is going to go world wide before we know it. Now the rest of the world has another reason to hate us."

"I have a strange feeling we're no longer talking about zombies here. Goddamn it! Why can't these assholes wise up?" He pulled a chair out and held it until she sat down. "We have the chance to get back what we lost, and now they want to play mad scientists again and screw up what we've accomplished. Good people died along the way to get us back this far."

"You're preaching to the choir, Chris. I've been through all this over and over again with these people long before you got here. No one had any answers before and now that they think they have those answers, they want to start something new. I'm sorry to say it because I'm supposed to be a life saver, but I'm with the CDC. All these pregnancies should be terminated. Nothing good is going to come of it."

They got up and went to the food line. Several minutes later they were sitting down to club sandwiches and soft drinks. Chris wiped his mouth and leaned back. "Thou shalt not kill. That doesn't bother you here?"

Marlene gave him an unexpected look and shook her head. "No it doesn't. This has nothing to do with God. These...atrocities against nature are not his children. I'm not going to sit here and preach a sermon, Chris, but unfortunately that's my view. These children are going to be deformed for life. Who knows what their mental capacities will be. Would you want one of your children playing with...?"

Chris smiled. "You don't have to finish. And the answer is, no. No, I wouldn't want my children anywhere around something like that. I just feel there's got to be more that can be done to save this planet. It's dying at a very fast pace, Marlene. An apocalypse brought on by nightmarish beings born of man. Maybe this is the new evolution. This may be the way we're supposed to look in the future."

"Progress turned against us," Marlene said. She smiled despite the truth of the matter and sat quiet for a moment. "I remember being a little girl and going to our beach house on the Maryland side of the Potomac River. We had a long pier that went quite a ways out into the water. Well, maybe about thirty feet. It was so peaceful there. I would sit for hours with a fishing pole. I even showed my brother how to put a worm on the hook. Those are days I wish I had back. I think I would have done things a little differently if I had the chance."

Chris pushed his thumb lightly into the soft metal of the soda can. "Something bad?"

She waited for a moment before speaking again. "My brother thought he had a monster fish on the line once. We reeled and reeled. I called my father to come and look. When he did come running, we already had our catch on the surface of the water. That's when I screamed and ran for the house."

"You were afraid of a big fish?"

Marlene shook her head. "No. I was afraid of the dead body that stared up at me from just under the water. A drowning victim. When I first saw Farin Taska's face staring at me from behind that small window, I saw that face again. I guess that's the price you pay for having a place designed for peace and tranquility."

Chris stood and picked up his scraps. "I have a meeting to go to. But I'll leave you with one final thought. There's a price for everything. The world is almost as a fragile as rising batter." He drank the last of his soda and headed for the door, throwing his waste into one of the receptacles. He turned and stood in the double-framed doorway. "I'd like to see you later on today or sometime during the week if you can get free."

Marlene smiled faintly. "I'll find the time. There's a moral to that batter thing, isn't there?"

Chris smiled back. "Yeah, someone left the cake out in the rain."

EPILOGUE

Eight months later.

The obstetrician once again placed the sonogram in front of him. The image wasn't as clear as an x-ray, but disturbing none the less. The head was grossly oversized for such a tiny infant, but it was the miniature hands that had him straining his eyes. Something in their structure wasn't normal for a baby about to be brought into the world.

But he let his concerns go. He was paid to keep quiet. Taking out a bottle of Early Times from his desk drawer, he poured himself a small amount. Glancing at the image once again, he tilted the bottle once more. His practice was on the line. His teeth were clenched as the whiskey slid down his throat. Office hours were closed, but he kept the woman secluded in another room with a nurse whom he felt he could trust. Splitting spectacular fees made people do things they would never have dreamed of in a million years.

He once again checked the skull structure. There was of course nothing there to see except a soft, oversized cranium with a white blur for a brain. He shook his head and poured himself another drink. There couldn't be a parasite attached. They weren't simply born along with a child. Anything about what he was paid to do was wrong. His mind raced back and forth between the Hippocratic Oath and the five hundred thousand dollars that would be laid at his feet when the job was complete.

It was a weekend, and no one else was scheduled for Saturday. Inducing labor was the way to go right now. The office needed to be open on Monday to avert any suspicion on his part.

Was that being paranoid? he thought.

Checking his schedule showed there were seven appointments for Monday. There were seven normal fetuses resting in the uteruses of each woman.

The doctor screwed the cap back on the bottle and stashed it away. There was no time for drinking anymore.

Steady! Steady! his mind shouted.

He needed everything to go just as planned. Putting the money into the bank would be the trick. The IRS was all but defunct, but there was still the law, or what was left of it.

The nurse poked her head in the room, cleared her throat to get his attention, and waited for him to acknowledge her.

"Doctor, the patient is dilated over seven centimeters."

He nodded. "I'll be there in a moment. Let me scrub up. While I'm at it, go ahead and get everything else ready."

An hour and a half later, his secret patient was screaming at the top of her lungs as she struggled to give birth. There was no epidural since it would be too risky without a regular team present. The head was visible, but the size was making it difficult to pass through the birth canal. He performed an episiotomy and the woman once again let out a blood curdling scream as he hadn't given her a local first.

The doctor cupped his hands around the child's head when it was finally fully extended and pulled lightly. The rest of the body slid out without incident. Immediately it started to make noises other than crying. They were more animalistic sounds than human and it sent chills up the spines of both caregivers.

"Jesus, God All Mighty!" The doctor gasped as he laid the child down on the small gurney. The hands and feet were claw-like with small talons that curled inward. "Why in God's name would someone want this abomination?"

The mother had passed out from the pain and was oblivious to the creature she had just given birth to. The nurse quickly sucked the fluids from the nose and mouth of the baby, wiping away any of the mother's bodily fluids still remaining on the body. She shook her head and glanced over at the physician, her face full of disgust.

"This is the Devil's work, Doctor."

She looked down once more on the small creature, and as it stared up at her with hunger in its eyes, she quickly noted it was void of any hair.

But not of teeth.

REVOLUTION OF THE DEAD

By Anthony Giangregorio

THE DEAD SHALL RISE AGAIN!

Five years ago, a deadly plague wiped out 97% of the world's population, America suffering tragically. Bodies were everywhere, far too many to bury or burn. But then, through a miracle of medical science, a way is found to reanimate the dead.

With the manpower of the United States depleted, and the remaining survivors not wanting to give up their internet and fast food restaurants, the undead are conscripted as slave labor.

Now they cut the grass, pick up the trash, and walk the dogs of the surviving humans.

But whether alive or dead, no race wants to be controlled, and sooner or later the dead will fight back, wanting the freedom they enjoyed in life.

The revolution has begun!

And when it's over, the dead will rule the land, and the remaining humans will become the slaves...or worse.

DEAD RECKONING: DAWNING OF THE DEAD

By Anthony Giangregorio

THE DEAD HAVE RISEN!

In the dead city of Pittsburgh, two small enclaves struggle to survive, eking out an existence of hand to mouth.

But instead of working together, both groups battle for the last remaining fuel and supplies of a city filled with the living dead.

Six months after the initial outbreak, a lone helicopter arrives bearing two more survivors and a newborn baby. One enclave welcomes them, while the other schemes to steal their helicopter and escape the decaying city.

With no police, fire, or social services existing, the two will battle for dominance in the steel city of the walking dead. But when the dust settles, the question is: will the remaining humans be the winners, or the losers?

When the dead walk, the line between Heaven and Hell is so twisted and bent there is no line at all.

RISE OF THE DEAD

by Anthony Giangregorio

DEATH IS ONLY THE BEGINNING!

In less than forty-eight hours, more than half the globe was infected.

In another forty-eight, the rest would be enveloped.

The reason?

A science experiment gone horribly wrong which enabled the dead to walk, their flesh rotting on their bones even as they seek human prey.

Jeremy was an ordinary nineteen year old slacker. He partied too much and had done poorly in high school. After a night of drinking and drugs, he awoke to find the world a very different place from the one he'd left the night before.

The dead were walking and feeding on the living, and as Jeremy stepped out into a world gone mad, the dead spotting him alone and unarmed in the middle of the street, he had to wonder if he would live long enough to see his twentieth birthday.

DEADFREEZE

By Anthony Giangregorio

THIS IS WHAT HELL WOULD BE LIKE IF IT FROZE OVER!

When an experimental serum for hypothermia goes horribly wrong, a small research station in the middle of Antarctica becomes overrun with an army of the frozen dead.

Now a small group of survivors must battle the arctic weather and a horde of frozen zombies as they make their way across the frozen plains of Antarctica to a neighboring research station.

What they don't realize is that they are being hunted by an entity whose sole reason for existing is vengeance; and it will find them wherever they run.

DEAD WORLDS: Undead Stories
A Zombie Anthology Volume 1
With a story by Pasquale J. Morrone
Edited by Anthony Giangregorio

Welcome to the world of the dead, where the laws of nature have been twisted, reality changed.

The Dead Walk!

Filled with established and promising new authors for the next generation of corpses, this anthology will leave you gasping for air as you go from one terror-filled story to another.

Like the decomposing meat of a freshly rotting carcass, this book will leave you breathless.

Don't say we didn't warn you.

VISIONS OF THE DEAD
A ZOMBIE STORY
By Anthony & Joseph Giangregorio

Jake Roberts felt like he was the luckiest man alive.

He had a great family, a beautiful girlfriend, who was soon to be his wife, and a job, that might not have been the best, but it paid the bills.

At least until the dead began to walk.

Now Jake is fighting to survive in a dead world while searching for his lost love, Melissa, knowing she's out there somewhere.

But the past isn't dead, and as he struggles for an uncertain future, the past threatens to consume him.

With the present a constant battle between the living and the dead, Jake finds himself slipping in and out of the past, the visions of how it all happened haunting him.

But Jake knows Melissa is out there somewhere and he'll find her or die trying. In a world of the living dead, you can never escape your past.

DEAD WORLDS: Undead Stories
A Zombie Anthology Volume 2
With a story by Pasquale J. Morrone
Edited by Anthony Giangregorio

Welcome to a world where the dead walk and want nothing more than to feast on the living.

The stories contained in this, the second volume of the Dead Worlds series, are filled with action, gore, and buckets and buckets of blood; plus a heaping side of entrails for those with a little extra hunger.

The stories contained within this volume are scribed by both the desiccated cadavers of seasoned veterans to the genre as well as fresh-faced corpses, each printed here for the first time; and all of them ready to dig in and please the most discerning reader.

So slap on a bib and prepare to get bloody, because you're about to read the best zombie stories this side of Hell!

THE DARK
By Anthony Giangregorio

The darkness came without warning.

First New York, then the rest of United States, and then the world became enveloped in a perpetual night without end.

With no sunlight, eventually the planet will wither and die, bringing on a new Ice Age. But that isn't problem for the human race, for humanity will be dead long before that happens.

There is something in the dark, creatures only seen in nightmares, and they are on the prowl. Evolution has changed and man is no longer the dominant species. When we are children, we're told not to fear the dark, that what we believe to exist in the shadows is false.

Unfortunately, that is no longer true.

BOOK OF THE DEAD
A Zombie Anthology
Edited by Anthony Giangregorio

This book is the most faithful, truest zombie anthology ever written and we invite you along for the ride.

Every single story in this book is filled with slack-jawed, eyes glazed, slow moving, shambling zombies set in a world where the dead have risen and only want to eat the flesh of the living.

In these pages, the rules are sacrosanct. There is no deviation from what a zombie should be or how they came about.

The Dead Walk.

There is no reason, though rumors and suppositions fill the radio and television stations. But the only thing that is fact is that the walking dead are here and they will not go away.

So prepare yourself for the ultimate homage to the master of zombie legend. And remember... *Aim for the head!*

FAMILY OF THE DEAD
A Zombie Anthology
by Anthony, Joseph and Domenic Giangregorio

Clawing their way out of the wet, dark earth, these tales of terror will fill you with the deep seated fear we all have of death and what comes next.

But if that wasn't bad enough to chill your soul, these undead tales are penned by an entire family of corpses. The zombie master himself, Anthony Giangregorio, leads his two young ghouls, his sons Domenic and Joseph Giangregorio, on a journey of terror inducing stories that will keep you up long into the night.

As you read these works of the undead, don't be alarmed by that bump outside the window.

After all, it's probably just a stray tree branch...or is it?

DARK PLACES
by Anthony Giangregorio

A cave-in inside the Boston subway unleashes something that should have stayed buried forever

Three boys sneak out to a haunted junkyard after dark and find more than they gambled on.

In a world where everyone over twelve has died from a mysterious illness, one young boy tries to carry on.

A mysterious man in black tries his hand at a game of chance at a local carnival, to interesting results.

God, Allah, and Buddha play a friendly game of poker with the fate of the Earth resting in the balance.

Ever have one of those days where everything that can go wrong, does? Well, so did Byron, and no one should have a day like this!

Thad had an imaginary friend named Charlie when he was a child. Charlie would make him do bad things. Now Thad is all grown up and guess who's coming for a visit?

These and other short stories, all filled with frozen moments of dread and wonder, will keep you captivated long into the night.

Just be sure to watch out when you turn off the light!

THE MONSTER UNDER THE BED
by Anthony Giangregorio

Rupert was just one of many monsters that inhabit the human world, scaring children before bed. Only Rupert wanted to play with the children he was forced to scare.

When Rupert meets Timmy, an instant friendship is born. Running away from his abusive step-father, Timmy leaves home, embarking on a journey that leads him to New York City.

On his way, Timmy will realize that the true monsters are other adults who are just waiting to take advantage of a small boy, all alone in the big city.

Can Rupert save him?

Or will Timmy just become another statistic.

THE PLACE TO GO FOR ZOMBIE AND APOCALYPTIC FICTION

LIVING DEAD PRESS

WHERE THE DEAD WALK
www.livingdeadpress.com

Lightning Source UK Ltd.
Milton Keynes UK
17 August 2009

142759UK00001BB/63/P